I0545397

THE
FUTURE
OF
SUPERVILLAINY

By C. T. Phipps

That was when a Mexican ninja threw a pair of katana at me.

"I'll defend you, Your Majesty!"

"Lucia, no!" Diabloman shouted,

Goddammit, was it so much to ask for a moment to think? I turned insubstantial and the katanas passed through me.

"No fair!" the ninja, Lucia, I presumed, said.

"Uh, who the hell are you?" I asked, wondering why my reunion with my ARCHNEMESIS was being interrupted.

"I am Diabolique, Scourge of Evildoers and Agent of Order!" Lucia said.

"She's my daughter, Boss," Diabloman said. "She's decided to go the route of the antihero."

"Ah," I said, really not giving a shit. "Well, consider me defeated. You really shouldn't throw katanas since you have to go pick them up, unless you have magnetic gloves to retrieve them."

"Right," Lucia muttered, embarrassed. She then jogged over to the other side of the building to get her swords.

It was like I'd died and gone to amateur-hour hell for D-List supervillains. I fully expected to see the Shadowmaster and the Darden Valley Guardian hanging around.

"Gary, what are you doing here?" Mr. Inventor asked.

"We're here to kick Nazi ass and chew bubblegum," I answered. "And I'm all out of bubblegum. Also, to rescue you guys."

Copyright © 2019 by Charles Phipps
ISBN 978-1-950565-53-5
Cover Artist: Raffaele Marinetti
All rights reserved. No part of this book may be used or reproduced in any manner
whatsoever without written permission except in the case of
brief quotations embodied in criticalarticles and reviews
For information address Crossroad Press at 141 Brayden Dr., Hertford, NC 27944
A Mystique Press Production - Mystique Press is an imprint of Crossroad Press.
www.crossroadpress.com

First edition

Foreword

Ah, Indiana Jones.

Oh, right, I'm not supposed to tip my hand as to what this book is going to be about. So I won't mention Indiana Jones, *Tomb Raider*, *Uncharted*, Edgar Rice Burroughs's Pellucidar, *Hollow Earth Expeditions*, or any other sources I'll be drawing from. I won't reveal this is meant to be a book of pulpy two-fisted action and adventure set in a Lost World like Marvel's Savage Land or DC Comics's Skartaris.

When last we left Gary Karkofsky, he was dealing with the fact that had just altered reality to make consequences stick in his comic book world. Death, if not final, was going to be a lot harder to overcome. Superheroes who had died would remain dead and that included Ultragod, the Nightwalker, Sunlight, the Prismatic Commando, and his wife Mandy. Yes, the bad guys would stay dead too but that was a small comfort compared to the loss of so many great heroes—and Sunlight. Worse, Gary also found out his life had been subject to numerous retcons that re-wrote his history and past for the benefit of a deranged child-like god who was obsessed with angsty heroes.

Yes, it was a commentary on the fandoms (or perhaps the perception of fandoms by comic book publishers). It was also very real to our protagonist. The fact it once more trashed all his existing relationships and sent him into a deep funk can't be denied. On the other hand, it meant that Gary could go forward and make a difference for his family. He had two children now, Leia and Mindy, for whom he was going to be the most overprotective father since Harry Dresden.

Still, I felt like Gary was in a spot where he needed to take on an adventure outside of his usual comfort zone. He'd already done battle with every permutation of supervillain, cosmic evil, and supernatural bad guy he could in Falconcrest City. It was time to take Gary to an exotic locale and see how he managed to adapt, in spite of being a geek ill-equipped for anything but a climate-controlled building with high-speed Internet access.

Which, yes, brings us to Indiana Jones.

Part of the fun of comic book worlds is they are not just one genre but every genre. You can have Superman fight aliens, wizards, gangsters, mad scientists, Zeus, and the Devil without ever breaking canon. There are no limits what is possible in their stories and that makes their stories all the sweeter. Indeed, whenever I make a reference to something insane (like Ultragoddess dating a flying werehorse) then you can bet that is a reference to something that actually happened in comics.

One thing I was always proud of when reading these sorts of books was when our heroes ventured to the Lost Worlds of their respective settings. Places where ancient temples, tribes, lost civilizations, dinosaurs, and more were all true. Arthur Conan Doyle invented the concept, but it took comic books to refine it. Explorers and adventurers in real life often brought as much misery as joy to the places they discovered but hopefully Gary will prove more Marco Polo than Cortez. At least our hero's adventures will be taking him against the one enemy we can all agree deserves not to have control over such a place.

One he and Indiana Jones share a loathing for.

CHAPTER ONE

A SUPERVILLAIN NO MORE

"So, yeah, it's been a year since I quit being a supervillain," I said, standing there with my hands in the pockets of my large leather coat. I had a Fedora on my head and was dressed like it was the 1930s, which apparently had come back in style as the men's fashion in Falconcrest City. I personally didn't like it because it made me look like a pick-up artist, but I had basically just been looting Arthur Warren's wardrobe for the past year. I couldn't be bothered to shop for clothes as I'd barely left the mansion.

Why?

Guilt.

I was standing over Mandy Anne Karkofsky's gravestone in the private cemetery built into the Warren Estate. I had no idea what had compelled the Warren family to build a cemetery for themselves on their home's property, but I supposed when you owned ten miles of land that it wasn't so much your home as the small country you ruled.

A year ago, I'd saved the entire multiverse from a crazy space god. That was something I could be proud of, but it had cost me everything in the process. I'd ended up in the future with my friends and meeting my two daughters (also from the future). They'd made me an offer I couldn't refuse and then I'd refused it. Disappointed, they'd brought me back to the past and I'd been without a purpose ever since. You see, I'd decided to hang up my cloak for good. It just wasn't fun playing dress-up anymore.

"It's weird adjusting to the quote-unquote lifestyle of a normal human being," I said, knowing that I was far from it. "I mean, I stole plenty of money from a bunch of bad guys beforehand, so that even after giving away ninety percent of it, I'll never have to work again. I don't really care; living like a drug lord or kingpin isn't really my thing. Money never mattered to me. It was all about making an impact on the world. To live before I died and change the world for the better."

I looked up to the sun. The light blinded me until I covered my eye with my palm. A trio of Exterminator-robots flew through the sky, painted with American flags. The new president had repurposed President Omega's army of Super-hunting death machines and re-branded them "Freedom Robots." They'd picked up the slack in keeping superhuman terrorism down as well as oppressing anyone on both sides of the superhero/supervillain dichotomy to keep them from doing anything good or bad. The world had become a safer, less interesting place if you sufficiently stretched your definition of *safer*.

"I'm not sure I've made a difference," I said, taking a deep breath. "I know, you'd say we both saved the world from being destroyed so obviously we did. But, well, maybe if I wasn't there then someone else would have been there instead and done it better. Maybe you'd still be alive."

I wasn't a sexist jackass. Mandy had known what she was doing when she set out to become a superhero. Her career had been short, at least as a living woman, but it had been important. Thousands of people were alive because of what she'd done during Falconcrest City's miniature zombie apocalypse. I knew she'd died protecting Cindy and that act had resulted in the former living long enough to have our child, Leia, but I was having myself a pity party. I wasn't in the mood to argue with Mandy's ghost, even if it wasn't here except figuratively.

"*Fine,*" I said, looking down at the headstone. It listed her full name, birthdate, and had a tiny carving of a black rose. "You were right. I did good and wrecked a lot of bad guys' shit in the time I was Merciless: The Supervillain without Mercy. Still, I can't do it anymore. I can't be the guy who runs around joking and blasting people knowing what the consequences might be. I'm a father now of two kids and I don't want to leave them without a father. I also don't want to be that parent who is always having to rescue them from supervillains."

The fact there were no guarantees anymore had caused substantial blowback. It had been my decision to make resurrection impossible in this world. What I hadn't realized was that it would affect all the quote-unquote genre conventions I'd secretly had propping up my superhero-filled world. Villains ended up kidnapping the children of superheroes, killing them, and then getting killed in return.

Heroes ended up broken down emotionally or quitting with no chance of returning. Each day the world got a little less magical and more mundane as the best and worst began not showing up for work. Why should they? No one appreciated their efforts and the masses actively opposed their attempts to make things better or worse. The Age of Superheroes had ended because of my actions and it had ended not with a bang but a whimper. *Wow,* had I screwed up.

There are some good things going on in the world. Doctor Aeon's clean fusion process has finally gotten out of the beta-testing it's been caught up in since the Sixties. No more global warming. For-profit space travel is a thing and we have the Mars Colony finally taking off. The Venusians are helping with that one. Elon Musk and Gizmo are competing for who will be getting the first functional human-designed hyperdrive into space. Personally, I'm on Leia's side, not just because she's my daughter, but also because it's likely to have fewer bugs.

I let out a half-bitter laugh. "What else is there to say? Relationship-wise? Well, I'm still in the penumbra of not being sure what I am to whom. Gabrielle gave birth to Mandy a few months ago in secret but refuses to name me as the father in public. No surprise there. Cindy is seeing Mr. Inventor now, not that she ever wasn't, but we've been a bit distant since I took up with Gabrielle. It turns out my best friend didn't like being considered not only second best romantically but third best since I proclaimed my undying love for you, then Gabrielle but not her. Mind you, she loves Gabrielle every bit as much as she loves you, so that just makes it weird. Well, in a *Dear Penthouse* sort of way."

I coughed into my fist.

"Kerri is continuing to help raise the kids, though Gizmo doesn't really need so much raising as reining in. I caught her building a death ray to threaten a dictator who was trying to execute his poorer citizens. Gabrielle ended up taking care of that anyway. It may be illegal to be a superhero in the United States for now, but our country's loss is the rest of the world's gain. Diabloman has been trying to get in touch with Spellbinder, his back-from -the-dead sister, and I haven't seen him since the Eternity Tournament. I hate that he seems to care about her more than our family but that's because she passed herself off as you. I can't forgive that."

The emotion of the moment overwhelmed me, and I got down on my knees before putting my hand on Mandy's gravestone. "I miss you so much. You were always more important to me than all of this. I didn't demonstrate it, and I screwed things up big time. No one can ever replace you, though, and I just have to keep faith that I'll see you again someday."

Well, not really faith. I'd met Death and seen countless ghosts. It's more like hope. Still, I also hadn't seen Death or any ghosts for months. The Death Orb remained an inanimate object I kept attached to my car keys. I knew Mandy was in a better place. I'd seen the better place. I just didn't think I would ever go there myself. So, I closed my eyes and prayed in front of the grave. I badly mangled the Hebrew, but I suspected God would get the sentiment. It was a good moment, ruined by the sound of automatic weapons being prepped behind me.

My eyes shot open. "Not now. Not here."

The Death Orb started glowing in my pocket. I reached in and grasped it, feeling it draw energy from my cold fury. It was one of the most powerful magical objects in the universe but, a bit like the One Ring of Sauron, was limited by the amount of supernatural juice a person already had.

In simple terms it worked a helluva lot better for Gandalf than it did for Sméagol, and I was a good deal more Hobbit-like than Istari. Unfortunately for whoever was defiling my wife's grave and interrupting my visit, the Death Orb was also capable of channeling anger in lieu of sorcery. Right now, it felt like the orb was rapidly reaching peak megawizards and I didn't mean Harry Potter.

I slowly stood and turned. Standing behind me was an African-American woman in a black U.S. military uniform with a colonel's insignia. She stood between two armored hard-suit-wearing soldiers with energy-blaster gloves. Two Federal agents, armed with machine guns and dressed in a Falconcrest City anachronistic style that made them look like G-men from the 1930s completed the immediate threat. They were dressed in gray suits that looked vaguely menacing even though they had badges hanging from chains around their necks. I didn't recognize the name of the organization they worked for, but it looked very official.

Mind you, these idiots hadn't come alone. There were over a hundred U.S. Special Forces and regular Army pouring out of stealth helicopters landing all around the cemetery. I also saw a dozen or so of the "Freedom Robots" land in a circle around me.

"Gary Karkofsky, a.k.a Merciless: The Supervillain without Mercy, you are hereby placed under arrest by the Anti-Paranormal Task Force of the U.S. Army. You will be interrogated and placed in isolation by the Department of Supernatural Security. We are operating here under the provisions of the Anders Act and with the full authority of the President. Your powers represent a clear and present danger to the citizens of our great nation. If you cooperate you will receive benefits and live in relative comfort, but you will never see the outside of a detention center again."

I took a deep breath then sighed. "Fine."

The African-American woman who looked like she was spoiling for a fight blinked. "What?"

I extended my arms and presented my wrists. "Fine. I'm not looking for a fight. If you want to take me in, I'll go."

The woman narrowed her eyes. "You realize what I said. You won't be able to escape from us like you have on so many other locations."

"What, you think I want to take on the entire U.S. Army?" I asked.

"You have before," the woman said.

I heard one of the soldiers in the back mutter, "He's cooperating. They never cooperate."

"It's a trick," another said. "That's what this guy does. He's tricky."

Clearly, I was not dealing with the finest of the U.S. military. These guys were not being all they could be.

"Colonel Jones," the white-uniformed Federal agent sneered, walking over to slap power-suppressing shackles on my wrists, "stop talking to this filthy assassin. He murdered the U.S. President and is a terrorist. The only thing he's going to find in an interrogation cell is a wet rag until we decide to put a bullet in his head."

"Charles Omega is not and has never been the U.S. President," Colonel Jones said. "The Supreme Court annulled his presidency on the basis of the fact that he was never a U.S. citizen but a foreign aggressor from the future."

"The attempted genocide of all Supers was also a big deal," I pointed out, amused at the fact these guys thought they could take me. I'd bitten off way more than it would take to chew up and spit these guys out. I'd fought demon lords, space gods, and A-list supervillains bigger than these guys.

I was tired, though. Tired of killing, tired of fighting in general really. I didn't want to resist, and it was my hope that if the government did toss me into a hole somewhere, then that would be the end of it. I had brought too much pain and misery to my family over the years to escape punishment for it. I needed to pay for what I had done and maybe this was my way to atone for it.

"Shut up," the man in the white suit said, punching me in the face.

"Reginald!" Colonel Jones said.

The man pulled back, shaking his fist as my face had clearly been harder than he'd expected. "Don't Reginald me. This subhuman filth has been menacing decent ordinary people for years. He's the reason why regular humans can't go out in the streets every day in peace. Supers are the enemy of the common man."

I blinked. "You realize I get my powers from magic, right? I mean, literally crack open a book and anyone can—"

"Shut up, freak!" Reginald said, putting all the contempt and hiss into his voice you might expect from a Saturday Morning Cartoon villain. Honestly, if the government was starting to recruit hyper-intelligent psychopaths into its ranks, things were probably going to get a helluva lot less peaceful.

"You're agitating the prisoner, Mr. Smith," the man in the gray suit said. His voice was cold and robotic and I saw little circuit patterns behind his eyes. "Our chances of successfully bringing in this Class-A target go down exponentially the more he is upset."

"We can't just let this guy surrender! He needs to be made an example of!" Reginald shouted, genuinely furious. He proceeded to shove his gun right in my face and pushed the barrel against the side of my nose.

"Reginald—" Colonel Jones started to say.

I was starting to regret my decision to surrender peacefully. "Can we just get on with this? I haven't had lunch yet and I have a real hankering for prison eggs. You know, the kind that are powdered then turned back into eggs in water? I don't know why I love those. I suppose they remind me of my poor, desperate upbringing."

Reginald pulled away and lowered his voice. "Do you know who we're going after next? Do you? When we bring you in, we're taking out your children. Both of the little shits and we're going to burn them—"

Oh no, he didn't. "You're threatening my kids?"

"You're damn right I'm threatening your kids!" Reginald shouted.

Colonel Jones' eyes widened as she perhaps realized she'd made a mistake slightly larger than attacking Pearl Harbor or playing with a bear cub next to its mother.

My shackles fell away, not able to do much about phenomenal cosmic power. "That was a mistake."

Reginald opened his mouth as if to scream some more obscenities.

I didn't let him. I placed my hand on his forehead and his

face began to melt like the Gestapo officer's in *Raiders of the Lost Ark*. He let out a gurgling scream that lasted far longer than the seconds it took for his skin and vital organs to slosh off his bones. Colonel Jones pulled back as did the man in the gray suit.

"Fire, fire, fire!" Colonel Jones shouted, pulling out an energy pistol and blasting a few times herself.

What followed was a series of energy blasts, machine gun fire, grenades, explosives, and a laser-targeted missile that ended up killing a few of the soldiers surrounding me. It was like the scene from *The Last Jedi* where Luke was hit with the entire might of the First Order. I could digress, discussing how much I hated that movie instead of discussing how none of this did a damn thing to me, but I won't.

In fact, that was the one scene in the movie I'd really enjoyed. Well, the throne room scene was cool, too, even if I don't understand where Rey became the greatest lightsaber duelist in the galaxy. Was there a secret martial arts school on Jakku? I mean, maybe they could insert that into her backstory as part of the comics. I think that would be neat. Oh, right, me killing the fuck out of these guys. Sorry, Mandy. I didn't mean to bring violence to your gravesite.

"I can turn insubstantial numbskulls," I said, walking out of the flames and destruction they'd used to assault my wife's memorial. "Did none of you even bother to look up my Superpedia entry before you came here? Oh right, no you didn't, because I deface it every day, so no one knows my weaknesses or strengths. Guess what, my secret weakness isn't aluminum and I'm not held back by four-leaf clovers. I am the wrath of gods."

I stretched out my fingertips, remaining insubstantial and blasted black hellfire from dark dimensions at the Freedom Robots, which were consumed completely. I waved my hand over the soldiers and their hands became frozen to their guns, now encased in heavy blocks of primordial ice harder than steel. Then I lifted my foot and stomped it on the ground, causing the helicopters to start sinking halfway into the Earth. I turned them substantial. They weren't buried, they were fused with the rock around them. What had been an enormous military force had become an embarrassment.

Colonel Jones, however, wasn't deterred. She lifted her pistol, clearly scared out of her mind. "You can't defy the government, Merciless! If you kill us, another group will come. Another group after that! The entirety of the world will unite—"

"Stop it," I said, interrupting her by looking at the Death Orb. "You threatened my kids. I've never hurt anyone's kids. Leia's seven and Mindy's a baby, for godsakes. You don't get to play the aggrieved party. You are permanently 'Colonel Child Murdering Asshat' as far as history is concerned."

Colonel Jones, who seemed to be not fully on board with the threaten-my-kids plan, didn't respond but looked to the man with the gray suit who was currently texting someone. Colonel Jones' reaction was an incredulous stare. "Really, Mr. Grey? Is now the time!?"

I shook the Death Orb. "You fully charged?"

The Death Orb crackled with unnatural power.

"Right," I said, lifting the orb into the air. "Time for a lesson in what exactly you're dealing with here."

It went dark despite being the middle of the day.

Colonel Jones stared as Mr.Gray stopped texting. A U.S. Army Ranger, his arm frozen to his gun, charged at me, leading with his head. He, of course, passed through me and landed on the other side. I had to give him credit, as well as to the other soldiers who were trying to get themselves free. They were tougher than the late Reginald Smith. Also, had balls of steel. I hoped they weren't in on the child-threatening plan.

"This is your brain on dark magic," I said, gesturing to the sky. "Wait, dammit, I've screwed up the entire thing. Okay, let's start over. This is reality, this is—"

"What are you doing?" Colonel Jones said, looking up. "What happened to the sun?"

"Oh fine!" I snapped, annoyed at being interrupted. "We'll do the short version. If you *ever* threaten me, my loved ones, or my children again then I will kill everyone who has ever had that thought. It will start with every single politician in Washington, D.C. then move through all the people who will have to have signed off on this mission. Furthermore, you've put me in a foul mood so I'm going to add a caveat that if I find out you've used *anyone else's kids against them* like this, then the result will be the same. I don't care if their parents are Charles Manson, Tom Terror, or Mother Theresa, unlikely as those individuals having children may be. In fact, if you have any in custody, then I expect them to be reunited with their parents or I will have the Earth swallow Congress whole."

I could do it too.

"You can't dictate to the United States government!" Colonel Jones hissed. "The U.S. army does not negotiate with terrorists."

I stared at her. "You are not the United States government or her military. They were the guys who liberated France and stopped the Nazis (props to the other Allies). The U.S. military is the group that fought P.H.A.N.T.O.M and the Taliban. You're not real soldiers. You're a bunch of toy soldiers threatening the freedom of your country's citizens. So, while I don't go after good guys in uniforms—*you do not qualify.*"

Colonel Jones looked ready to go after me despite the odds. I had to give her props for her courage, even if it was going to get her killed. "You do not scare me."

"My threat isn't to you," I said, coldly.

There was a pleasant beeping noise from the man in the gray suit's cellphone. He looked down on it. "We're to withdraw."

"What?" Colonel Jones asked. "Is he going to nuke the site?"

No," the man in the gray suit said, who I mentally just named Mr. Gray for lack of a better term. "The Chief of Staff has determined Merciless is a myth."

Colonel Jones opened her mouth and looked to the injured soldiers and damage around her. "A myth? Are you serious?"

Mr. Gray looked up and bowed his head. "We're sorry for disturbing you and your wife's resting place, Mr. Karkofsky. If you'll excuse us, we won't bother you again."

"Good," I said, dissipating the darkness I'd simultaneously conjured for an acre around the graveyard and the White House.

The outrage on Colonel Jones' face was beyond belief. Still, there was something about her expression that told me she thought the late Reginald Smith had it coming. I wouldn't have been surprised to discover if she had children of her own. Nevertheless, she and the rest of them departed on foot toward the estate's east wall, leaving me alone with my wife's now-destroyed grave. I'd had no idea if I could have lived up to my promise of using the Death Orb to slaughter everyone who threatened Leia and Mindy. I would have, though, and that kind of power terrified me. I stood alone for close to an hour before turning back to the mansion. It seemed that the world wasn't going to leave Merciless alone.

So Merciless couldn't leave the world alone.

CHAPTER TWO

BACK IN BLACK
IS NOT JUST AN AC/DC SONG

I walked back to the Warren mansion, which was its own little Versailles constructed by the late Uther Warren way back in the 19th century. It was sort of like Charles Foster Kane's Xanadu except not a complete waste of money (and you just thought I made *Star Wars* references). The place was ridiculously large and frankly looked like it was something someone had created with CGI when they needed to show someone was super Old Money Rich types.

The place had a West Wing, East Wing, North Wing, South Wing, and Central Manor with a courtyard stretching behind it that led to a hedge maze, pool, guest houses (as in plural), plus its own 18-hole golf course. That wasn't including the secret nuclear bunker that also had its own separate mansion formerly used as the headquarters for the Society of Superheroes back in their pre-moon base days.

Personally, I thought the place was a victim of changing social standards since it had been constructed *Downton Abbey* style with the implication that something like a hundred servants would be living there full-time. Lancel Warren, a.k.a The Nightwalker, had devoted himself to fighting crime, evil wizards, aliens, and Nazis for a century, so he hadn't really done much to expand the family line. His nieces and nephews had also gone on to build their own little mansions. The whole thing had come to me in an estate sale after the city finally acknowledged the legendary hero was not only merely dead but really, most sincerely, dead.

I missed Cloak.

Most of the mansion remained uninhabited and covered in white sheets to keep it from turning into a dusty cobweb-filled haunted house owned by an evil necromancer. My home was meant to be a clean and perky haunted house owned by an evil necromancer. Enough space existed in the place so that I could live there, along with my sister, my niece (when she wasn't crashing with her fellow Texas Guardians), Diabloman, Cindy, my two kids, and a bunch of freeloaders from alternate realities.

To show how much I valued security, I walked up to the back of the mansion and immediately opened the unlocked door to enter one of the halls. Agent G, a Ryan Gosling-looking cyborg from a *Blade Runner* universe, as well as one of those aforementioned freeloaders, was lying on an expansive couch in his underwear. He had a half-empty bottle of scotch lying beside him and looked about as drunk as a robot with a fleshy covering could be. The ornate carpet on the ground was being vacuumed by a trio of foot-tall yellow robots with one eye that my daughter had made in homage to a certain movie's mascots.

"Nyaaaaah, boop, blah!" a Henchbot said.

I made the Vulcan peace sign. "Live long and prosper to you, too."

"Nah, nah, nah, beep boop!" the Henchbots said, saluting me together. There were God knows how many of these things moving around the house and serving as a substitute for the servants I neither wanted nor could afford. Being a billionaire barely covered the estate tax on this house. By the way, even supervillains fear the IRS. That's how they took down The Bootlegger King ya' know.

"Case," I said, referring to G by his chosen name. "You know where Gabrielle is?"

Most people were only lucky to find love once in their lives and sometimes not even then. I'd been lucky enough to fall in love three times, though each was a very different kind of love. Gabrielle Anders, a.k.a Ultragoddess, was the mother of my youngest child. She rarely had time to spend with me but I treasured each second we were together. She'd walked past me when she'd arrived this time and told me to give her an hour.

I was pretty sure that meant she wasn't visiting for fun—which was a shame. I had no idea how I was going to explain, "By the way, I just scared off the child-threatening dregs of the U.S. army at the cemetery. Oh, and I also killed a Federal agent. That won't have repercussions, I'm sure."

Case woke up with a start and pulled out a high-tech gun from under a pillow, aiming it every direction in a quick sweep. Thankfully, he didn't fire.

"Ah, morning PTSD," I said, pausing. "How did they even program that into a robot?"

Not my nicest statement but I was having a spectacularly crappy day. It wasn't even noon yet and I'd made an enemy of the U.S. government. Because, really, I wasn't stupid enough to buy that they were backing off. They were just waiting for me to let my guard down and I was pretty sure they wouldn't wait more than a few hours. The last time I'd been an enemy of the state they'd blown up a good chunk of the mansion. This time? This time would be worse.

I could feel it.

Case glared at me and put the gun away. "No one pro-grammed my nightmares. I've earned them the same way other people have."

"Shouldn't you be going back to your magical world of mega-corps, holographic babes, cheese-in-a-can, and super-slums?"

Case was from Earth-C, a reality where pretty much every William Gibson and Ridley Scott movie was real. Okay, not *Robin Hood*. It was a cyberpunk world without superheroes but sport-ing plenty of villains. Life was cheap there and it had been Case's job to charge for it. Much to my surprise, he preferred to live in my world. The thing was, I wasn't sure that it was possible for him to stay indefinitely. I would have let him if it was up to me.

"Cheese-in-a-can is what stuck out about my world to you?"

"I miss it so much in this world and yet cannot find it at my local grocery store anymore!" I said, raising my hands. "I lived off that stuff in college."

Case felt his head with both hands. "Your priorities are deeply skewed. Also, I remind you there's a thing called the Internet you can order it off of."

"I note you're dodging the question about returning home." Case and Jane Doe had been brought from their respective universes by Death to fight in the Eternity Tournament. Strangely, unlike me and my group, they'd been taken in astral form. In simple terms, their bodies were lying back on their homeworlds. Jane was in a sweat lodge and Case was hooked up to a virtual reality simulator. Theoretically, when and if they decided to go home, they'd return to the exact moment they'd left with a whole bunch of new memories.

You know, like the Chronicles of Narnia. Neither of them expressed much of a desire to do so. For Jane, it was because she'd bonded with my daughters as their nanny (God, I had a nanny— I was officially part of the bourgeoisie) while Case stayed here for Jane. Both had romantic partners they'd left behind, which would have appalled me, were I a massive hypocrite.

Case stated his reluctance to leave upfront. "Even if it's getting nastier and grimier, your world is still a colorful world of superheroes, magic, and super-science. I'll take that over my hellhole Earth any day."

"Said someone who has never lived through a zombie apocalypse followed by their evil twin coming to kill them."

"My evil twin *has* tried to kill me," Case pointed out.

I ignored his response. "Come on, you can come back anytime you want to. I'll even help you settle back into your world. We can do some Runner missions where we rob big corporations, kill the evil executives out to bulldoze the slum, and steal vital information for shadowy employers only to be double-crossed."

"You're describing my Tuesdays, Gary. Also, you don't get talk to me about retiring from being a badass mercenary while you're retired."

I raised my hand and made a shadowy cloak appear around me with my regular magic. I wasn't anywhere near the world's strongest wizard, not even in the top 100, but I had my PHD in sorcery. Powers, Hexes, and Deviltry.

"I'm not retired anymore," I said, simply. Then I faked excitement. "Merciless is back, baby!"

The Henchbots all released a cheer and started running around the room. Two of them collided and knocked each other out. I wasn't sure if Leia had programmed them to be endearingly clumsy or there were just limits to what level of balance a seven-year-old could install in downloaded open source artificial intelligence.

"Are you sure we're not going to be sued for those?" Case asked. "I mean I love the *Despicable—*"

"Shh, don't mention the name," I said. "We can defend against any foe except the copyright office. Besides, Leia has a plan."

"Your seven-year-old has a plan?"

"Yes, nuke the studios if they object."

"*Does* she have a nuke?" With anyone else, I'm sure Case would have assumed I was joking.

I looked sideways. "She doesn't *not* have a nuke."

"Gary!" Case said, fully believing my joke.

"What? I needed to give her something for her birthday! She only uses it to threaten people!"

"I literally don't know whether you're joking!"

I threw out my hands. "Of course, I'm joking! She built her own! She got the nuclear material from one thousand glow-in-the-dark Ultragoddess stickers!"

"Oh, Jesus."

"Yeah, I think someone needs to sue that company for potential health hazards. I may own it, though." The scary thing was, I was only half-joking. I'd managed to stop her before she built the launching mechanism.

Case felt his face as one of the Henchbots handed him his finely pressed clothing. He started getting dressed. "Okay, okay. So, what inspired you to get back into the supervillain game? I mean, I thought you were done-done."

Case, once dressed, managed to look more handsome than most Hollywood stars after hours of makeup. All his cybernetic enhancements were below the surface, so he was more like a Terminator than Darth Vader. Honestly, I wasn't anxious to kick him out of my home since it was good to have someone around who had gone through something similar to my own experiences… at least in terms of being the bad guy until you were honestly sick of it. I just hoped that I could knock some evil back into him the way the Feds had just done to me.

"Well, a bunch of government stooges from the Department of Harassing People came to Mandy's grave and blew it all to hell," I explained. "I may have killed one of them and scared the President into declaring I don't exist."

I wasn't a big fan of President Karl Trust. He'd been elected in the emergency following President Omega's declaration of war against everyone and everything. He was a celebrity media mogul and ex-Governor of Florida that embodied the worst of the Right and Left. His only platform was to make sure things ran smoothly, and if that included pretending problems like me didn't exist, then so be it. I'd heard he'd done the same for other supervillains as well as a few heroes. Most of his platform consisted of declaring superheroes a menace, but at the same time protecting their rights, which strangely made him a moderate.

"You killed a Federal agent!?" an angry female voice spoke from down the hall. "Goddammit, Gary, you can't do things like that!"

I turned around and blinked as I saw Cindy Wackowski wearing an avocado mask, a bathrobe, a weird set of clippings in her hair, and a necklace of life-crystals bought from the most expensive Useless New Age Medicine stores. She'd also had her nails and toes done by the look of cotton and red around them. Standing behind her was Jane Doe, a.k.a Weredeer, holding the tiny form of my daughter Mindy.

Jane Doe was a short, svelte, bowl-cut young woman who still looked like she could win a few Olympic events thanks to the fact lycanthropy (cervidthropy?) gave you tight abs and muscular thighs. She looked, basically, how Chun Li would look if she was Anglo-Odawa American instead of Chinese. That meant she was part Native American, part Canadian, part deer. It explained where all my organic maple syrup kept going. Seriously, the girl drank it out of the bottle with a straw.

"It just happened, okay!" I said, throwing up my hands.

Jane shook her head. "Seriously, you can't just kill a Federal officer. On my world, that brings down reprisals, arrests, investigations—"

"Not without me, you can't!" Cindy interrupted.

"Wait, what?" Jane did a double take.

"Do you know how boring it's been just lying up here surrounded by endless stolen millions, my every need waited on, and adored by millions of Internet followers?" Cindy asked.

"Oh, you poor thing," I muttered.

"I've had three reality shows while you've been lying around, doing nothing! I had to hire a couple of Gary impersonators to do evil stuff in the background," Cindy said.

"I wondered who those guys were," I said, rubbing my chin. "What about Mr. Inventor?"

Cindy waved a hand. "He has to go help people. What about helping me? I would have invited the Backstreet Boys to seduce, but I know your policy of killing all boy bands."

"It's for the greater good," I said.

"The who?" Jane asked.

"Before your time, Jane," Case said.

"Is that why you're getting, uh, all beautied up?" I asked, waving at her.

"Pfft," Cindy said. "Spoken like a man who doesn't have to spend twenty-four/seven focused on making sure she looks presentable in a villainess costume. It's nonstop calorie management, electrolyte treatments, and Jazzercize."

"Jazzercize?" I repeated, surprised anyone still did that.

"How do you and Case keep looking like you do? You live off doughnuts and him Jack Daniel's?" Cindy asked.

"Well, I'm a machine," Case said.

"Eh, I use magic to stay young and beautiful," I said, shrugging. "Magic is the cheat code to the universe and I freely take advantage of it."

Cindy muttered something about science catching up with me someday. "What about you, Jane? You live off Mountain Dew. Not the kind of mountain dew deer drink either."

"Weredeer burn ten thousand calories a day," Jane said, shrugging. "I have to eat piles of salt and fries with every meal."

Cindy glared at Jane. "No one asked you."

"You just—" Jane started to say.

"Well, I've decided to get back into supervillainy! I shall rob from the rich and give most to the poor! I shall humiliate the

corrupt and prank the peerless! As for the really evil? I will horribly murder them and laugh at any consequences."

"Great example you're setting for your kid," Jane said, rolling her eyes.

"Kill Nazis," Mindy said, cheerfully.

"Please tell me those aren't her first words," Case said,
grimacing.

"Why?" I asked, knowing they weren't, but very proud they
were her sixth or seventh. "It's the best sign of Cindy's parent-
ing yet. I can't wait to see what she teaches our grandchildren."

"That's it," Cindy said, waving her hand. "I am no longer
going to age! Gary, contact me a vampire."

I stared at her. "Cindy, we're not contacting a vampire."

The mental trauma I'd suffered watching what I'd thought
was Mandy become a soulless abomination was something that
still haunted my nightmares. Vampires were not cool or attractive creatures to me but horrible monsters. Because they had
about as much sex appeal as a walking corpse.

"I'm aging, Gary!" Cindy said, looking at me. "I used to be
twenty-something Julia Stiles hot. Now I'm—"

"Thirty-something Julia Stiles hot?" I suggested.

"Who *is* Julia Stiles?" Jane asked. "Is she an actress?"

Case shook his head.

"Jane, be less young," I said, sighing.

"Yes, do that!" Cindy snapped. "Wait, do weredeer live
forever?"

"No," Jane said.

"You still age slowly," Cindy said, stretching out her arm.
"Bite me and infect me with your lame shifter disease."

Jane's eyes narrowed and there was a look of pure supernatural fury behind them.

"Lame shifter disease? We are not diseased!"

"Well, I don't have anything cool around like a werewolf to
bite me!" Cindy snapped. "Werewolf women can still be hot.
Anna Paquin was one."

"Anna Paquin is a werewolf in this world?" Jane asked, confused. "Sweet."

That was the problem with having conversations with my

friends. No matter how urgent a topic you might be discussing, everything rapidly degenerated into nothing more than a series of digressions. It was like *The Life and Opinions of Tristram Shandy, Gentleman.* That was a literature reference to Thomas Jefferson's favorite novel about an author who could never get to the point. Consider yourself to be slightly more educated.

I raised my hands in the air and whistled for everyone's attention. "Listen, everybody, I need your complete and undivided attention."

"I need to change Mindy's diaper," Jane said.

I sighed in defeat. "Yeah, you do that. But, seriously, all I want is to know if anyone has seen Gabrielle. I need to tell her that I've decided to become a supervillain again. Given she's only at the mansion maybe a quarter of the time, it's important to catch her while I can."

Gabrielle was legally forbidden from superheroics in the United States, not that it prevented her from diverting nuclear missiles fired at it or fighting alien invasions. She instead devoted her time to building hydroelectric dams, stopping famines, and punching out other nations' collections of supervillains. It turned out most people didn't have the love/hate relationship with superheroes the U.S.A. did and were just happy to have people help out. Really, the only places she wasn't welcome were Russia and China. It turns out if you are pro-democracy and freedom of speech that those two places don't much like you trying to talk about them. North Korea, well what was left of it at least, had learned that the hard way.

Case looked at me. "Oh, is that what you were asking about?"

"Yes!" I snapped.

"She's in the living room," Case gestured with his thumb.

"Pppft zip zoop blah!" the Henchbots said, doing circles around us.

"Don't let them change Mindy's diaper," I said. "Even if she's an indestructible baby, as Cindy has demonstrated."

"I only dropped her a few times," Cindy said, looking guilty.

"She's meeting with the Pulp adventurers from Cthulhu world," Jane said, walking over to a door leading to one of the house's forty bathrooms.

"Cthulhu world?" I asked, wondering if we were having to deal with another alternate reality.

"Yeah, John and Mercury, they're a pair of superheroes I met in the tournament," Cindy said. "They're from a post-apocalyptic world where the Great Old Ones destroyed humanity. Basically, their world is like ours but what it would look like if we didn't have superheroes punching the giant godlike aliens."

"Ah," I said, grimacing. "Don't tell me they want to move in, too."

"No," Case said. "They want your help invading a lost kingdom."

"Oh, great," I said, rolling my eyes. "Because that's what I want to do with my day—go on one of those weird side-treks storytellers send their heroes on when they've run out of stories in the Big Cities."

"Apparently, the kingdom is overrun with Nazis," Case said. I blinked. "I'm in."

CHAPTER THREE

NAZIS IN THE CENTER OF THE EARTH

"Nazis. I hate these guys," I muttered.

Part of it is because I'm Jewish. Part of it is because I'm not a fan of white supremacists in general. But the thing that irritates me most about them is that they just won't frigging die out already. I don't throw around the Nazi label lightly either. On my world, it's not just an Internet insult.

There's a bunch of actual WW2 supervillains out there still partying like it's 1939 and have a distressing number of fanboys. People who fail to realize whether you do it "ironically" or not, waving the red and black flag is pretty much a declaration of intent. Either way, I have a simple rule when it comes to the *Sieg Heil* crowd. I kill them. I've even gone to multiple parallel Earths and killed Hitler dozens of times. Usually, that just meant someone much smarter took his place (Tom Terror and President Omega were the usual candidates) but I still consider it a net positive activity.

"Wait for me," Jane said, following me around with Mindy in hand.

"What, you want a piece of the action?" I asked, hoping it was a bloody and vicious mission Gabrielle brought to me.

"I'm a part-Native American, so yes," Jane said.

I blinked. "Did the Nazis do anything to the Native—"

Jane glared at me.

"Welcome aboard," I said, raising my hands in surrender.

Cindy waved me off while G followed at a discreet distance. My sister Kerri was at the supermarket. As mentioned, I hadn't seen Diabloman in a year and it was bothering me that he hadn't even tried to stay in touch. I knew his guilt over his sister's death—okay, murdering her—was a big deal but she was back now, so hopefully he'd get over it. Yeah, maybe it wasn't the best logic, but I missed the big guy.

I pushed open the doors to the Warren Estate's study and found myself in a room that looked like a movie set. There was a huge six-foot-in-diameter globe next to the door, two stories' worth of bookshelves, framed maps, and some black-and-white photos from Uther Warren's days adventuring with Allan Quatermain. Uther Warren was the least racist Great White Hunter who ever lived (that was serious damning with faint praise) and the architect of the Warren Family fortune.

The room had numerous leopard-print sofas, couches, and chairs that were, thankfully, all fake. Apparently, either Uther Warren wasn't really that good of a hunter (though a genius at negotiating trade deals) or his descendants didn't like sitting on murdered exotic animals. I say that as a carnivore by the way.

There were four people present in the room, only one of whom I recognized.

The first of them was Gabrielle Anders, the mother of my second child and one of the three women I'd loved in my life (yes, I'm aware that's selfish). She was a beautiful brown-haired woman of mixed African and Latino descent. Gabrielle wasn't wearing her Ultragoddess outfit, but a sweater, headband, and skirt that made her look like a grad student from the Sixties. She was the daughter of the late Ultragod and ace reporter Polly Perkins, as blue a blood among superheroes as you could get. Why she was with me, if she was with me, was anyone's guess.

The other three individuals were, indeed, characters out of Pulp novels. Well, characters who looked like movie characters based on old Pulp novels. The first of them was a tall, muscular black man with a Stetson hat and a duster. There was an aura about him like I'd sensed in the Death Orb and his shadow had tentacles that moved on their own. Basically, he was something magical and terrifying like the Great Beasts that lived between dimensions.

Standing beside him was a black-haired woman who very

much resembled an Asian Lara Croft, the reboot version versus original shorts and tank top version. I sensed an aura of magic coming from her equivalent to my own (i.e. a solid B-lister). Finally, there was a muscular blonde woman dressed in animal furs and face-paint who looked like Frank Frazetta had drawn her, and then given her more clothes. She had a feathered spear in hand.

"Hello, Gary," Gabrielle said, looking at me as if she half expected me to be covered in someone's blood.

"What?" I asked, wondering why I was getting the stink eye.

"Ahem," Gabrielle gestured down to my feet.

Then I looked down at my shoes and saw they were covered in gore. "Oh, right. I should have cleaned off the guy I murdered before I came in."

Gabrielle felt her face. "Oh, Gary."

"Believe me when I say he had it coming," I said, raising my hands.

"Killing people is—"

"He threatened Mindy and Leia," I said. "He said he was going to put them down."

Gabrielle stared. "I'm not going to say you did the right thing, but I'm not going to say you did the wrong thing either."

Ultragoddess was a bit more hardcore than her father, Ultragod. Most superheroes believed the Ultragod Family were paragons of "Thou Shall Not Kill." The truth was that they tried hard not to kill people, but if it was a choice between killing someone or saving innocent lives, they chose the latter. The difference between them and me was that they weren't *executioners*. If you were subdued, be you misguided antihero or monster, they left you alone. It's the only reason Tom Terror is still breathing. I consider that unfortunate.

"I take it those are your kids?" Asian Lara Croft asked. Wait, was that racist? Woman who *looked* like an Asian Lara Croft? Okay, I just needed to ask her name.

"Her kid and a half," I said, shrugging. "Mindy is her child with me and she's Leia's stepmother except for the part about not being married to me. We're a modern Space Age family."

I wasn't even sure how our relationship presently stood

since she stopped by for booty calls and the occasional date but was soon off to cap volcanos or knock meteorites off their course. It wasn't exactly the most stable relationship and had disrupted just about every other one I was involved in. I still loved her.

"I love Leia like my own," Gabrielle said.

"You can have her at a reasonably low price!" Cindy said, walking in. She was wearing her full Red Riding Hood costume and her hair perfect. I did a double take.

Jane stepped away from Cindy, holding Mindy protectively. Gabrielle then snatched her away with a glowing Ultra-Force energy field that gently levitated her daughter into her arms.

"You are like the worst mother ever," I said, shaking my head.

"Not true as long as my mother is alive and suffering in the shitty nursing home I've got her under guard at," Cindy said. "That reminds me, I need to borrow the car so I can go down there to gloat over her paralyzed form. I also need to whip up the drugs to make sure she stays that way."

Cindy didn't like her mom. I don't know if you, the audience, picked up on that. Something about selling her into prostitution as a pre-teen. Yeah. Her backstory is surprisingly dark for such a fun gal.

"Real bunch of winners you have here," the tall black man with the creepy shadow said. Okay, seriously, I had to introduce myself.

"Hello, I am Gary Karkofsky, a.k.a Merciless: The Supervillain without Mercy! I make the villains fall down! Also, heroes."

Okay, not my best introduction.

The newcomers exchanged a glance.

"Yeah, we know that," the Asian woman said. "That's why we came here to get your help."

"And you are?" I asked, wondering who my new fans were.

"They're John Henry Booth and Mercury Halsey Takahashi," Cindy said, as if this was perfectly apparent.

"Wait, the protagonists from the *Cthulhu Armageddon* books?" I asked, surprised. "The cheesy post-apocalypse fantasy novels?"

"Protagonists?" Mercury asked.

"Everyone's fiction is real somewhere," Case explained to them. "It's weird but an actual idea in string theory."

"A sure sign of why most quantum physics is probably the result of copious pot use," Cindy replied. "I'm dating like two physicists right now."

"The *Cthulhu Armageddon* books by C.T. Phipps?" I continued, surprised. "I *hate* that guy! He just makes cheesy one-liners and sets his books as parodies of other, more interesting works. Like H.P. Lovecraft and you guys."

"Huh?" John asked.

"Cthulhuworld," I pointed out. "That's where you're from, right?"

Both Mercury and John flinched at the name of Cthulhu.

"Oh, right, because he's real in your world," I said, making finger guns. "He's not a guy you adapted to plush toys and house slippers."

"Cthulhu is a monster. It's killed billions," John said, dryly.

I grimaced. "Right, I'll try not to mention him, Yog-Sothoth, Azathoth, Shug-Niggurath, Nyarlathotep—"

Mercury and John looked ready to duck under the nearest table.

"Hastur, Hastur again, Hastur for a third time and yet he doesn't appear. I always thought that was cool, even if Beetlejuice and Candyman stole it. The Color from Outer Space, shoggoths, the Elder Things, the Deep Ones—"

John pulled out his sidearm and shot in the air. Little bits of plaster from the room's ceiling rained down on us.

"Oh," I said, pausing. "Is this bothering you?"

John narrowed his eyes.

"I'll take that as a yes," I said, shrugging. Yeah, it's true I just can't stop being a jackass no matter how hard I try—which usually isn't very hard.

"I absolutely love the works of H.P. Lovecraft except for the racism and sexism. At least he had the presence of mind to marry a Jewish woman."

"You seem oddly familiar with a semi-famous writer from the early twentieth century," John said.

"I'm a white male tabletop roleplaying gamer who played in the early Nineties," I said, shrugging. "He casts a big shadow in my circles even if he never made it mainstream. Mindy sleeps with a little doll of him."

"I find that horrifying," John said.

"Idols help ward off evil spirits," the girl dressed like central casting's idea of a sexy primitive tribeswoman said.

Gabrielle held Mindy close. "They need your help, Gary."

"I didn't think they were dropping by here for a social call," I said, frowning. "Only my friends do that. Then they never leave. By the way, Jane, Case, I'm referring to you."

"Yeah, I got that," Jane said, rolling her eyes.

"So, what do you want, and how does it deal with Nazis I can kill?" I paused. "I'm up for anything involving getting out of the country and killing fascists. Mostly because I'm probably going to be a fugitive here soon."

"Are you sure this is the guy you want to help us?" John asked Gabrielle.

"He's usually less...murdery," Gabrielle said.

"I'm not complaining, just asking," John said. "Fuck Nazis."

Okay, I was starting to like these people. Even if they did come from a silly world.

"So who are you?" I asked the blonde woman with the spear.

"I am Reyan," the blonde woman finally spoke. "I am the Champion of Nub'Ab'Sul."

"Not familiar with that locale, Swedish-looking tribal person," I said.

"They're the descendants of Vikings who descended the tunnels of Hel to the Hollow Earth," the woman said.

I blinked. "The Hollow Earth?"

"Yes, the center of the Earth is actually a big glowing orb that is surrounded by a hollow sphere that has its own ecosystem built on the interior. It's a place full of dinosaurs, jungles, lost civilizations, and alien peoples that predate the evolution of humanity."

"And why haven't I heard of this place?" I asked, blinking. "I mean aside from the fact that it violates everything we know about geology."

"Now you're complaining about the laws of science?" Case asked, glancing at me. "In a universe where people fly?"

"What's weird about people flying?" I asked, confused. Case shook his head.

"So, the Nazis are invading the Hollow Earth?" I asked, confused. "Also, how do the Cthulhu people fit into this?"

"Please stop calling us that," Mercury said.

"I'm just asking—why me?" I'm not exactly the kind of person you'd go to for most of your heroics. Hell, Gabrielle is at the top of the list and she was right there. It's not like any superhero ever turned down a round of Nazi bashing. Even with the death of Ultragod, the Nightwalker, Nighthuntress (oh, Mandy), Sunlight, the Prismatic Commando—okay, I was just starting to realize that a lot of heroes were dead.

"We'll get to that. First, you have to know what the situation is," Reyan said. "Five years ago, our world was invaded by P.H.A.N.T.O.M. Our people managed to drive off the Nazis when they invaded during WWII, but they made random incursions in between. This time, they came to stay. They brought tanks, gunships, rocket-packs, and energy weapons. Close to ten thousand warriors set themselves up in our land before enslaving city after city. They put the people to work in mines and dig sites, attempting to unearth the ancient Pre-Atlantean ruins in search of something. We think it might be ancient Ultranian technology."

P.H.A.N.T.O.M was the world's largest terrorist organization. They were composed of ex-Nazis wielding weapons provided for them to by aliens like the Tsavong and Thran. The group had been kicking around since 1945 and never quite managed to be completely wiped out despite the entire world standing against them. Several times their defeat had been declared, only for them to slither off into their hole and rebuild. The Society of Superheroes thought they'd really been wiped out, five years earlier. I wasn't surprised to find out they'd just relocated.

"The Ultranians created the Hollow Earth as a refuge for dying peoples," Gabrielle explained. "Also for species that might otherwise be lost to history. They abandoned the facility centuries ago but left behind much of their advanced equipment.

Some of this equipment is capable of visiting parallel worlds."
Jane and Case exchanged a glance.
"Which is where you guys come in," I pointed to John and
Mercury.
"Yes," John said, his voice deep and heavy like James Earl
Jones. "Our world is a devastated wasteland, but it has power-
ful magical relics they're utilizing to harness the power of the
Smoky God, their miniature sun. They've also taken a lot of
slaves from our world. We followed them back through their
portal to rescue our people."
"It's also an opportunity," Mercury said. "Once we've dealt
with P.H.A.N.T.O.M, that world would be a perfect place to settle
the survivors of our own. There's not many left and this planet
isn't overrun by the Great Old Ones."
"I'm pretty sure the locals will object," Gabrielle said, perhaps hoping to head off the Age of Imperialism 2.0.
"We will be happy to let some of them stay," Reyan said.
"As long as they don't bring smallpox, venereal disease, or false
religions. We worship the one true god Odin and his relations."
"Yes," Jane interjected. "Make sure you give any and all
European-descended people hand sanitizer. You won't regret
it."
"Right, so Nazis in the center of the Earth, stealing crap, and
doing their usual Nazi thing. Go kill them. So far, this is very
straightforward."
"You have a different definition of straightforward than I
do," Case said, looking over at me.
I waved him away. "What's the catch? Why are you coming to me? I mean, this seems like a typical job for the Society
of Superheroes. They are, after all, a literal army of good guys
meant to take down threats no one hero can accomplish."
Last I checked, the Society of Superheroes had been taken
over by Ultragodling. Ultragod's foster son and boy sidekick
(now a man in his late forties) had replaced Guinevere and taken
the organization in a more militant, pro-government direction. He hadn't gotten superheroes authorized to operate in the
United States yet but was close. I didn't like the guy, since he
considered me to have stained Gabrielle's honor or something.

Gabrielle played with Mindy's nose before answering. "That's the catch. We didn't come to you first, Gary. The Society of Superheroes went to liberate the Hollow Earth last week. I was there. We lost. They've all been captured by P.H.A.N.T.O.M."

CHAPTER FOUR

ON OUR WAY TO THE HOLLOW EARTH

"Say what?" I asked, stunned. "The Society of Superheroes has been captured?"

"Is that bad?" Jane asked.

"On a scale of one to ten, it's about a million," I said, trying to wrap my head around it. "Are they missing or dead?"

Ever since the day I'd won the Tournament of Supervillainy, I had harbored a very real fear that this day would come: the day when the superheroes lost completely. Before I'd made my stupid wish to make death permanent, the Primal known as Destruction had kept the war between good and evil a stalemate. Villains would always escape imprisonment and heroes would always rally back after defeats. Even death was a minor inconvenience (for "interesting" people at least). No one could win and the only people who would permanently suffer were those caught in the crossfire.

I thought things would get better once consequences were real. That good would triumph over evil and we could make the world a better place. I hadn't really thought the bad guys would get the upper hand. I was, in simple terms, a complete moron for thinking this.

"Missing," Gabrielle said, sighing. "Ultragodling led the Society of Superheroes straight into a P.H.A.N.T.O.M ambush. It was a hard fight, but the Smokey God is a kind of giant magical battery that saps the power of any non-mystical heroes. The rest put up a valiant fight, but P.H.A.N.T.O.M has its own mystical corps in the Ghostappo."

Jane lifted her hand. "Hold on a second, it's actually called the *Ghostappo?*"

"Yes," Gabrielle said. "It's a play on Gesta—"

"Yeah, I get that, but it's only a pun that makes sense in English," Jane interjected.

"Technically, it would be *Geistappo* in Germany," Case said, speaking dozens of languages thanks to his built-in Babelfish. "Which sorta works I guess, but—"

"Are we actually arguing about puns here?" Gabrielle asked, shaking her head.

"Puns are serious business for weredeer," I pointed out. "They're like garlic to vampires."

"It is the stupidest weakness of all time," Jane pointed out. "However, we can't resist them. They call to us like...puns to a weredeer."

Yeah, Jane isn't very good at speaking in metaphor. She could, however, make puns out of words like rutabaga. No, I'm not sharing it. You had to be there.

"So, you were there?" I asked Gabrielle. "I mean, fighting alongside Ultragodling in the Hollow Earth."

Gabrielle nodded. "He prefers to be called Captain Ultra now."

"I'm sure he does," I said, genuinely hurt by her actions. "Not the point."

Gabrielle looked confused. "What *is* the point?"

"You were going to risk yourself against an army of P.H.A.N.T.O.M goons and didn't think to take me? I know you can handle most things, Gabby, but maybe you should have your partner when the big team-up events happen."

Jane leaned over and whispered to Case, "Does it weird you out that they talk like they're in a comic book even though they're real people?"

"Everything about this world weirds me out," Case said. "It's why I love it."

"Hush, you two," I said, not turning to face them. "Comic books are high art on my world."

Gabrielle looked guilty. "You haven't been yourself for a while, Gary."

"Yeah, mourning a dead wife will do that," Cindy said, crossing her arms. "So, Nubile Savage Lady, if we save your kingdom, do you have any awesome statues of gold or magical doohickeys that bestow eternal youth on beautiful educated professionals like myself?"

"We don't need to be paid to fight P.H.A.N.T.O.M, Cindy," I said, looking at her. "Punching fascists is its own reward."

"No," Cindy said, pointing. "Uh-huh, Gary. We're not going down that road."

"What road?" I asked.

"I've put up with a lot of selfless altruistic bullshit over the years. Fighting bad guys, giving away more than a tax write-off's portion of our loot, and hanging around superheroes, but we're not doing anything—even fighting P.H.A.N.T.O.M—for free. We have standards to uphold," Cindy said, pointing at me. "Or violate. We are villains, goddammit and that means something."

"They actually call themselves villains here?" Mercury asked, looking at John.

"They live in mansions, eat regularly, and don't have to worry about monsters eating them," John said, shrugging. "The rich have always been a little strange."

"It's the least strange thing about this place," Jane said.

"The strangest thing is when cartoon animals show up," Case said. "Though we were all being poisoned by Doctor Feelgreat at the time."

"Good times," Cindy said, smiling.

"Do not mock Mouseless," I said, pointing at them. "The Mouse without Mercy™ is a dear friend."

"Cindy, you're better than this," Gabrielle said, her voice soft and reassuring. "You want to help us for free."

"I'm really not," Cindy insisted. She then pointed at Jane. "Do you know how pathetic I've become because of my looming old age? I've considered letting myself get infected by the weredeer disease!"

"Weredeer are not diseased!" Jane snapped.

"Who knows what ticks and weird stuff you carry in that short brown hair of yours!" Cindy said. "No, if I'm helping, I want some of that Ultranian underground super-science to make me young and sexy forever. I need to avoid lime disease if I'm going to be around Jane."

"That's it!" Jane grabbed a two-hundred-pound cheetah-print couch and swung it at her. Case, in the way, ducked.

Cindy, being absurdly acrobatic, dodged out of the way with a backflip.

"Is this normal around here?" Mercury asked.

"I dunno," I said, ignoring their antics behind me. "What generally happens in your world when you meet new and untrustworthy people?"

"I shoot them in the face," John said.

I blinked. "Okay."

"Sometimes I hex them," Mercury said. "A few even like it."

I waved. "Anyway, we'll work on the payment issue later. I'll pay Cindy myself if I have to."

John raised his hand. "Don't. I wouldn't ask you to go on a mission like this for free. We're not savages who depend on the kindness of strangers."

I nodded. "Bust a deal, get the wheel. It's the law of Thunderdome."

Gabrielle looked offended. "Surely, we can persuade them to act out of the kindness of their hearts."

"I love killing slavers back where I'm from, but I still charge for it," John said, having the same attitude toward them I do toward fascists. "P.H.A.N.T.O.M has assembled a vast treasure of stolen loot from temples, palaces, and other worlds. We split it four ways. Half of it goes back to its original owners. The other half we can divide between our two groups."

"So, you and Mercury get twenty-five percent and my entire gang gets the same?" I asked, looking over at Cindy and Jane. Case was filming their fight with his cellphone.

"SPINNING DEER KICK!" Jane shouted.

"TASER!" Cindy replied, equally loud.

"That's cheating!" Jane said, following a shocking noise.

"Villain!" Cindy gloated.

"Could you do some more hair-pulling?" Case asked. "Maybe tear at each other's clothing? HEY! WATCH WHERE YOU THROW THAT COUCH."

I looked back at them. "Sounds good. I can assure you we have nothing but the best people here."

"Uh-huh," Mercury said. Under her breath she added, "This is a horrible mistake and we are all going to die."

Clearly, she was the brains of this outfit.

"I do not care about the trinkets of gold and jewels that P.H.A.N.T.O.M has looted," Reyan said, narrowing her eyes. "I only ask that one item be returned to my people: The Eye of Odin."

"Like his literal eye? The one he sacrificed for great wisdom?" I asked, just wanting to be clear.

Everyone looked at me.

"What? You think I can talk at great lengths about the works of H.P. Lovecraft but don't know basic Norse mythology?" I asked.

Everyone continued to look at me, giving me my answer.

"You guys suck," I said.

"The Eye of Odin is my people's most sacred relic," Reyan continued, apparently not aware that I'd heard a lot of similar stories over the years. Every tribe had a sacred relic the Nazis were after, including my twelve tribes and a certain ark. "It bestows the wearer with great mystical might and allows him, or her, to dominate lesser wills completely. It can also open doorways to other worlds. Their leader, the Supreme Phantom, is using it to prepare for something—"

"Probably something nasty," I said, interrupting her. "They're *Nazis*. Of course, it's global or universal domination. You'll get your eye, don't worry. I'll just pry it out of their leader's socket once I've killed him."

That was the only good thing about fascists. You could kill them in horrifying ways, and nobody cared. Well, maybe their parents did, but then again, they raised fascists, so who cared what they thought?

"Killing the Supreme Phantom may be harder than it sounds," Gabrielle said, sounding concerned.

"You remember I've beaten Space Gods, right?" I asked, referring to Entropicus. "Also, my own version of Cth-Not-Mentioning-The-Rest-Of-The-Guy's-Name-Thulhu in Zul-Barbas the Great Beast. I think I can take on a magically empowered terrorist leader."

"It's Tom Terror," Gabrielle explained. "The Supreme Phantom is Tom Terror."

"Ah," I said, sucking in my breath. "That does change things."

Tom Terror was the O.G. supervillain. *The Supervillain* in many people's eyes. While there had been Moriartys and Fu Manchus before, he was the archetype all others would be compared to. The original mad scientist out to conquer the world, Tom Terror had tried hundreds of times to kill Ultragod and bring the world to its knees. He'd come pretty close on multiple occasions and had often only been undone by time travel or other "cheating." I'd encountered him only once before and he'd come within inches of killing me, Ultragod, and every other hero in the Society of Superheroes.

"You still in?" John asked, clearly not knowing me very well.

"You bet I am," I said, looking at him.

"There's more," Gabrielle said, sounding like she didn't want to tell me the next part. It wasn't the kind of attitude I expected from the World's Strongest Woman.

"More than a bunch of Nazis have captured the world's greatest superheroes and rule over Edgar Rice Burroughs' Jurassic Park?" I asked.

"What else am I missing?" I said, knowing it had to be bad if Gabrielle hesitated to tell me. She'd come to me when her father had been killed, when the Society of Superheroes had turned against her, and when she'd discovered she was with child—admittedly, the last one because I'd helped with that.

"It wasn't just the Society of Superheroes down there. It was an Alpha Protocol level attack. All hands on deck. So the Texas Guardians were there with us. That means—"

"My niece," I said, realizing what she was talking about. "My niece, Lisa, was with your team that got themselves captured by Nazis. My Jewish niece."

I fell back into a chair behind me. The magic inside my form spilled out, rotting and corroding the chair until it was black and desiccated. I closed my eyes. I was feeling a tranquil fury now, arguably one even more intense than when the dumbasses outside threatened my children.

Lisa Karkofsky, a.k.a Sparkler, was the daughter of my late brother Keith. Keith had been Stingray the Underwater Assassin. Unlike her father and uncle, she hadn't become a supervillain. Instead, she'd become the superhero Sparkler and was working with their teen superhero branch.

"You left her?" I asked, sounding more like an accusation than I intended.

"I left a lot of people," Gabrielle said, looking down at the ground. "She was still alive when I saw her, but there nothing I could do."

I kept my mouth shut. No matter how much I wanted to berate her. "Alright, then," I said, "let's get going."

"It's a seven-day journey to the North Pole and down through the Tunnel of Freya," Reyan said. "At least the way we traveled."

A week. Great. Lisa had been in the hands of Nazis for a week. This just kept getting better and better.

"What about Mr. Inventor? Alex?" Cindy asked, having stopped her ridiculous behavior.

"He was there, too, along with Diabloman," Gabrielle answered. "Galahad Alexander Warren was badly injured, though. He took the brunt of a concussion grenade while trying to save my life."

"Yeah, he's always doing stupid stuff like that," Cindy said, frowning.

"It wasn't stupid," Gabrielle said.

"Were you still invulnerable?" Cindy asked.

"Err, yes."

"Then it was stupid," Cindy said.

I was smart enough not to agree. "I don't suppose there's any way we could speed up our way to the Hollow Earth?"

"I can cast a teleportation spell, but I don't have the juice to

take us all there on my own," Mercury said. "Got any powerful magical artifacts I could borrow some power from? I mean,
just in case human sacrifice is off the table."

Everyone looked at her.

"I said off!" Mercury said, defensively. "They'd be bad people anyway."

"Will this do it?" I asked, lifting the Death Orb. My car
keys jingled beneath it, along with a little cartoon version of
the Super-Duper Splotch.

Mercury stared at it with the kind of hungry gaze a villain in an Indiana Jones movie did when confronted with the
McGuffin.

"Yeah, that'll do it," Mercury said.

"Case, Jane, I need you to look after the kids while I'm
gone," I said. "And my sister when she returns from the store.
If she doesn't, you will probably have to go to war with the
U.S. government."

Case nodded. "As you wish, Gary. It's not the first time I've
gone to war with them."

"Are you serious? You're going to leave us while you go off
to Tarzan-land to all the guys who look like Chris Hemsworth
in loincloths?" Jane asked, appalled.

"Vivid image," Cindy said.

"Thank you," Jane said.

I stared at her. "I only trust you two to take care of my
children."

Jane took a deep breath. "But I'm charging a share of the
treasure."

"Oh, dear," I muttered "However will I afford it."

"This deal gets worse all the time," Cindy muttered "I wish
I'd gotten vast amounts of treasure for babysitting."

Mindy reached out to Cindy.

"Stop being adorable," Cindy said, covering her face. "It
invokes weird and unnatural feelings like caring for babies."

I smiled then turned to Cindy. "Are you coming?"

"To a place with no indoor plumbing, electricity, and for
no certain reward?" Cindy asked. "Of course I am, Gary.
Someone's got to watch your back. I would never abandon

Lisa, Diabloman, or Alex either. I may be a terrible mother, but I am an incredibly good lover. Plus, Galahad is loaded. If he dies down there before we're married, I'm not going to get a cent."

Oh, Cindy, never change.

CHAPTER FIVE

JOURNEY TO THE CENTER OF THE EARTH PART DEUX

It didn't take much effort for Mercury to conjure her portal to the Hollow Earth. Indeed, I made it a point to memorize the magic she displayed. I didn't know if I could duplicate it, but the Death Orb allowed me to cheat and cast well beyond my level, so to speak.

"It's beautiful," I said, whispering.

"It's a living world," John said. "Of course, it's beautiful."

I stared at the glowing portal through space and time that had been conjured in my study. It showed a beautiful jungle-filled land with an enormous sun four times the size of "ours" hanging before a skyline that contained more verdant paradise behind it. It was like being in the interior of a globe only the continents were surrounding the glowing center.

Pteranodons flew as I saw brachiosaurs and hadrosaurs eating the leaves of long-extinct trees. An active volcano was smoking in the background and, in the distance, I could see a stone city rising from the ground that was a little bit Aztec mixed with a little bit Egyptian. It was like Edgar Rice Burroughs had married the crazy Ancient Aliens guy and had a science baby.

"What's wrong with the dinosaurs?" Cindy said, squinting as she looked through the portal with me.

"What do you mean?" Mercury said, her hands glowing with the energy necessary to conjure the portal. The Death Orb hovered in front of her, enhancing her powers a dozen-fold.

"They have feathers," Cindy said.

"Yes, dinosaurs have feathers," John said, loading his revolvers.

"So, T-Rex is just a big chicken?" Cindy said, shaking her head. "Lame."

"Given they're still nine tons of feathered death, I'm going to say you may not quite appreciate how dangerous they are," John said.

"I once rode a cyborg T-Rex," I said, cheerfully. "I used it to fight Amazons."

"Did you know, historically, that the great monuments of ancient society were all garishly painted? Instead of the somber and stately grays we duplicated for the buildings in Washington, D.C., they were reds, yellows, and oranges," Leia said, standing beside me. She is the world's smartest six-year-old and probably the world's smartest everything. She was dressed in a little red jumpsuit with an M on the lapel. I'd had her henchgirl costume made specially for her and they doubled as her pajamas.

"So, the government screwed up even its buildings meant to look cool," Cindy said, surprise.

"You know the builders of the Washington Monument completely missed that obelisks were actually sacred monuments to the Pharaoh's penis," John said, pointing at me. "The Founding Fathers completely missed the ancients were not nearly as uptight as later Europeans."

"Please, not in front of my daughter," I said, looking at John. "Even though she's a telepath and probably has an utterly filthy mind at prepubescence."

"Guilty," Leia said, raising her tiny hand.

"What are you doing here?" I asked, turning to Leia and kneeling. "We're about to go someplace dangerous and I was going to leave without telling you."

Leia frowned. "You can't go to *Jurassic World* without me!"

"*Jurassic Park*, honey," I corrected her. "*Jurassic World* was the not-so-cheap knockoff they made to cash in on a classic film."

"But it had Chris Pratt and Bryce Dallas Howard," Cindy pointed out. "Which makes the movie twenty percent yummier."

"I'm sorry, honey, but it's too dangerous," I said, looking down at Leia. "That's why I'm going with the perfectly expendable people from a book series way less cool than mine."

"You have a book series?" John asked. "In my world, you're just a really lousy comic book that is filled with nothing but bad puns and incomprehensible pop culture references. Also, mysteriously being attractive to multiple beautiful women out of your league who don't mind sharing."

"He does have a point," Cindy said.

"He does not!" I snapped before realizing what he said. "Wait, my comic books survived the apocalypse?"

It was one of the weird elements of the Multiverse that everything that was fiction in one universe tended to be reality in another. Part of this was the manipulation of the Primals but another part is that fiction was inspired by everyone unconsciously picking up elements from other worlds. As such, in Jane and G's world I was a popular fictional icon while the same was in reverse for them in my world. Apparently, that applied to John and Mercury here. I wondered if I could tell them Idris Elba and Olivia Munn had been cast as them for the third Cthulhu Armageddon movie. Personally, I didn't see the resemblance.

"Unfortunately, yes, you do survive the apocalypse as a fictional character," John said, shaking his head. It was like he was embarrassed I was a cultural relic in his time. "One of my daughters really loved reading the fifteen or so that remained after the end of all things."

Huh, they were family men. "What do they think of you going out and risking your life to save the world?"

"They'd prefer not to die horribly so they approve of my saving the world," John said.

That was remarkably effective logic. "Are you guys going to be much longer?" Mercury said, sucking in her breath. "Because bending space and time to open a portal through reality is not actually that simple."

"Sorry!" I said, raising my hands. "I promise you, Leia, I'll be back safe and sound."

"But what if the government comes to murder me?" Leia asked, a question that I unfortunately couldn't lie to her about the ridiculousness of.

"They won't," I said, lying anyway.

"But I can nuke Washington, D.C. if they do, right?" Leia asked.

"No," I said, simply. "Only Congress."

"Gary!" Gabrielle said, walking in and having changed into a pair of clothes more appropriate for a safari. Sadly, they didn't include short-shorts like video games had taught me. We'd just have to leave that to Mercury.

"No WMDs before you're thirty," Cindy said, simply. "We've already bent the rules about you creating life without God. Don't make us take away your science privileges."

The Henchbots complained a little. I wondered if G also felt like that statement was racist since he was an Artificial American.

"Ah, shucks," Leia said, frowning. "I wish I was in the future with Big Leia." Big Leia was my daughter's future self who sometimes babysat herself as a child. It was a relationship that was, even by my standards, damn weird.

A year ago, I'd had an encounter with adult versions of Leia and Mindy. They had rescued me from my encounter with Entropicus following my very-very narrow victory. They'd asked me to do something, something that I couldn't do. Wouldn't do. Big Leia had created a mental block in my head so not even younger self could know what the request was they'd made.

"No time travel either," I said, only half-kidding. "Only I am allowed to break the laws of casualty for petty gain."

"We tried to use time travel once to save the world from the Great Old Ones," John said.

"It didn't take," Mercury muttered. "On the other hand, I rediscovered the bra. Very useful in the future."

"I'm sure it is," I said, turning to Gabrielle. "Are you sure you're ready to go back to the Hollow Earth? You won't have any powers there."

Gabrielle hoisted a rifle over her shoulder. "I was one of the leaders of the team. I got your sister and Diabloman captured."

"Also, Mr. Inventor," Cindy said. "He's my second favorite person in the world. Well, third after me. Well, fourth really with Gabrielle."

I looked at her. "After Leia?"

Cindy blinked. "Oh, right, fifth."

"I take it I'm the first?" I asked, deadpanning.

Cindy looked at me with true love in her eyes. "Gary, you gave me something more precious than anything anyone else has ever given me."

"A child?" I asked.

"Money!"

"Would it be wrong to rewrite your personality to make you a decent mother?" Leia asked, looking up.

Cindy knelt by Leia and smiled, putting her hand on her shoulder. "It's okay, Leia, because you *have* a decent mother. Gabrielle! Also, Kerri. The second-best part of being with Gary in our weird Abrahamic era relationship is that he comes with all sorts of people who can compensate for my many shortcomings."

"Wow, Mom, just wow," Leia said, disappointed.

"Remember, motherhood is all about blaming your children for your own screw-ups," Cindy said. "Pass that down to your own kids."

"At least I have a Freudian justification for when I overwhelm the world and establish my New Gizmo Order." Leia looked down at the ground.

"There's Freud in this house, Leia. We're Jungians. Freud leads to marrying your mother and killing your father and vice versa." I pulled Cindy back. "Let's get going."

"Finally," Mercury muttered, starting to sweat from maintaining the force of the spell. It was rather artful as if she'd been sprayed during a photo shoot. I had to wonder if she was using glamour or if it was just a side effect of the fact my world made every superhero and villain unreasonably pretty.

"Well, it gives you more time to steal my magic orb and become all-powerful," I said, causally. Personally, I was hoping she did steal it. The Orb of Death had brought me nothing but trouble and a part of me wished I could get rid of it.

Reyan narrowed her eyes. "Are you in the habit of accusing your allies of being thieves?"

There was something about Reyan that bothered me, aside

from the fact she looked like a *Sports Illustrated* swimsuit model dressed up as a tribal princess. She glowed with magic from head to toe, which was something that only mystical beings like demons or elves did. It made me think her body was fake— and no, not in that way.

"No, Gary never accuses us of being thieves. That would imply we didn't admit to it," Cindy said. "Except for G who is an assassin and Jane who is just annoying."

Jane glared at Cindy, holding Mindy tight. "I hope you get eaten by something."

"Or the Jungle Clap," G suggested.

"Don't suggest that," I said, shaking my head. "That would spread rapidly through the population and kill us all."

Cindy slapped me across the back of the head and walked through the portal.

"We're not thieves," John said, walking to the portal. "We kill everyone we take stuff from first."

"Uh, I don't think that actually precludes you from being a thief." I started to say.

He disappeared through the portal. It didn't seem to be an exact representation of where we were going since he didn't appear on the portal image. A part of me briefly considered this was an extremely clever way to teleport me into a black hole or sun, but I figured that whatever evil genius would come up with such a plan was probably a friend of mine.

Mercury chuckled as Gabrielle and Reyan went through the portal. "Believe me, I planned to steal it. Unfortunately, the Orb of Death is linked to your body and soul. It's impossible to say where one of you begins and the other ends now. It's actually elevated you to godhood."

"Really, godhood?" I asked. "While a monotheist, I find that enticing."

"Well, sort of."

"Sort of?"

"Yeah, imagine most gods like Zeus or Cthulhu are ten million. Nyarlathotep and Azathoth are like thirty million."

"This is getting very *Dragon Ball Z*."

"I'll pretend I know what that is. You're about a ten."

"Ten?" I blinked. "Is this a system where lower is better?"

"No."

"Ah," I said. Somehow, reality always schemed to make my accomplishments seem lamer than they were. It was as if they were deliberately setting out to make my being a god as unimpressive as possible. "So, best not send out any fliers for my new religion just yet."

I was joking. My rabbi would kill me.

Mercury shook her head. "You're like the god of rusty door hinges or infomercials no one watches unless they have insomnia."

"That's a very odd example for someone who grew up in a post-apocalypse wasteland."

"The things we had to watch in our library were VHS tapes of what people had recorded before the end of the world."

"Truly a hellish nightmare world. VHS tapes?"

"Get through the goddamn portal!" Mercury said, rolling her eyes.

"Right!" I said, realizing I was still on the wrong side of the portal. I waved to Jane and G on my way out, the Henchbots waving to me as well. I also blew kisses to my daughters who stared at me with a look that made me wonder if Mindy was going to use her super-strength to steal an ice cream truck again. As for Leia? Well, I fully expected to return to adorable pictures hanging from banners over the burnt-out ruins of the White House, because, don't all parents want to see their children exceed them? I mean aside from Cindy?

Stepping through, I found myself in a lush and verdant paradise that had enormous blooming orange flowers growing from trees I couldn't recognize. The Hollow Earth was warm but tropical heat rather than something boiling. The air was fresh and clean, which briefly caused me to cough as I was used to a forty-five percent smog, fifty-percent nitrogen, five percent oxygen mix. We were next to a forty-foot-tall waterfall pouring down into a nearby lagoon that had a triceratops drinking out of it.

Cindy pulled out my cellphone and took a picture of it.

"Really, Cindy?" I asked.

"Instapost demands I document all of my adventures," Cindy said, taking a selfie as well. "I brought a floating camera so we can get real-time footage of our Hollow Earth expedition for *Where in the Multiverse is Cindy Wachkowski?*"

"That's not a real show," I said, raising an eyebrow. "Also, if it was, you'd still get sued."

"It's a working title. I'm still trying to pitch it," Cindy said, pulling out a small ball that she tossed in the air. It floated up and popped out a tiny camera that started looking her up and down. "I figure it'll be like *Mary Poppins* and appeal to both kids *and* their dads."

"Excuse me?" I asked.

"You know, you watch Mary Poppins as a child and it's this cute magical adventure, then you watch as an adult and you realize how hot Julia Andrews is."

I opened my mouth then closed it. "You've ruined that movie for me."

"Ruined it *or made it better?*" Cindy asked.

"Ruined."

"This is a fantastic place," Gabrielle said, walking over to the waterfall pond and scooping a handful of water to drink.

"You realize dinosaurs probably pee in that, right?" Mercury asked.

Gabrielle shook her head. "Cast-iron alien-power infused stomach."

"Which you don't have," John explained. "The Great Old Ones killed billions of people when they rose from power, but that wasn't what killed most of humanity. It was the disease, starvation, thirst, and other daily evils that destroyed us."

"Are you human?" Reyan asked, looking at John. "You do not feel human."

"No," John said. "I'm a monster in human form."

"You'll find the definition of monster is a bit different on my world," I said, reassuring him. "Being a monster is what you do, not what you are."

"My father said that," Gabrielle said, looking down.

I'd gotten it from *The Witcher* video games, but truth was truth. "So, Reyan, do you know which way to head from here?"

"Vaguely," Reyan said. "We're about a hundred miles from the city of Nur'Ab'Sal. That is near the border of the Nazi territory."

"Wait, *a hundred miles*?" I asked.

CHAPTER SIX

NAZI SUPER-SCIENCE IS THE WORST

"A hundred miles?" I asked, repeating what I'd just said. "On foot?"

"That's a bit of a forced march," John said, nodding. "An average adult human can walk three to four miles per hour so potentially ninety-six miles in twenty-four hours. However, we'll probably have to spread that over a week's time, given you are civilians. Obviously, we'll have to consider water, food—"

"Yeah, I think we need to just cheat," I replied, not happy about the prospect. I worked out an hour a day, to maintain my distinctly non-nerd physique. However, bluntly, that wasn't any real training for hiking and (ugh) nature.

"Yes," Cindy said, raising one foot wearing an expensive boot. "These boots were made for walking...down a runway."

"You are terribly unprepared for a jungle journey," John said.

"Yes," I said, nodding. "Yes, we are. However, preparing would have required me to think clearly when my niece was endangered and there's Nazis to punch."

"Fair enough," John said. "I've gone a little crazy when my loved ones were threatened, too."

I blinked. "Okay, this is going to seem like a very personal question but... do you have kids?"

"Yes," John said. "Many. Some with my ex-wife, some adopted, and a few with other partners. It happens in the future. Not much to do but hook up, kill monsters, and hope your off-spring don't die."

"And you're an alien," I pointed out. "Just to be clear."

"Sort of," John said. "I'm half-human."

"Kind of a big tentacle slime-monster," Mercury explained. "Lots of eyes, mouths, and multi-dimensional space-time distortions. He can just shapeshift into a gunslinging cowboy. His guns draw matter from other dimensions that can rip through most supernatural beings like they're made of paper."

I grimaced. "Aside from telling you that you would make an awesome anime protagonist, I have to ask: how does that work?"

I didn't actually want to ask this guy too much about his sex life, but I was always curious how so many alien-human hybrids popped up across various dimensions. I mean, there are plenty of things that don't make much sense in my world, but that just means you have to try harder to understand them. Even God just qualifies as an extra-dimensional hyper-geometry being when you get down to it.

Or so my theoretical physicist rabbi says.

"How does *what* work?" John asked, making me spell it out.

I waved around my hands. "Just saying, crossbreeding slime-monsters with people confuses me. I mean, it feels like a bad *Dungeons and Dragons* supplement. Half-elves? Yes, I can buy it. Half-dwarves, not a problem. Half-ooze or gelatinous cube? A little confusing."

"Magic," John said, clearly irritated by the entire line of conversation.

"Just magic, huh? No further explanation?" I asked.

"Do you want specifics?" John asked, his voice taking on the slightest bit of an edge.

"I do!" Cindy piped in.

Gabrielle felt her face. "Some shapeshifting species have tri-dimensional DNA that allows them to be simultaneously whatever species they breed with as well as their original one."

"Uh-huh," I said, not saying that sounded like gobbledygook. "What I was actually asking is maybe you could turn into a dragon or giant bat and fly us there."

"No," John said. "I'm not going to let you ride me. Not even after a few drinks."

"Aww," Mercury said.

I looked at her.

"What? Cindy's not the only pervert here," Mercury said. "Don't worry. We won't have to do the lengthy death march with woefully unprepared mortals."

"You're going to magic us there again?" I asked. "Whip out a *Mordekain's Magnificent Mansion* for us to stay in between walks?"

"See, it *sounds* like you're speaking English, but it comes off as gibberish," Mercury said, looking at me sideways.

"I can control animals," Reyan said, simply. "I will summon mounts from the local wildlife to carry us across the jungles of Pait'an and through the valleys of Unkunda. It will not be a comfortable ride, but as heroes of the Surface World, I am assuming you are used to struggle."

"You would be wrong," Cindy said, making finger guns. "I am a perfect example of a woman who will do everything in her power to avoid discomfort."

"Then why did you even come Cindy?" Gabrielle asked, exhausted.

"Fame," Cindy said. "If you disappear for a few months, the public forgets you exist and then you get replaced with cheap knock-offs using your codename. That's how we got White Ultragoddess in two-thousand and eight."

"I thought we all made an agreement never to speak of her again," Gabrielle said.

"So, you can control animals or talk to animals?" I asked.

"Both," Reyan asked, looking at me. "Why do you ask?"

"Just wondering," I asked. I was a big animal lover, but my dogs had passed away while I was off on a caper and I'd never forgiven myself for it. People who hurt poochies and cats were just below Nazis in my view. I'd never killed anyone for animal abuse but that didn't preclude breaking their legs.

"I primarily control dinosaurs. I have mastered almost every single kind to be found in the Hollow Earth," Reyan put her hand to her forehead and stared at the triceratops. "Gotta catch 'em all."

"Wait, what?" I asked, wondering if I'd heard that correctly.

A glow surrounded Reyan and then the triceratops before it lifted itself up from where it was drinking and sauntered over. The creature proceeded to flop down on the ground. Cindy crawled up on its back and took a deep breath.

"Not my favorite type of barebacking, but it'll do," Cindy said.

Gabrielle felt her face. "Oh, for the love of the Primals."

"I'll walk beside it," John said. "I don't get tired."

"I'll be fine, too," I said.

"Really, Gary?" Cindy asked. "You complain about getting drinks from the fridge."

"Because I am exhausted from my *strenuous workout* every morning," I snapped.

"Uh-huh," Cindy said. "The one you achieve with an IV drip of Mountain Dew and vitamin water that consists of ninety percent sugar and ten percent water."

"Sugar is a vitamin," I argued. "The best kind."

Reyan and Mercury joined Cindy on the back of the triceratops while Gabrielle walked behind me. "You sure?"

"Gary, I've had survival training on the moon," Gabrielle said. "I'm fine."

"Sorry," I said, taking a deep breath. "So, anyone want to share their life stories as we begin our journey to Mount Doom?"

"No, Mount Doom is the other way," Reyan said, pointing to a volcano east of us.

She kicked the side of the triceratops and it started walking west. Well, as much as east and west mattered when you were walking on the interior of a sphere.

"That means you go first, Blondie," I said.

Reyan frowned. "My parents were archaeologists. They discovered the secret entrance to the Hollow Earth at the Tomb of Sigurd and Brunhilde. My brother and I were playing with the artifacts there when we were bestowed the power of the Aesir."

"Really?" I asked. "That's fascinating."

"Not really," Reyan said, frowning. For a moment she didn't sound like the stoic woman she had for our short acquaintance but an upset teenager. "P.H.A.N.T.O.M turned out to be the sponsors of the expedition. They killed both my parents and took my brother hostage. They also killed our dog."

"Oh, those sons of bitches!" I snapped. "I didn't think I could hate those guys more. What breed was it?"

"Malamute."

"Bastards," Cindy said.

"I like dogs," Mercury said. "Very good for hunting down game. I hated when the famine happened, and we had to eat mine."

Well, that was a conversation stopper. The triceratops smashed down trees and crushed them as it continued onward. There was a clearing nearby and we were soon walking through the tall grass.

"So, what about you, Shorts and Tank Top? What's your story?" I asked Mercury.

"I was a torturer for a fascist city-state that executed anyone they suspected of having nonhuman DNA or mutations."

I blinked. "Huh. Must have been a problem for a mixed-race woman and black man."

"Why?" Mercury asked.

"Oh, right, apparently in the future the authoritarian military governments are pro-racial tolerance," I muttered, sarcastically.

"The black and the white gang up on the furry and clawed," John said. "Mind you, that didn't stop people from still hating on the black."

"It never does," Gabrielle muttered.

"So how did you stop being, uh, a torturer?" I asked, regretting even inquiring.

"I saw a chance to get out and I took it," Mercury replied. "The Wasteland and almost certain death seemed a better opportunity than a long life while my soul was sucked out of me. Along the way I encountered more than my fair of wizards and Old Earth knowledge. I used that to become a witch. As for the shorts and tank top, it's hot in the desert. Also, I look good in it."

"I live my life by that credo," Cindy said, nodding.

"You're very well preserved for your age," Reyan said, smiling.

Cindy pulled out a hand-held death ray from under her cloak and aimed it at Reyan.

I glared a her.

Cindy begrudgingly put it back under her cloak.

"Sensitive about your age?" Reyan asked.

"There's a lot of places to dump a body here," Cindy said.

Reyan blinked rapidly.

"What about you, Great and Powerful Blog the Gunslinger?" I asked, trying to divert the story.

"Call me that again and we'll test Cindy's statement," John said.

"Sorry," I said, taking a deep breath. "It's all this nature. There's something unnatural about so much green. I can't wait until nightfall."

"There's no nightfall," Reyan replied.

"Oh. How about seasons?"

"Nope."

"Huh," I said, thinking about the economic possibilities. "You know, we could build some seriously awesome resorts down here."

"Just ignore the giant monsters, wasps, and the indigenous culture," Cindy said.

"*Et tu*, Cindy?"

"I'm not saying we shouldn't, but we should cut the locals in and leave the first guests to be eaten," Cindy said. "We can make sure the guests are idiots, too, like investors in Objectivist anarcho-paradises and bitcoin."

I didn't tell her I'd invested heavily in bitcoin. "Yeah, sure. Come on, John, tell us a bit about you."

"I was a ranger back on my world."

"Army or Aragorn?" I asked.

"A little bit of both," John explained. "Gamma Squad was a collection of the fiercest, toughest, and most heroic humans of my age."

"What happened?"

"The fiercest, toughest, and most heroic humans of an age were still only human. They died in an assault on a wizard's temple and I did my best to avenge them. Along the way, I found out my heritage wasn't entirely human. I had a choice between life as a monster and merciful death as a man."

"And you chose life as a monster," I said.

"I've seen too much evil done by humanity to have any particular attachment to them," John said, his voice low. "Besides, being a monster allowed me to do things that other people couldn't do and make the world slightly less horrible for those who weren't."

"I'm on Team Human until I get an upgrade," Cindy said.

"On our world, trying to make the world a better place despite the evils afflicting is what's called being a hero," Gabrielle said.

"And look how much good being a hero has done," I said, more bitter than I realized. The Society of Superheroes was on the verge of being snuffed out, while trying to defend the oppressed of a land most people had never heard of, but the governments of that world were completely unaware of it. Hell, some would be glad when the superheroes were gone. Supervillains they understood. We wanted, took, and had. Altruism was alien to the governments of the world.

It was why I could never be a superhero. I might save people when I was inclined, but I'd never feel obligated to the ugly, nasty side of humanity. I helped people because I wanted to help them, not because I had to. Also, because some people needed to be torched or frozen.

"So, you became a blob in a cowboy hat."

"Pretty much. Mercury kept me sane or at least insane in a way that could be pointed at people trying to kill humanity's last remnants," John said. "The Hollow Earth is a last refuge for us. All we have to do is take it back from P.H.A.N.T.O.M."

"And the local potentates are okay with this?" I asked, still not sure about this. There was a pretty big difference between imperialism and immigration. I just wanted to make sure it was the latter rather than the former.

"The Night Empress has empowered me to make the offer. She is ruler of ten city-states and the last of the Great Rulers who has not been conquered by P.H.A.N.T.O.M. As the guardian of Odin's Spear and the Golden Apples, she is also the holder of the sacred relics that determine who is ruler among humans."

I processed that. "The Night Empress, huh?"

Odin's spear Gungnir was only slightly less famous than Thor's hammer Mjölnir in Norse mythology. The Golden Apples were far more important, though, because they were the secret to the gods' immortality. I hesitated to mention that, though, because Cindy would almost certainly freak out over the possibility.

"She's the one who summoned us," Gabrielle said. "I chose to respond to her request because I'm ninety-nine percent sure it wasn't a trap."

I blinked. "You know, Gabrielle, when you say things like that, it puts me on edge."

"I don't like people who are referred to by titles rather than names," Cindy said. "You can't trust them."

"You mean like superheroes?" I asked.

"And supervillains!" Cindy said. "Look at us."

I didn't have time to respond to that because there was the sound of a roaring engine over our heads. Looking up, I saw a P.H.A.N.T.O.M hover pyramid about the size of a small house pass over us. If you wonder what a hover pyramid looks like, it's self-explanatory; P.H.A.N.T.O.M just made a bunch of geometrically precise objects and slapped alien technology onto them.

Rather than have planes, trains, and tanks they had floating cubes, battle spheres, and pyramids. This one had dozens of laser cannon emplacements on its side as well as an enormous P.H.A.N.T.O.M Skull and crossbones in a circle. The hover pyramid aimed its weapons at us and fired dozens of energy blasts with the intent to not so much kill us, as to obliterate us.

"Ah hell," I said, seconds before the blasts struck.

CHAPTER SEVEN

FLASHBACK TO (SORTA) BETTER TIMES

Even though the ground beneath us was destroyed in the torrent of laser fire, we didn't die. If we were the kind of superheroes (villains? people?) to get killed by guns, then we wouldn't have lasted very long in our chosen careers.

I summoned my Death magic and surrounded us in a bubble that caused us to turn intangible. My powers with the Reaper's Cloak had been moderate, at least by superhero standards, and were now extra-moderate. It was enough to keep us from being obliterated. It also triggered a flashback.

That was the price for using the Orb of Death. Perhaps because people associated death with anger, regret, grief, and remorse—those were the emotions that empowered it. Calling upon that power meant I was plunged deeply into those feelings.

One moment I was standing in the middle of a massive grassy field by a dinosaur and the next I was wearing a white button-down dress shirt, black slacks, and a pair of reading glasses I barely needed. I was lying on the couch of my old home, the one the government demolished while cleaning up after the zombie outbreak in Falconcrest City (seemingly out of spite), with a rerun of *Friends* on the television.

Yes, I was having a flashback.

"Tough day at work?" Mandy asked, coming from the kitchen. She was a beautiful half-Korean, half-Caucasian woman with long curly black hair and piercing dark eyes. She was dressed in a black Judas Priest t-shirt and sweatpants.

"Define tough," I said, sighing. "Today the Society of

Superheroes Fought P.H.A.N.T.O.M as they tried to drop a plague bomb on Paris that would wipe out all non-white people in the city. The Nightwalker also beat up the Ice Cream Man as he held a grade school hostage with poisoned dessert. Compared to that, the fact my boss is a prick and we're expected to cover the costs of recent layoffs doesn't seem like a big deal."

"Super World Problems," Mandy said, simply. "No matter how bad the economy is, how many people struggle, you can always depend on politicians to talk about how it could be worse. This despite the fact they're not the people who are keeping the chaos at bay."

"The chaos at bay?" I asked, looking up at her. "Who are you, Ultragoddess?"

"You should know, you dated her."

I rolled my eyes. "I did not date Ultragoddess."

"Your theory that Gabrielle Anders is Ultragoddess is ridiculous."

"Why? Because she wears glasses?"

"No, because I've been saved by Ultragoddess like a dozen times. I think I could tell the difference."

In fact, I'd once had a hook-up with Ultragoddess in college (Gabrielle and I were briefly broken up at the time). It happened after she'd saved me from a fire started by the Arsoness. Strangely, the next day Gabrielle had acted like we hadn't broken up. I wasn't about to share that with Mandy, though. Believe me, I would have been able to tell the difference between them unless I was incredibly unobservant.

"Maybe she brainwashed you with Ultra-hypnosis into not being able to tell you were dating her until she wanted you to know."

"First of all, that would be a gross violation of my free will. Second, Ultra-hypnosis? That's a ridiculous power. Like Ultra-basket weaving or Ultra-knitting."

"Ultragod has both those powers. My mom's Silver Age comic books say so."

"Yes, let's get our knowledge of how the world works from comic books," I said, sitting up and turning the channel.

"Don't be a dick, Gary."

"I'm pathologically incapable of not being one."

"Yes, but you usually aim it at someone other than your wife."

"Sorry."

One of my bull terriers, Arwen, walked up to me as I patted her head. I turned around to change the TV channel. There was a screen-shot of a funeral being held in Texas with large numbers of citizens, the National Guard, and an ex-President in attendance. The Texas Guardians, minus a couple of members, were also present.

"Oh shit," I said, looking at the service. "Did you know Spellbinder died?"

"Yeah," Mandy said, frowning. "It was all over my media."

"Damn, really?"

Spellbinder was a dark and Gothic-looking superheroine who had the powers of empathic healing, witchcraft, and the ability to possess people. She was apparently half-god or half-demon (a rather nebulous distinction for non-Jewish religions according to my rabbi) and an escapee from an evil cult. Mandy had always been a big fan of hers and drew inspiration from her example—I personally didn't see the draw. Well, aside from the fact she wore a lot of black and was the snarky angry member of the team. Qualities I admired.

"Crazy how our lives are superhero adjacent," Mandy muttered. "If we were still with our exes, we might be in the crowd of mourners there."

"Yeah."

It was strange how my life had gotten so much simpler once Gabrielle dumped me. Mandy had been dating a supervillain, until the Black Witch had gotten herself sent to prison for accidentally killing someone, the final straw for my wife. Now both of us had lives that were largely supervillain and superhero free. All the craziness of the world was something that happened to other people.

"Do you know how she died?" I asked, having remembered the Guitarist had died just a few months earlier.

"She was killed by Diabloman," Mandy said, scrunching up her nose in disgust. "Her own brother."

"I could never hurt a member of my own family," I said, thinking of departed brother and my still-living sister. "Do you think she'll come back?"

"Excuse me?" Mandy said, doing a double take.

"Superheroes sometimes come back," I said, as if it was the most natural thing in the world.

Mandy walked to the kitchen and opened the fridge door. "Sometimes they do. Most times they don't. Your brother stayed dead. Some of the Sunlights. Most heroes we don't remember. They just die and stay dead."

"Would you want to come back?" I asked, unaware of just how ironic my question would be.

"Excuse me?" Mandy said.

"Let's say something crazy and we both get the superpowers we've been dreaming of," I said, pausing.

"Are we bitten by radioactive dogs? If so, I want to be called the Bitch Queen."

I rolled my eyes. "I'm pretty sure that wouldn't work unless we had metagenes influenced by dog saliva. Which you shouldn't take as a sign I've researched this. I mean, let's say we're superheroes and one of us dies—what would you want done?"

"You mean, would I want you to hope I'd come back from the dead? Is this a serious question?" Mandy pulled out a beer. "You want one."

"Yes and no."

Mandy popped open the top of the beer bottle with her fingers, a trick I'd never understood and took a deep breath. "No."

"No?"

Mandy took a drink. "Your family talks to ghosts, Gary. You deal with the supernatural on a daily basis."

"Correction: my sister talks to ghosts. So did my grandmother, and she had a lot of them to talk to because she lived in Poland during WWII. I am just an ordinary average nobody who thinks a lot about death."

"Don't go Hot Topic on me, Gary. You're not fifteen and listening to Linkin Park anymore. That's was decades ago."

"I haven't felt this old since I talked about how much I loved

Shakira and the teller beside me at work only knew her as the girl from *Zootopia*."

"Who is Shakira?" Mandy asked. "I only know music that involves screaming and people dressed like it's Halloween."

I smirked. "You were saying?"

Mandy walked over and sat beside me. "I'm a Wiccan, Gary. I believe there's a natural order to things. People are born, they have children, they grow old, and they die. If death is to have meaning, it needs to be permanent. I don't think you believe that."

It was kind of an ironic statement for her to make, because Mandy had made it clear she didn't want children. She just didn't see herself as a mother. I tried not to be bitter about it, but we'd rushed into marriage and hadn't completely worked out the details. I did want to be a father and

"You're damned right I don't," I said, letting my face droop. "Maybe death doesn't have a meaning. Maybe it's only life that does."

"Then I'm glad you aren't a superhero."

I laughed. "No, I'd suck at that. Super*villainy*, though?"

I didn't get a chance to dwell on the memory, because I was punched in the face with the force of someone hitting me with a car. The blow sent me flying through the air. I did an unintentional somersault before I landed on the soft ground.

"I really hope that's mud," I muttered, feeling like I'd suffered three concussions and a broken jaw at once. Ow! And why did I speak with a punched jaw? Oh right, I'm pathologically addicted to snark.

That was when I realized that, though my flashback had taken only a couple of moments, the entirety of my surroundings had turned into a warzone. The hover pyramid had been knocked out of the sky and was half buried in the ground with smoke coming out of one side.

John, or what I at least believed was John, had become a hulking, slimy, ink-black monster with an enormous mouth and white iris-less eyes. A dozen tentacles stuck out of his back, and he used them like an octopus crossed with a spider, throwing aside P.H.A.N.T.O.M soldiers before leaping at a woman dressed like a Nazi Valkyrie.

Mercury was surrounded by a glowing force shield as she fired energy blasts and hex bolts at the soldiers attacking her. Gabrielle fired two pistols as she ran, ducking under the attacks of a T-Rex-human hybrid in a lab coat with a big Imperial Japanese flag on the back of his lab coat. Reyan flew above our heads with the triceratops having grown a pair of glowing wings as she wielded an energy sword twice as large as her body like an anime heroine.

And Cindy?

Cindy had become a werewolf.

Yeah, that was surprising. My on-and-off lover for the better part of my adult life had become an eight-foot-tall tall brown-furred killing machine that looked less like the Wolfman and more like someone had stuck one of Tolkien's Wargs on two legs before putting it in Cindy's cape. This entire experience was so surreal that I didn't have time to react when a big skeletal hand encircled my throat.

The owner was a figure who was difficult to describe. He looked like a skeleton in a superhero uniform, with the typical "heroic build" associated with capes. It was jet black, the cape red, and the P.H.A.N.T.O.M black Skull and Crossbones were his emblem. Strangely, I could feel flesh around the skeletal fingers and remembered who this jackass was from my WW II history course.

Death's Head.

Victor Totenkof had been one of the many Waffen-S.S. *Ubermensch* Project volunteers who had been experimented on by Tom Terror during the Second Great War. After Hitler was taken down by Ultragod, the supervillains had free rein and had made use of alien super-science and demonic magic to create an endless horde of destructive but tactically useless super-villains to throw at the Allies.

Death's Head had been given super-strength, super-dura-bility, and the power to jump hella high for the small price of having his skin turn invisible. He also developed a toxic breath that could melt the skin off people. This meant, yes, that he was a Nazi poison gas power. Ugh. Israel's Defense Team Prime, the Zealot, and a time-traveling Jesse Owens working with the

Bronze Medalist, had all killed this guy at one time or another. Unfortunately, P.H.A.N.T.O.M's cloning labs and necromancers had always succeeded in bringing him back from the dead. I'd been really hoping he'd be one of those who'd stayed dead after I won the Infinity Tournament.

"You, Merciless!" Death's Head cried out. "Enemy of all Nazis!"

"Wait, really? That's kind of flattering," I said, struggling to keep him from choking me. "Do I have any other nicknames?"

"Killer of Hitlers! Destroyer of Reichs! Jewish vermin!"

"Okay, you were doing so well until that last one," I said. "Wait, does the fact I've killed so many of you guys mean you aren't the Master Race? Not that you're looking particularly blond and blue-eyed. Does that mean you're out of the fan club or do they give you the one-testicled freak exception they gave Hitler?"

Yes, I know Hitler didn't actually have one testicle, but historical accuracy doesn't matter when insulting Nazis.

"ARGGHH!" Death's Head opened his mouth to breathe his poisonous breath. Unfortunately, I'm not immune to poison gas, even if I turn intangible. Don't ask me how that works.

I slipped through his grip, ducked under the cloud of toxic gas, and punched him in the groin. Unfortunately, it turns out that punching someone who is invulnerable is actually a pretty stupid idea if you don't have super-strength. Breaking two bones in my fist, I remembered there was a reason that superheroes and villains trained—so they didn't end up doing these things by reflex.

"Ow," I said, knowing it would take a few minutes for me to heal.

That was when Totenkof kicked me like a football and I flew through the air, again, and banged against the side of the hover pyramid. I slid down the side, my cloak slowing my descent a bit as I silently wished Cloak were still alive. Well, around, as he was a ghost by the time I met him. He'd been very good at preventing the worst of my stupid mistakes.

Death's Head wasn't the first of the small group of Nazi supervillains we were fighting to reach me. A woman with long blonde braids, a horned helmet, black wings, and a ridiculous set of armor with a metal brassiere reached me first. She grabbed me by my snow-white hair and lifted me up. "Pathetic *erbsenzähler*, Brunhilda shall now slay you and avenge all the losses ve hafftaken at your hands!"

"Did you just call me a pea counter?" I asked, confused at her insult.

"It sounds better in German," Brunhilda said, defensively.

"It'd have to."

Brunhilda hissed and pulled her fist back, but before she could drive it into my face, Totenkof grabbed it.

"Nein! He is mine!" Death's Head shouted. "The glory of his death belongs to the foremost of the Overlord's Generals!"

"*Hosenscheisser!*" Brunhilda hissed. Hosen meant pants and scheisser, well, you can figure that one out.

That was when Gabrielle came up behind both, aimed her pistols at the backs of their heads, and fired. "Dodge this."

Whatever was in the guns, they weren't bullets. Glowing energy blasts blasted them in the face. The results weren't pretty. Both supposedly invulnerable Nazis ended up with their brains splattered against the hover pyramid's wall, right beside me. I even had to wipe a little Brainhilda off my cloak. I had to give Gabrielle credit; she'd made her witty retort after killing them. That was just good common-sense tactics, even if they probably hadn't heard it in hell.

I looked up at Gabrielle. "Aren't you against killing?"

"Nazis don't count."

She had me there. I was mostly upset she hadn't let me blast them first. "What are you using for ammo?"

"Ultranium," Gabrielle said.

"So….the one thing in the universe that can kill you normally is the thing you're carrying around," I said, trying to follow the logic.

"Yes," Gabrielle said. "I have one magazine of Ultranium bullets for each pistol. The rest of the time they just draw from the nuclear generators in my pistols."

I blinked. "Who made your guns? Satan?"

"No, the Space Angel Varkel. He's the forgemaster of God."

Ask a stupid question, get a stupid answer. "How is the fight going?"

That was when Cindy's werewolf form landed against the side of the pyramid.

"Not well," Gabrielle admitted.

CHAPTER EIGHT

ME VERSUS A SUPER(IOR) BOY

The field before us was littered with the bodies of dead Nazis, something I'm always in favor of.

Unfortunately, dead Nazis were not the only thing on the other side of the hover pyramid. Instead, I saw a pounded-up and doughy-looking black blog that I presumed was the still-living (albeit barely) form of John Henry Booth.

It was curled around the badly injured, but glowing form of Mercury Takahashi. She was muttering healing spells to try to keep her body together after someone had tried to tear it to pieces. The triceratops lay dead to one side, decapitated, and Reyan was collapsed on the ground. Well, maybe just collapsed. I could only see her blonde hair and smaller-than-normal hands sticking up from the ground.

"Bastards," I said, looking at the dead triceratops. "They killed Dave!"

"You named the dinosaur?" Gabrielle said.

"You'll be avenged, Dave. This I vow," I said, searching for whoever had torn through the team like they were nameless mooks facing the Nightwalker. "For both this and three of the five *Jurassic Park* movies. Plus, all the crappy games."

"Gary, look!" Gabrielle said, pointing it at the sky above the massacre.

Hovering above my beaten associates was a fourteen-year-old kid wearing a P.H.A.N.T.O.M Youth uniform. It was identical to the kind possessed by Hitler's murderous band of Anti-Boy Scouts and child soldiers but gray colored with a black cape.

Oh, and they'd given the guy an actual set of pants, which was a good thing since a flying Nazi kid sidekick didn't need a pair of shorts to make him look ridiculous.

The Japanese dinosaur woman was getting up. The rest of the fascist force (that would also be a good codename for this group) wasn't. It couldn't have happened to a nicer bunch of people but, apparently, the kid had managed to trash the rest of my team thoroughly.

"*Uberjunge,*" Gabrielle muttered, not aiming her guns at him. "Superior Boy? Really? That's his codename? Not Nazi Kid? Fascist Lad? I mean, P.H.A.N.T.O.M is really slipping in their efforts."

"Silence!" Uberjunge shouted. "I am Ubermensch, not Uberjunget! I am the ultimate warrior of P.H.A.N.T.O.M! No one calls me boy."

"Right," I said, looking at him. "Because that's what I'm worried about now."

"Argh!" Uberjunge screamed before turning to fly at me, zipping at supersonic speed. I, unsurprisingly, had expected this and turned insubstantial. He smashed into the side of the hover-tank.

Uberjunge passing through me caused me to feel like I'd been punched in the gut. His body was made of magic, like Reyan's, but my powers prevented it from liquefying me. Instead, it just sent me to my knees. The boy, meanwhile, smashed into the side of the hover pyramid and came out the other side.

"He's as strong as I normally am," Gabrielle said. "His powers are magical, too. He tore through much of the Society of Superheroes by himself."

"Great," I muttered, clutching my stomach. "You could have told me this. My genius plan now needs some more steps."

"Your genius plan being to have him smash into something?" Gabrielle asked. "Do you get all your plans from Looney Tunes?"

"It's worked so far," I said. "I'm ninety percent Bugs Bunny in my fighting style. The rest is evenly divided between Wile E. Coyote and Evil WizardTM."

Werewolf Cindy proceeded to get up on her hind legs and

stretch out her claws. "Grrrr.... He's coming back around... grrooowl."

Gabrielle paused a second before looking to her side. "By the way, Gary, is Cindy a werewolf?"

"It seems so," I said, keeping my eye on Uberjunge as he came back around.

"Is this a new development?" Gabrielle asked. "Do we need to get you laser hair removal?"

Cindy turned her wolf-head toward her and snarled.

"Down, girl," Gabrielle said, pointing at her.

Cindy involuntarily sat down on her buttocks.

"Good girl," Gabrielle said, pulling out a treat from her pocket and tossing it to her.

"Maybe there was a crossover comic she got infected in that readers will have to shell out twenty bucks to pay for the trade paperback."

"You are so goddamned weird," Gabrielle said, holding her guns up at the sky. "He's back!"

Seconds later, Uberjunge came back around as there was a crack of thunder. The child soldier descended, and I sensed the magic radiating off him. It was more than I'd ever felt from any-one save Entropicus, Zul-Barbas, and maybe the Nightwalker. It was energy different from my own, tainted by something vile. There was more going on than him just being another Nazi supersoldier. He was the product of something older and more terrible. Lightning crackled up and down his body as he stared down at me with pure hatred in his eyes.

Cindy returned to her human form. "Yeah, I don't suppose you still have that teleporting scythe?"

"No," I said.

"I wonder if he likes older women," Cindy muttered.

"No, Cindy," I said. "Just no."

Gabrielle surprised me by speaking to the monster descend-ing from the sky. "Ken, don't make me destroy you!"

"Ken?" I asked. "I thought we were just calling him boy. Also, since when do we not kill Nazis? Teenagers or not?"

"You don't have to be Uberjunge!" Gabrielle said. "We remember who you really are."

I had no idea who he was. Why is it that everyone in my world has a deep and complicated backstory with one another except me? You know, ignoring that I grew up with Cindy, was friends with the Nightwalker's ghost, was the chosen of Death, and had a child with Ultragod's daughter. Okay, I needed to stop thinking about these things. I needed instead to figure out how to beat a supervillain with the power of ten thousand Nazis.

"I am Superior! Not Uberjunge." the boy shouted. "The man who will kill Merciless: The Superhero without Mercy!"

"Oh, sweet Moses," Cindy said, looking on in horror. "He just said your name without any irony. You're screwed."

Uberjunge then grabbed me by the back of my hood and began flying toward the glowing orb above us. "Let's see how much of a smartass you are when I toss you into the Inner Sun!"

"Gurk!" I said, trying to say something snarky but prevented by the fact I was being throttled by my own cloak.

The two of us rose through the air, growing closer and closer to the Sun at the center of the Hollow Earth. It wasn't anything like the real Sun and you didn't need a degree in nuclear fusion to figure that out. However, it became incredibly hot as we got closer and closer. My flesh began to blister and regenerate while Ken seemed unharmed.

"The Supreme Phantom will reward me greatly for this!" Ken shouted. He was slowing down despite his approach of the Sun and I remembered he'd not actually killed any of my friends.

Maybe he was regretful? Maybe he wasn't entirely onboard with Neo-National Socialism? Well, it sucked to be him because I was fully prepared to kill him to survive. If you were old enough to kill, then you were old enough to die.

"Sorry, kid," I said, turning my hand intangible and putting it into his brain. "This hurts you more than it hurts me."

It was at this point I realized Ken wasn't a physical human being. He was purely composed of energy and I didn't actually put my fingers through his brain. Instead, it just caused him to rear back and grab his head like I'd given him an ice cream headache. I was prevented from falling by my power to levitate that, oddly enough, felt like actual flying now.

"Ha!" Ken said, triumphantly. "The Sun is the source of magic in this land! An infinite battery of unlimited power!"

"First of all, that's redundant," I said, fully aware of my own hypocrisy as Merciless: The Supervillain without Mercy. "Second of all, do you have any idea what a really stupid thing that is to tell me?"

"What?" Ken asked.

I unleashed a storm of black lightning that was the nastiest and most dangerous magic I knew. I felt the warmth of the artificial sun pour into my body—an unimaginable stream of mystical power that I channeled into the superpowered teenager's body. Ken screamed as his artificial body was disrupted and flickered like a bad WiFi signal.

That was when I charged him like M. Bison in Street Fighter, forced him away from the Sun, and slammed him into the ground at around 1000mph. I turned insubstantial at the final moment and thus avoided the force of the blow, leaving a two-foot-deep crater where we struck. I floated up and stood above him.

"Ten points!" I said, throwing two peace signs in the air. Then I did the Ric Flair stylin'-and-profilin' dance (props if you know what that is). "Woo!"

Ken proceeded to get up.

"Oh shit," I said.

Ken took a swing at my head. I ducked. He spun around and missed wildly. He was completely untrained in fighting and relied on brute strength. Like most people who were faster than a speeding bullet, more powerful than the United States antiquated rail system, he also was as slow as his brain allowed him to fight. Unfortunately, that was going to get faster as soon as he shook off my earlier attack.

That was when a dinosaur in a lab coat grabbed me from behind. "I've got him, Herr Masterson!"

Ken grabbed me by one of my legs and before I could turn insubstantial, smashed me against the ground left and right. I felt bones break in my arms and legs and my head rang like there were church bells clanging around inside it. He then tossed me into the crater I'd created and lifted his foot to crush my skull.

Gabrielle proceeded to shoot him in the leg twice and then kneecapped him, sending him to the ground. "Stay away from my boyfriend!"

"No!" the dinosaur doctor shouted.

Werewolf Cindy tackled it and started tearing it to pieces. Ken slowly stood up, bleeding badly from his injuries but looking furious. That was when Reyan grabbed him from behind in a bear hug, looking decidedly worse for wear. She then shouted into the sky, "By the Might of Asgard!"

A bolt of lightning flashed from the sky and struck them both, driving them to the ground into the tall grass. I would have just watched what happened, but I'd just gotten my ass kicked. I wasn't about to let myself lose to a fascist Generation Z loser. I struggled to get up then fell to my knees and then landed on my chin.

Not my finest moment.

"Got you," Gabrielle said, helping me to my feet. "I think we won."

"Are all the Nazis dead?" I asked, spitting out a tooth that would take a couple of hours to regenerate.

"No," Gabrielle said. "Just most of them."

"Then we haven't won yet," I said, feeling my body slowly beginning to heal. Ken's blows were among the hardest I'd taken outside of Entropicus beating my ass during the Eternity Tournament.

"Take a deep breath," Gabrielle said. "We can get Mercury to heal you."

I started slurring my speech. "You know I'm not entirely feeling the whole 'Ultragoddess with Guns' thing. You should be harmlessly punching people with the force of a moving train, not using pistols. Either that or smacking them around with house-sized fly-swatters. What happened to the Silver Age, man?"

"Gary, you're rambling."

"Also, why does your costume have a skirt? You fly. Do you put bicycle shorts underneath or what? I mean, it's a good look but—"

"I think you may have a concussion," Gabrielle interrupted.

"Pfft!" I said, blinking rapidly. "Superheroes don't get concussions. We're right and ready by next month's issue!"

I then collapsed face first into the mud.

Gabrielle picked me up again. "You've got a concussion."

"I might have three," I muttered. "But what does not kill you makes you stronger. Discounting traumatic brain injury, maiming, permanent injury, or all the other ways that quote is dead wrong. Damn, Nietzsche! Why couldn't you stay as relevant to me as you were in high school!"

Cindy walked up to me and Gabrielle and spit out a chunk of the dinosaur lady. "Wow, I think I've solved one of history's greatest mysteries. They are birds. That thing tasted just like chicken."

"Cindy, when the hell did you become a werewolf?" I asked, feeling my mind clear.

Cindy shrugged. "I dunno."

I blinked. "Okay, good to know."

"We'll find out and get you a cure," Gabrielle said, earnestly.

"Hahahahahaha," Cindy said, letting out a peal of high-pitched laughter. "Oh, wait, you're serious."

I rolled my eyes and stumbled over to where the others had fallen. Mercury was almost fully healed but looked like I felt. John was slowly convalescing into an ink-black humanoid shape that started to look like his previous self. Cowboy hat and all.

"Huh," I said, looking at him. "Are you actually wearing clothes or are they part of your body? I've been wondering."

"Yes," John answered, pulling out an oversized .45-caliber Magnum that was as Clint Eastwood as the rest of his outfit but a different movie. "Now, where's the little superpowered shit, so I can put two rounds in his head?"

"Over there," Cindy said, pointing to where Reyan had tackled him.

"I'll enchant the bullets," Mercury muttered. "They'll be able to pierce any magical defenses he has."

"No, you can't kill him!" Gabrielle said.

Literally all four of us looked at Gabrielle and said, simultaneously, "Why?"

"He's a child!" Gabrielle said.

"A bad child!" I snapped. "Damien Thorne! King Joffrey! Some other bad kids—"

Gabrielle looked at me. "Gary, please, be the better man for once."

My expression lost all its mirth. "This is a mistake."

"It's not," a teenage girl's voice spoke as a slightly chubby sixteen-year-old blonde girl walked through the tall grass after getting up from where she fell. The girl seemed familiar. She wore a pair of glasses, a white button-down t-shirt, and a long brown skirt with Crocs. "My brother is brainwashed by P.H.A.N.T.O.M. He's not guilty of the Uberjunge's crimes."

"Who the hell is she?" Cindy asked.

Gabrielle rolled her eyes.

"Reyan?" John asked, looking down at her. "But she's uh... well, not at all like that."

Apparently even the human-blob monster had thought she was hot in her other form.

"The shapeshifter shouldn't comment on appearances being deceiving," I said, shaking my head.

"The power of Odin gives me the beauty of a Valkyrie," the girl said, adjusting her eyeglasses.

"I've got my eye on you," Cindy said, pointing at me. "Pervert."

"I'm sixteen," Reyan said. "I just look twenty-eight when I change."

Cindy looked at me with contempt. "You're a sick man, Gary. How could you even think of a child that way!?"

I did a double take. "What the hell are you talking about?"

"I'm blaming you for what I was thinking," Cindy said.

"Ah," I said before turning back to Reyan. "Sixteen is way too young to be adventuring down here. You're purely side-kick material. Go join the O-Men or the Texas Guardians. They accept child-soldiers."

"*I* was a Texas Guardian," Gabrielle said.

"Leave the real fighting to us adults," Cindy said. "Shoo-shoo. Fly away, be free."

I walked past Reyan and looked behind her. What I saw was

the collapsed form of a fourteen-year-old boy who looked completely different from the child Nazi I'd fought. I mean, completely different. For starters, he was black.

"Uh—" I started to say.

"P.H.A.N.T.O.M also changed the way he looks," Reyan explained. "He normally looked like a black Viking in his twenties."

"Obviously," I said. "And you?"

"I was adopted," Reyan said.

"Ah," I said.

"We need to figure out how to get the hover pyramid going again," Reyan said. "The Reichmen were the primary team of P.H.A.N.T.O.M in the Hollow Earth. Destroying them and recapturing my brother means they're going to be weakened. That will allow us to rescue the Society of Superheroes, Texas Guardians, and your niece."

"Assuming any of them are alive," I said.

"They are," a new voice spoke behind us. "You're also the only ones who can save them because this is where they are meant to die."

I turned around. "Oh, great. You two."

"Who are they?" John asked.

"Our daughters," Gabrielle said.

CHAPTER NINE

REUNION WITH THE FAMILY

I had a lot of weird things in my life. My wife being killed by a dragon, my raising her as a vampire, and then a dead superheroine possessing her while still claiming to be the original Mandy. My brother Keith was a supervillain killed by a vigilante psychopath, my sister could see ghosts, and my niece was a superhero. Even my relationship with God was crazy. Death had made me her chosen one and used to send me on missions. But the weirdest thing in my life? The fact I had *adult* children from the future.

Nothing says that you live in a world where normal has no meaning better than your children traveling back in time to visit. In some ways, it was flattering. In other ways it was terrifying. It implied something terrible must have happened to you as they used time travel instead of texting their present-day dad.

Standing just to the side of the group were the adult forms of my two daughters. Leia was a late-twenties beautiful woman with snow-white hair like my own (I was the only platinum-blond Jew I knew aside from my sister and called it our "Targaryen blood at work"). Leia had a superficial similarity to Cindy but hadn't gotten the nose job Cindy had at sixteen. Leia wore a pair of orange-red overalls that had the word "Gizmo" over the right breast. Around her waist was a toolbelt of various devices and gadgets that I only recognized half of, as well as her mother's ray gun.

Mindy, having a different mother than Leia, obviously

looked a great deal different with shoulder-length curly hair and chocolate skin slightly darker thanher mother's. Yeah, that sometimes happens in genetics. She was dressed in a bright blue overcoat and fedora that made me wonder if the future had retro-1940s fashions, or she'd been raised by Carmen Sandiego. She glowed with an aura that I recognized as the Ultra-Force, despite the fact this place should be draining it away.

"Your daughters?" John asked, raising his gun.

Gabrielle pushed the gun down. "Yes. Gary's and mine."

"And mine!" Cindy snapped. "I'm their mother, too! One of them I totally gave to Gary's sister to raise! I also gave up drinking for eight months."

Mindy pinched the bridge of her nose. "How do you not die of embarrassment?"

"My telepathic abilities reveal that she really does love me," Leia said softly. "Under many, many, many layers of selfishness and arrogance."

"Add a few more layers there," Cindy said.

"I agree," I said.

Cindy swatted me. "Only I get to admit how horribly I screwed up."

"I forgive you for my many, many, many years of therapy," Leia said.

"Thank you," Cindy said. "I'm sure Gary played a role in that, too."

"No, not really," Leia said, smiling. "Best father ever."

"We even got him the mug!" Mindy said, smiling.

I admit I chuckled at that.

Reyan stared at them like they were a ray of hope. "You're from the future? That means you know how things turn out? Does it get better?"

"Nope!" Leia said.

"What?" Reyan said, blinking.

"Sorry. The future sucks. That's why we're trying to change it," Mindy said, speaking with an Atlas City accent. Apparently, that was where I was going to move sometime in the near future.

"This must be very confusing for you," Gabrielle said to John and Mercury.

"Not really," Mercury said. "It gives me a warm sense of comfort that our reality isn't the only crappy one in the universe."

"How did the future end this time?" I asked, taking this less seriously than I did last time. "Zombies? No, we did that. Time-traveling Nazis? Nope. Also done. A war between the Muggles and the Supers? Actually, that seems to be a running theme around here."

"We can't use the word Muggles," Cindy said. "Joan Rowling copyrighted that. I think."

"Come on!" I snapped. "It's so perfect for referring to them."

"True," Cindy said. "Now that I have superpowers, I feel an overwhelming disdain and dislike for inferior beings. Perhaps I should infect everyone with werewolfism—"

"Lycanthropy," I corrected.

"Whatever," Cindy said. "Then I shall be their Wolf Queen! All shall love me and scratch behind my ears!"

"You stopped being a supervillain," I pointed out.

"I did?" Cindy asked.

"Yes, because Mandy sacrificed her life and inspired you to reform," I mentioned.

"Yes, but then she came back and...oh wait, she didn't. Dammit!" Cindy snapped. "Okay, forget the whole plans for world domination. What do our Brats from the Future want from us, anyway?"

"For me to take over the world," I deadpanned.

"Wait, what?" Gabrielle and Reyan asked simultaneously.

"Is there an echo in here?" Cindy asked. "Also, no fair! I want to rule the world. This is sexist!"

Leia made a strangling gesture before putting her hands behind her back and smiling. "It's complicated—"

I felt a headache coming on and soon found myself suffering another flashback. I was getting sick of those. While making my life more like the Highlander films (watch the first one and pretend the others don't exist) was cool and all, this was not helpful to my present-day social status.

One second, I was in the Hollow Earth and the next I was standing in a cabin in the future. Both daughters, dressed similarly but not identically, were sitting down at a table in front of me. It had happened a year in the past, though the three of us were in the future, and Mandy had just been revealed to have been replaced by an imposter. The original Mandy, my Mandy, had been dead for years and I'd never noticed. Worse, there was no reset button. The consequences of the superhero world couldn't be reversed and could never be again.

Whee.

Man, did I long for the days when death was an inconvenience for the good guys.

"It never was," Leia said, frowning at me. "Death only was reversed when it amused the hidden masters of the universe. Unfortunately, it was permanent and traumatizing for most people."

I blinked at her.

"Telepath, remember?" Leia said, pointing at her head.

"I thought I said never to read my mind," I said, pointing at her. "No ice cream for you."

"I'm lactose intolerant," Leia said. "You should probably learn that."

"I wondered why Cindy ordered a hundred gallons of special non-milk-based alien cheese for our pizzeria," I said.

Leia smirked.

"So, what do you want?" I asked, trying not to fall over. I'd literally just escaped the End of the Universe and was still reeling from the world's most epic beatdown. While my enhanced powers had kept me alive, I still felt like Rocky after his fight with Ivan Drago at the start of *Rocky V*. You know, the one we don't talk about? Oh wait, you might not have seen every piece of media I mention in my asides.

You should fix that.

"We need you to try to take over the world," Mindy said, nonchalantly. "Like really try to take it over, not just say you're going to take it over but do nothing to actually make it happen."

I walked over to the wall and leaned up against it so I wouldn't collapse. "I'll have you know that I own one of the world's largest soft drink and pizza joint firms! Your stomachs belong to me as does your caffeine intake!"

Mindy rolled her eyes. "This is serious, Dad."

"I'm not actually a big fan of taking over the world now," I said, taking several deep breaths. "I thought I'd be able to share it with Mandy. Now I know I won't be. Plus, did you know that I probably will have to kill innocent people to take over? I mean, no one pointed that out! It makes evil so permanent!"

"We're serious, Dad," Leia said.

"So am I," I said, looking between them. "I was really hoping you'd take after your mother, Mindy. She's a hero and someone I wish I could be like in the entirely not-hot Afro-Latina superheroine sense but the moral person way. I don't think I could pull off the former. As for you, Leia, I was hoping you'd not take after your mother in any way whatsoever. Well, except for the fact she's brilliant. I've never seen someone with such a high IQ concoct so many ways of avoiding work and responsibility. Well, except for me, obviously."

"We're not supervillains," Leia said, sounding increasingly annoyed. "We're police."

"Take that earlier disappointment and magnify it by ten," I said, shaking my head. "Where did I go wrong with you? It's not too late! Turn back from your police ways and embrace the path of criminality! I'll even accept you as superheroes! Some of my best friends are heroes! Just don't disgrace your family like—"

"*Time* cops," Mindy interrupted, as annoyed as her sister.

"Oh, that's different," I said, immediately relieved. "Do you know Jean-Claude Van Damme?"

"Who?" Leia asked.

"I'm going to give you a pass on that one," I said. "Even if the movie *Street Fighter* should have been part of your education growing up."

"We're the *last* Time Cops," Mindy said, with a sense of gravity. "All of the others have been killed by the Thordrax."

"Who are they?" I asked.

"Evil mutant robot aliens," Leia said. "President Omega made them with technology from the planet Abaddon."

"Entropicus and President Omega? Great, two shitty tastes that taste worse together. Wait, I thought I killed President Omega."

"You did," Mindy said. "He's so terrified of you now that he refuses to go to any point of history where you're still alive."

That was both flattering and terrifying. Mind you, President Omega was a coward at heart like all fascists. Entropicus, despite my winning against him through sheer dumb luck, I expected was more annoyed at having been beaten by a B-list supervillain. Like that time Ultragod lost to the Leapfrog. Everybody has their off days.

"I obviously need to work on that immortality thing," I said, frowning. "I'm not sure how my taking over the world helps, though."

Both girls exchanged a glance. "In the way history was meant to be, Ultragod, the Nightwalker, and Guinevere were meant to inspire the next generation of heroes who inspired the next and so on."

"I take it that doesn't happen now?" I asked, noting two of those three were dead and the third had become an angry antihero.

"No," Mindy said. "The revelation of the Nightwalker's involvement in the Brotherhood of Infamy and Ultragod being killed by, well, you did a number on the way they were remembered. Guinevere is now a *quotix* and has lost much of her symbol of hope status."

"A what?"

"It's a non-gendered slang term from the future. It basically means people think she's a bit—"

"Yeah, I get it," I said, interrupting. "What about Gabrielle? I mean, she's every bit the hero her father was. More so I'd argue since she just saved the entire multiverse from Entropicus. With my help, of course."

I'd always thought Gabrielle was the greatest hero on Earth. I admit to bias, but this was before I was sleeping with her, she carried my child, and shot two Nazis in front of me. Whereas Ultragod was a shining example of morality and as close to a real-life paladin as you could get, he was also a little too conservative in his beliefs.

When crises happened, Moses Anders always tried to do the lawful thing *as well as* the righteous thing. He worked well with the courts, governments, religions, and scientific community as a result. Gabrielle? Gabrielle never let anything get in the way of doing good. She'd single-handedly ended civil wars and dealt with the fallout afterward.

Mindy frowned. "Our mom is…controversial."

Cindy grimaced. "For a lot of reasons."

"Like what?" I asked, assuming it had to do with me.

They instead listed all the various opinions she'd spouted on every subject ranging from women's rights to American socialism.

I blinked. "Wow, there is something in there to offend everyone. Where does having a child out of wedlock with a supervillain rank?"

"Not even top fifty," Leia said.

"Ouch."

"Just under it's right to punch Nazis," Cindy said. "We accept that's right in the future."

I processed that. "Good. I have to ask, is it really appropriate to go from 'we need a hero to unite us' to 'Gary, you should be the dictator of everything.' I feel like we're missing a few steps."

"You don't have to take over the world, just try," Cindy said.

"There is no try, do or do not," Mindy said.

"Now I'm confused," I said.

"Superheroes aren't the only people who advance the world," Leia said. "In addition to hope, there's also fear. New alliances are formed in the face of threats, technology advances, and funding of large-scale infrastructure changes. As the top rises, so does the bottom."

"Yes, Leia, because I am the most terrifying supervillain of them all," I said, dryly. "Oooh."

"You could be," Mindy said. "Either way, Entropicus is going to invade sometime in the next fifty years. Depending on how weak humanity has made itself by dividing itself between Supers and humans, it could be worse than when President Omega took over. Worse, without humanity to provide the lion's share of superhuman defenders in the coming Galaxy Wars, well—"

"Well, what?" I asked, having no idea what the Galaxy Wars were.

"Well, it's like if the U.S. fails to show up for WWII. The war may or may not be lost but the results sure as hell are worse in the long run."

I sucked in my breath. "I can't do this. Don't ask me to."

"What?" Both my daughters said simultaneously. "Are you serious?"

"Don't Doublemint Twins me," I said. "You can't pull it off. As for the rest? I... I just can't. Mandy is gone. Again. Maybe I knew it on some level. Maybe I knew I was deluding myself. But, well, it just isn't fun playing dress-up anymore."

Cindy and Mindy stared at me.

"What?" I asked. "I was thinking of retiring from supervillainy before I saved the entire multiverse. I'm out."

"Oh, Dad," Mindy said before sighing. "You're never out."

That was when I woke up from my flashback to Cindy snapping her fingers in front of my face. She grabbed in a headlock and gave me a noogie. "Hello, McFly! Wake up!"

"Gah! What the hell!" I snapped, throwing her off. "You do not do that to the future ruler of humanity!"

Mercury looked at John. "Wow, we picked a real bunch of winners to side with here."

"Eh, they killed a bunch of superpowered monsters and their minions," John said, shrugging. "That makes them okay in my book."

"Sorry," I said, blinking. "My magic rock is making me see the past."

Mindy and Leia stared at me.

"He also has a concussion," Gabrielle said.

"That is completely irrelevant!" I raised my hands in the air. "So, what magical insight can you provide me from the future now that I've decided to actually follow your advice a year too late?"

"The President has declared you an enemy of the United States and sent the entire U.S. Army to your house," Leia said.

"Oh," I said, realizing I may have screwed up back there. I was suddenly terrified for the younger version of my kids, Jane, Case, and Kerri.

"It gets worse," Mindy said.

"How?" I asked.

"The President's Chief of Staff is behind P.H.A.N.T.O.M down here."

Cindy turned to me. "You know, they've got a serious problem with fascists in Washington, D.C. Next time, I'm voting Independent."

CHAPTER TEN

WAR FOR FUN AND PROFIT

"Seriously?" I looked at them before putting my hand over my face. "The Chief of Staff is a P.H.A.N.T.O.M agent? Didn't we just do this plot? People are going to think I'm anti-American."

"You *did* kill the President," Cindy pointed out.

"He wasn't the President," I snapped. "They removed that title from him retroactively. I'm not even sure he's still in continuity."

"I have no idea what you're talking about," Cindy said, shaking her head.

"He is, unfortunately," Mindy said, ignoring the weirdness of all this or perhaps just thriving in it. "P.H.A.N.T.O.M has always had their Crimson Elite agents that have infiltrated the highest levels of government. The majority were rounded up when President Omega was killed but a small number still operate in high levels of the government."

"Now we're ripping off G.I. Joe?" I asked.

"Shh," Gabrielle said, staring. "If the Chief of Staff is a P.H.A.N.T.O.M agent then this might explain why superheroes are outlawed in the United States. We can get that law overturned."

I sighed. "Yeah, I feel that's a bit more complicated. The world used to be all capes, jet packs, and talking gorillas. Now it's antiheroes, social commentary, and fantastic racism. I feel like we should just call it quits with the Society of Superheroes and join the O-men."

"I like the O-Men movies," Cindy said. "Mmm, Hugh Jackman and Ryan Reynolds."

"Famke Jansen and Hallie Berry for me," I muttered. "*Anyway*, I'm not sure what benefit even a rogue branch of the U.S. government, accent on rogue, has to benefit from sending a bunch of Nazis to the center of the Earth."

"Orichalcum," Mindy said, saying the name of a mineral every government on Earth would kill to possess.

"Sounds like a sex game," Cindy said. "But that's not possible since I've never heard of it."

Leia gagged, apparently having lost her tolerance for parental sex thoughts upon hitting puberty.

"Nope, that's not it," Cindy said, tapping the side of her head with one finger. "Maybe this one. No wait, that's a Dirty Cindy."

Leia looked disgusted.

"Oh hush, you've seen worse in my brain," Cindy said. "You wouldn't believe some of the sick and perverted—"

"It's crystalized magical energy," Gabrielle, thankfully, interrupted. "One of the most valuable substances in the universe. Ultranium is the refined plutonium version."

I nodded, knowing what it was. "Orichalcum is a basic component of pretty much every super-science invention or accident that grants superpowers. If you want to build something like a cold fusion device, perpetual motion machine, or other physics-defying object then you should include orichalcum. Orichalcum radiation is also the stuff that causes people to get superpowers when they're dumped in toxic waste or bitten by radioactive llamas rather than developing cancer."

"Radioactive llamas?" Gabrielle asked.

"You don't want to know," I said, shaking my head. "Almost led to the alpacalypse."

Man, I missed Niki Tesla.

"Chief of Staff Steve Duck sent P.H.A.N.T.O.M down here to kill the locals and enslave them before sending all of the orichalcum back to the U.S.A.," Mindy explained.

Gabrielle narrowed her eyes at the mention of the Chief of Staff's name. Steve Duck sounded familiar to me too. Not just in an 'I don't know the names of all the President's staff but have probably heard them somewhere' way either.

"Why take all the orichalcum?" Cindy asked. "What's the government going to do with it?"

"Make their own army of superhumans," Gabrielle said, horrified. "That will kick off an arms race between various world powers. It's what my father always feared. He believed the militarization of superpowers would be the end of humanity."

"All governments depend on the monopolization of force," John said, sagely. "They were never going to be friendly to independent superhumans. Any group that opposed their will becomes an existential threat."

"That was surprisingly erudite," I said.

"Why surprisingly?" John asked, narrowing his eyes. He'd misread my meaning.

"Uh, because you're from a post-apocalyptic wasteland?" I said, grimacing.

"Listen, I know Tom Terror," I said, exaggerating my knowledge of the world's most famous supervillain. "If he's the Phantom Leader then there's no way in hell he's going to be taking orders from the United States. Chief of Staff, President, or even an animated Statue of Liberty. The moment he takes over the Hollow Earth, he'll try for the rest of the planet then the star system, and then the galaxy. From there, the universe."

"That seems like a lot of work," Cindy said. "He should stop at the planet or maybe a tiny island nation where you have an unlimited supply of naked people and piña coladas."

"I support this plan," Mercury said.

"The Hollow Earth seems to support scantily-dressed native peoples," Cindy said, looking down at Reyan. "Even the ones who are a trap!"

Reyan looked confused, which was probably for the best.

"The Hollow Earth is the source of all the Earth's native superpowers," Leia said, pulling out a device that resembled a PKE meter from *Ghostbusters* and aiming it at the Sun. "The Inner Sun is pure raw mystical energy and it pours out its energy through ley lines. All magic not filtered through the Primal Orbs or from gods comes from here. Exposure is what causes them to develop the powers here. It's why the locals are nearly immortal, beautiful, and strong."

"Sweet!" Cindy said. "Even more reason to build an evil day spa down here."

"Why does it have to be evil?" Gabrielle asked.

Cindy shook her head. "You just don't get it, Gabby, and you never will."

"Is that why Cindy is a werewolf now?" I asked, wondering what other kind of effects this world might be having.

"No," Reyan said, surprising me. "She has been touched by Fenrir."

"Sweet!" Cindy said, cheerfully.

"It's a dreadful curse. Only the most evil and selfish souls are afflicted by his power," Reyan said. "It's an ominous sign that we have drawn the Ragnarök Wolf's attention."

"Can't hear you over my new superpowers," Cindy said, raising one hand and making the "shh" gesture.

"We don't know what Tom Terror is planning but he's already figured out how to start draining the power of superhumans into the Inner Sun while leaving his own forces untouched," Mindy said, disgusted. "Gary, only magic coming from a different source is safe like yours, Reyan's, or the alternate universe soldiers'."

"The Ultra-Force is universal but draws on wellsprings like this," Gabrielle said, as if what she said wasn't a further layer of nonsense.

"So, Tom is going to turn off all the world's superpowers and conquer the world," I said, figuring out his plan. "It's what I would do. "Then he can turn the entirety of the Earth's people into superhumans and unleash them on the rest of the universe. With no one to stop him, since no superhuman will have any powers but by his leave."

"I always liked 'by your leave'," Cindy said, distracting the conversation. "It sounds so sophisticated."

"Probably," Mindy said. "While you were kicking around for a year, doing nothing, we've been trying to keep the future from becoming a complete disaster. Whatever happens here is going to have a major effect on the world."

Cindy raised her hand. "Okay, you're time travelers. How

the hell does it work that Gary spending a year in a funk over his dead wife *for the second time in a row—*"

"Hey!" I snapped.

"Let me go with this," Cindy said. "How does that work? Can't you just return to when he wasn't in a funk?"

Leia looked at her mother. "Mom, do you have a Doctorate in Quantum Cross-Temporal Mechanics? A subject that didn't exist until your daughter created it?"

"No," Cindy said.

"Then shut the hell up," Leia said, smiling despite her words. "I won't tell you anything about how to bilk the medical system, or dad how to be John Simms Master, only on the side of the good guys."

I blinked. "Yeah, that's fair."

"Who's John Simms?" Reyan asked.

I glared at her. "His first televised appearance on *Doctor Who* happened recently! In...when was that...2007!"

Reyan blinked. "I was *four.*"

"Ugh," I said, sighing. "Why can't life be like *Ready Player One* and pop culture forever cater to my love of the Eighties?"

"You can do that when you take over the world," John said.

"Thank you," I said, nodding. "I'll do that."

"Also, if you can swing it, try to provide clean water and food to people. We need that in the future more than pop culture," John said.

"Do you?" I asked. "Do you really?"

"So, what do you want exactly?" Cindy asked. "I mean, we were already heading down here to Donkey Kong Country to kill the *Undermensch*. What's new?"

Mindy and Leia exchanged a look.

"We've moved down our younger selves to Nur'Ab'Sal along with the rest of the mansion residents," Mindy said. "We'd rather avoid a paradox where we're killed as children."

"Yeah, that's an automatic game over in *Metal Gear Solid*," I said.

Leia sighed, losing her patience with me as well. "We also think now is the best time for you to seize control over the

Ultranian technology here. If you can take it from Tom Terror then the world will fall quickly."

"Gotcha," I said, making finger guns. "We're going easy mode on world domination. Funny, I thought it would be difficult."

"You seriously want Gary to take over the world?" Gabrielle asked. "A guy who can't even keep up with how many mistresses he has?"

I looked over at her. "I don't sleep with that many women other than you."

Everyone looked over at me.

"Wow, that was a crappy defense. I'll be quiet now," I said, making a locking gesture over my mouth before throwing away the key.

"As ironic as it sounds, we're running out of time," Mindy said, checking a futuristic wristband. "We're always just a few steps ahead of President Omega and his minions. He may not be willing to come here around you or even disrupt your timeline too much but that doesn't mean we're safe."

"Good luck," Gabrielle said, staring at them. "We'll find some way to resolve this morally."

Neither of our daughters looked impressed.

"One last question," Reyan spoke up. "Are the Society of Superheroes and other superheroes still alive? Is Gary's niece?"

I regretted not asking that myself, but the answer was, well, I wasn't sure I wanted to know the answer.

"They're alive," Mindy said as both she and Lea started to fade. "But if you don't save them, they'll all wish they had been killed."

Then they were gone.

"Well, that was ominous," Cindy said. "So, who is up for BBQ-ing some dinosaurs? I feel like I need to eat my body weight in meat or you guys are going to start looking delicious. I call it the Big Bad Wolf diet."

I tried to ignore the implications of that. "Hey, John, do you think these hover pyramids have life boats?"

"Yes, probably," John said, looking at them. "The Reichmen used one to get down here and attack us. I suspect it probably has at least one more."

"Then I think we have our ride to the city," I said, suddenly much more interested in getting there.

"Only one problem with that," John said.

"Yeah?"

"Do you know how to fly a Nazi super-science bathtub?" John asked.

He had a point there. "No, I don't."

"I do," Gabrielle said.

I looked at her. "What?"

"You don't think I have other skills than punching people and flying?" Gabrielle asked.

"I just figured your flight skills were restricted to personal," I said, admittedly not having given it much thought.

Truth be told, there were still plenty of areas where we didn't know each other very well. Ten years earlier, when I was still her boyfriend in college, the two of us knew every little detail about the other. You know, except for me not knowing she was Ultragoddess but that doesn't count since that was a big detail. When we had time together, it was mostly spent talking about superhero business. I knew Ultragoddess very well, but I wasn't sure I knew Gabrielle as well as I used to. Mind you, these days I'm not sure I know Gary Karkofsky that well either.

With that, Ken Masterson got up from the grass beside us and groaned. Immediately, John pulled out his pistol and aimed it at his head.

"Ow," Ken said, feeling his head. Then he looked at the gun aimed at him. "By the Might of As—"

Reyan grabbed him and cover his mouth with her hand. "Don't."

"What's going on, where am I, and who are these people?" Ken asked, looking around confused. "Wait, is that Red Riding Hood?"

Reyan blinked. "Wait, she's the one you recognize?"

"She is pretty memorable," Ken said, looking up with an obvious crush.

Cindy rolled her eyes. "You wouldn't even know where to begin, kid."

"You've been brainwashed by P.H.A.N.T.O.M so that

whenever you turn into your god avatar form you become a white blond killing machine for evil," Mercury explained.

Ken looked horrified. "I become *white?*"

Gabrielle shook her head. "We'll figure out a way to cure you of your condition but don't try to use your powers until we've figured out just what they did to you. Until then we'll have to do without Viking Lad and Valkyrie Girl."

I stared at them. "*Those* are your codenames?"

"Wait," Ken said, pointing at me. "I know you, you're Cindy's sidekick! Mercy Man!"

"I can still shoot him if you want," John said, dryly.

"Don't tempt me," I said.

"Move sidekick!" Cindy gestured to the hover tank. "Fetch me my chariot."

This was going to be a long trip.

CHAPTER ELEVEN

ON OUR WAY TO THE EMERALD CITY

The hover pyramid turned out to have two car-sized open-cockpit flying saucers that were its equivalent of lifeboats. I had no idea how to operate the controls, and both had been damaged during the battle. Gabrielle, however, just casually restored the least damaged one with parts from the former. Apparently, being an alien technology mechanic was another of Gabrielle's abilities I hadn't been aware of.

"Well if you don't get your powers back, we can always rename you Wrench Wench," Cindy said.

"I'm getting my powers back," Gabrielle said, wiping the sweat off her brow. "I just need to spend a couple of weeks away from the Hollow Earth."

"A couple of weeks is a long time for the world to be absent Ultragoddess," I said.

Gabrielle paused as she screwed the last of the panels in place on her work. "Honestly, it's a relief, even if I'm spending it fighting Nazis and dinosaurs. The last time I had a vacation from my responsibility to the world was when Spellbinder removed my powers for a weekend in the Nineties."

I stared at her.

Gabrielle grimaced, having temporarily forgotten what a sore subject her friend was.

"I remember Spellbinder," Cindy said, sighing. "I used to love her for introducing Gothic Lolita fashion to white people. I was a teenager when she first did it and just couldn't get over the combination of dressing like a schoolgirl and adding corsets that emphasized your bust. You know, so you knew any guys you hooked up with weren't pedophiles."

"Merciful Moses, Cindy."

"What? I said *used* to love her," Cindy said. "I stopped after she impersonated Mandy and had sex with us both. That was wrong. Hot but wrong."

"I didn't know Red Riding Hood was bi," Ken whispered to his sister, though not softly enough I couldn't hear it.

Cindy, too. "I'm more heteroflexible, kid. There's a spectrum of these things. It's like when Gary confessed his love of Ewan McGregor."

"You asked me who I wanted my cellmate to be when I was next in prison," I snapped. "I didn't get the implications!"

"Sure you didn't," Cindy muttered.

"Do you have any idea what they're talking about?" John looked at Mercury.

"Apparently, people in the past have a lot of free time on their hands," Mercury said. "In the future, sex is want, take, have. The only rule is no one gets killed. Otherwise, everything is a go."

"Sounds nice," I said, nodding. "And by nice, I mean potentially but not definitely horrifying."

"Sometimes," Mercury said, her expression even. "It's more a question of whether or not what you're sleeping with is human or not."

"And whether that matters," John said, gruffly.

"Personally, I've always wondered how Gary and Gabrielle can have sex without breaking him. Even my experiments haven't given me much insight," Cindy said. "Really, you'd think—"

"Cindy, you do realize I can throw buildings, right?" Gabby interrupted.

"Right, right, I'll leave off details," Cindy said. "I'll cancel all the interviews I had set up."

"Wait, what!?" Gabby asked, horrified.

Ken looked at Cindy and Gabrielle with a blank expression that clearly indicated the former had broken his brain.

Reyan waved her hand over his face.

No response.

"Is he okay?" I asked, believing it was more than teenage hormones.

I was proven right when he fell to his knees clutching his head. "P.H.A.N.T.O.M is...argh, sending a signal to all of its operatives. I feel compelled to say the magic words and summon Odin's power."

"Don't or we'll kill you," John said, dryly. He put his hand down over on his revolver.

Ken looked up, still clutching the sides of his head. "Uh, that's a big inspiration not to."

"Look!" Reyan said, pointing to the sky.

I followed where she pointed and saw a deeply disheartening sight. Above our heads were a dozen more hover pyramids. Thankfully, they weren't flying in our direction and ignored the sight of their downed fellow P.H.A.N.T.O.M vessel. Instead, they were going due west.

Toward Nur'Ab'Sal.

"Ah, crap," I said, watching them go. "It looks like the Jerries here were the vanguard for an invasion."

"Who is Jerry?" Reyan asked.

"Everyone hop in!" Gabrielle gestured to the flying saucer's interior, which only looked as though it could hold eight. "We can catch up with them and maybe help in the city's defense."

"Assuming we don't get shot out of the air for flying around in an enemy UFO," I said.

"Hey, Gary," Cindy said, chuckling. "Wanna hear a joke?"

"Not particularly."

"What do you call a bunch of dead Nazis?" Cindy asked.

"What?" I asked, wondering what was wrong with her.

"A work in progress," Cindy said, bursting out laughing.

As funny as that was, I was worried. "Are you okay?"

"You mean aside from the hunger for violence and flesh?" Cindy asked.

"...yeah."

"I dunno," Cindy said, wiping sweat off her brow. "I feel weird."

Mercury walked over to her and pulled out a monocle, of all

things, to examine her. "The lycanthropy is inducing changes in the rest of her body. This usually takes an entire lunar cycle if it's anything like our world. It's accelerated here. If you want to reverse the process, you'll have to exorcise the wolf spirit soon."

"Why would I want..." Cindy said, stumbling to her feet. "You know, I just realized I can't complain when people call me a bitch now. Haha. Because female dogs—"

"Yes, Cindy, we get it," I said, worried.

Cindy proceeded to collapse on the ground. I rushed over to her side as Mercury took her pulse.

"Is she going to be alright?" I asked.

Mercury stared at me. "You mean, aside from being a hungry monster?"

"Hangry," Cindy moaned. "Don't make me hangry. You wouldn't like me when I'm hangry. Mmm, humans."

Yeah, that wasn't a good sign.

"I'm kidding," Cindy said. "Probably."

"Load her up, Gary," Gabrielle said, Mercury standing beside her in the machine's circular cockpit.

"She's not in any shape to fight," I said, feeling a little betrayed.

"Hopefully that will change," Gabrielle said. "That city needs us. Remember, our daughters were taken there by...our daughters...for their own safety."

I couldn't help but wonder if that was an oh-so-subtle way of my future children manipulating events, so we were guaranteed to defend the city. You wouldn't think they would put children at risk to do that, but I suppose they might think that was just self-sacrifice on their part. Man, I hated time travel.

"Alright, let's go," I said, less than happy about all this. "Hopefully, we can put a dent in their forces."

"I'm not sure how much help I can be," Ken said, looking down at his fists. "When I can call upon the power of Sigurd, I'm a demigod, but now they've put something in my head. I become someone else when I use the power and—"

"Yeah, yeah we got that from you kicking our asses," I interrupted him. "Muggles do it better, though. Don't doubt you can find some way to contribute."

"We can't use the term Muggle..." Cindy moaned, looking feverish.

"Do you believe that?" Ken asked.

"Not really," I said, looking down at him. "But sometimes lies are the only thing that get us through the day. Get a shield belt and a laser gun from the dead fascists on the ground. Let's hope they work better for you than they did for them."

Ken nodded and jumped out of the UFO, just as Cindy was loaded in by John.

"Gary, we can't use a child soldier," Gabrielle said. "We need to keep him from the front lines."

"I've been fighting since I was eight," Ken said, simply. "You didn't know my age when we fought together and were happy to have me punch out bad guys as Viking Lad."

"Because I didn't know your age," Gabrielle explained.

I'd killed my first man at age fourteen and it had resulted in my brain never quite being the same. Killing Shoot-Em-Up in a dirty hotel with shaking hands, a stolen gun, and hate in my heart meant I wasn't ever going to be someone who could live a normal life. I also understood that we didn't have time to play the game of when someone was old enough to fight for their life. I'd seen way too many dead gods as a psychopomp working for Death.

While I wasn't as up on superhero lore as I used to be, I had heard of Viking Lad and Valkyrie Girl. They were a black and white brother and sister team who both appeared to be adults. They could fly, punch through walls, and wield magical weapons. They had only appeared about two years earlier, but had made quite the splash.

They'd also fumbled missions, smashed things, and had very cheesy interviews. Them being fourteen and sixteen respectively helped explain that. Mind you, their codenames should have tipped me off, but I'd figured they were being ironic. Still, it made me wonder just how much Reyan actually knew about the Hollow Earth since it seemed unlikely she could split her time between it and her adventures on the surface.

Certainly not without a teleporter.

Who had sent her to my house? Why? I had assumed it was

Gabrielle, but if she'd gone to fight in the Hollow Earth with the Society of Superheroes, then that meant Reyan must have rescued her rather than the other way around. There was a sense that something else was going on, and the fact I didn't know *what* bothered me to no end.

"Ken, I've got a job for you," I explained, deciding to take the path of least resistance. "I need you to help find my kids and protect them."

"Is this a transparent attempt to manipulate me by giving me a job that will take me out of the fighting?" Ken asked.

I blinked. "Yes, because you don't have superpowers, and if you use yours then we'll have to kill you for you become a Nazi."

"Right," Ken said. "Sis, you handle things until I'm cured."

"You got it," Reyan said, taking a deep breath. "Step aside."

Ken did so.

"BY THE MIGHT OF ASGARD!" Reyan said, stretching out her arms.

Another bolt of lightning descended from the sky, which was kind of amazing since we were in the middle of a closed system with no sign of any storm clouds nearby and the miniature sun visible above our heads.

When the bolt struck Reyan, she transformed from her slight sixteen-year-old self into her more curvaceous but muscular alter ego. This time, she was no longer wearing skins but ornate battle armor with a glowing rune-covered battle ax in her hands. Her hair had also changed from golden blonde to braided platinum white like my own.

"Nice look, *Khaleesei*," I said, pointing at her. "You look like Barbarian Queen Elsa."

"That reference I got," Reyan said, unwittingly stealing another superheroes' joke.

"We should probably get going if we don't want to come across a city that has been completely burned to the ground," John said, continuing to serve as the voice of reason and sanity here alongside Gabrielle. Which was a shame since I used to have that role.

Hahaha, sorry, even I can't pretend that was true.

We piled together into the UFO and took to the sky with Gabrielle piloting. There were two sofa-like seats in the circular center of the flying saucer as well as a single seat for the pilot. There was no dome or top for the vehicle; it functioned like a flying convertible as it took to the air. There was even a little invisible energy field that kept the wind and bugs from flying into our faces. In simple terms, it was one of the most impractical designs ever made, but I had to admit it looked cool.

"I feel like I'm in the Jetsons," I said, getting absolutely no reaction. I really had to stop worrying about how dated my references were getting. Some things would remain nostalgic forever: Sherlock Holmes, Disney movies, and everything I liked growing up.

Feeling the warm winds of the Hollow Earth against my face, I sat back and enjoyed the atmosphere of the world around me. The strange and wondrous environment was unlike anything I'd ever experienced. Growing up in New Angeles and later Falconcrest City hadn't given me much time to look at pristine verdant wilderness. The closest thing to a rainforest I'd ever experience was driving through the Pacific Northwest with my brother to Seattle once.

It wasn't just the dinosaurs down below either. There were other signs of life. Huge farms where people had domesticated hadrosaurs pulling ploughs (okay, that was still dinosaurs), small cities with giant statues being constructed with brachiosaurs doing the heavy lifting (okay, still dinosaurs), and stone highways where people were rode wooly mammoths (ha! Not dinosaurs). This was a living civilization and it was a place that deserved to be protected from the psychopaths above us.

I had no doubt that, even if we did successfully repel P.H.A.N.T.O.M, it would not be the last invasion this place suffered. There were simply too many resources and possibilities for profit down here. Forgetting the orichalcum, there were Ultranium ruins that stood out as crystal spires rising from the depths as well as the endless paradise that hotel chains would want to exploit. Cindy had made jokes about opening a resort down here, but I could see everything from Starbucks to Marriot wanting a slice of the place.

When I had used my wish to drive away Destruction and allow change to affect my world, I had unwittingly set off a chain of events that wouldn't stop even if I wanted them to. Technology was advancing, society was altering, and tensions that had been controlled by the Primal's desire to keep the world stable were boiling over. It was very possible that isolated pockets of wonder like this, kept so superheroes could fight over them, were going to disappear now. It made me sick as it was a world without room for magic in it.

"I'm going to have to protect...ACK, ugh!" I said, having planned to make a big speech only to swallow a bug.

"Are we there yet?" Ken asked, looking over at Gabrielle.

Thankfully, we were. I could see the city of Nur'Ab'Sal coming up on the horizon and it was a magnificent metropolis that put Alexandria to shame. It was a combination of Ultranium crystal spires, the cultures of a hundred ancient civilizations. Combined with a few modern ones, judging by the radio towers I saw. It was also under siege. The hover pyramids were blasting it with lasers from the sky. Whole city blocks were burning.

Gabrielle narrowed her eyes. "Ramming speed."

I did a double take. "Huh?"

CHAPTER TWELVE

BATTLE FOR THE CENTER OF THE EARTH

"Ramming speed?" I asked, stunned. "It's a lifeboat. We're lucky it has regular speed!"

"I made a few modifications," Gabrielle grunted as the flying saucer started picking up speed. The blinking lights and controls in front of her also started making a variety of threatening noises. "Is everyone buckled in?"

Everyone was but me. "Uh—"

"This is meant to be a seven-seater," John explained.

"Grab Gary," Gabrielle said.

He put his arm around me.

We were heading straight toward the nearest of the hover pyramids, which was raining fire down onto the multi-ethnic crowds of toga and robe-clad people. It was a pointless, militarily useless massacre that just showed the attackers had no regard for human life.

"Sorry, Gary," Gabrielle said, before pushing a big shiny red button.

Why did those never do anything good?

An alarm blared and the top half of the lifeboat shot out of the flying saucer, showing that it contained an ejector seat fitted with a parachute. We landed with a gentle thud on top of one of the nearby buildings while the lifeboat UFO became a rocket and smashed into the side of the P.H.A.N.T.O.M war machine.

The hover pyramid wasn't destroyed by the action, but Gabrielle had aimed it at one of the machine's four base engines and its stability was damaged. The enormous battle fortress swerved out of control and smashed into another hover pyramid, knocking them out of the sky. The two machines collapsed into the middle of a mostly-empty city park. Internal explosions tore through them, leaving little doubt they'd been taken out of the fight.

"Wow," I said, blinking. "Did you mean to do that?"

"Obviously," Gabrielle said, blinking. "Did you think I would shoot them down without accounting for how they would land on civilians?"

Honestly, I'd never actually given much thought to collateral damage during battles between superheroes. Generally, whenever I'm fighting someone it was either one on one or something that was an existential threat to life itself. When the Behemoth raged out and punched monsters through buildings, it was mostly up to other superheroes to make sure everyone managed to get out safely. In retrospect, that was a terrible attitude to have.

I didn't have much time to process that, though, because taking two of the hover pyramids down caused every other unit of the P.H.A.N.T.O.M forces in the city to converge on us. The hover pyramids launched dozens of jetpack-equipped commandos and I also saw their weapons charging up. It didn't appear they were worried about friendly fire but these were Nazis and P.H.A.N.T.O.M was notorious for having an inexhaustible supply of idiots ready to die for them.

"This was a terrible idea," I muttered.

"Get to blasting them!" Mercury shouted, summoning a glowing green dome above us to deflect the dozens of energy blasts that descended upon us. I felt her drawing on the energy of the Inner Sun and realized that was still an option for me as well.

"You got it," John said, becoming an inky-black humanoid monster about eight feet tall with hideous teeth that occupied a quarter of his head. He ran out of the shield and started jumping from building to building before smashing into the side of a hover pyramid.

Reyan zipped into the air, generating a glowing pair of wings around her back and flying at the jetpack soldiers with battle ax in hand. It was like seeing a heavy metal video come to life. I also wondered if she could generate wings around anyone as we'd seen with the triceratops or if it was just restricted to herself and animals.

"Yeah, I don't think I'm going to be much use here," Ken muttered. "Unless you think maybe if I summoned my powers this time that—"

"No!" Gabrielle said. "Just stay safe."

Ken looked frustrated.

Cindy, meanwhile, transformed into her enormous giant wolf form and leapt down to the streets below us. She tore into enemy soldiers rounding up locals and shook them in her mouth like a wild dog with a rabbit. The viciousness of her new-found form was something she'd fully embraced, and I couldn't help but be terrified by it.

As for me, I wanted to know where in the city my children were. I sensed Leia and Mindy's presence, possibly because they were close by, or maybe just because I'd put a tracking spell on them. One time when I'd left the pair to watch *Game of Thrones* for an hour, Mindy had generated an indestructible Ultra-Force Teddy Bear to battle Leia's latest Murderbot. They'd followed the fight to Atlantis and there were still warrants out for their arrest in four countries.

I couldn't focus on them, though, as much as I wanted to. Instead, I gathered my strength and tried to focus all the supernatural energy around me. I wasn't a very good wizard, whether because of genetics, or just not having the knack, but right then I had to be. I channeled all the energy I could absorb into the Death Orb.

The entropic forces swirled around me until they crystalized into the white-hot sparkling orb, which suddenly felt like a miniature black hole in my hands. It threatened to swallow me whole and I worried I'd unleashed something worse than the monsters around me. Focusing my hate, anger, and frustration I then blasted the ball of death forward at the nearest hover pyramid.

"HADOUKEN MOTHERFRICKERS!" I shouted as the ball struck the pyramid, caused it to shudder, and then sucked it into an astral abyss where it was completely consumed. "Motherfrickers?" Mercury asked, still maintaining the force field around us despite the onslaught of laser blasts. "I'm trying to cut down on my swearing for the kids," I explained, collapsing to my knees.

John managed to down the pyramid that he was attacking, the machine unfortunately crash-landing it into a fountain and probably taking out a few civilians trying to escape from beneath it. It was soon joined by a fifth pyramid as Reyan smashed all the engines of one and hurled the enormous metal fortress into the ground so hard it collapsed into a pile of scrap. We'd managed to take down almost half of the enemy forces by ourselves.

The Nur'Ab'Sal proved to be capable of defending themselves as well. Much to my surprise, I saw dozens of pteranodon-borne warriors carrying laser spears that shot forth energy blasts as they attacked the remaining hover pyramids. They were soon joined by a stegosaurus-Tyrannosaurus hybrid creature that spewed radioactive fire and stomped down the streets, tearing open the enemy with ease.

"Is that Godzilla?" Ken asked, blinking.

"It sure looks like it," I said. I'd gotten a decent look at something very similar to the real thing during the Eternity Tournament.

"That's Kaijufornia," Gabrielle explained exasperated. "Camilla Watanabe is a Valley Girl who belongs to the Texas Guardians. She's your niece's bestie."

I blinked. "And she becomes a giant radioactive monster?"

"Yeah," Gabrielle said. "Do you know what this means?"

"Superheroes just became twenty percent cooler?"

"The Society of Superheroes still has members who are alive!" Gabrielle asked. "You know, confirmedly and not just on the word of our time lost evil-ish children."

"They're not evil. They just want me to conquer the world," I said.

"Get back to killing things!" Mercury shouted, clearly struggling to keep up her shield spell under the stress of the attacks. We'd managed to take out most of the enemy forces but there were three more hover pyramids descending on us.

I had a stupid idea. I felt barely able to stand after casting my last spell and hadn't entirely recovered from the beating that Superior Boy had given me. Still, I knew where I could get a LOT of magical energy quickly.

"Ken, I want you to say the magic words," I said.

"Please and thank you?" Ken asked.

"No, the ones I told you not to say!" I snapped.

"Gary, what are you doing?" Gabrielle said, lifting her pistols to shoot at jetpack soldiers who were descending on us.

"Magic!" I snapped.

"Hurry it up then!" Mercury said, falling to her knees as the dome above us began to crack and an energy blast went through, blowing a piece of the roof beside us away.

Ken took a deep breath and looked up to the sky. "BY THE MIGHT OF ASGARD!"

A lightning bolt descended from the heavens, carrying a nightmarish evil energy that I wondered about the origins of. Lifting the Death Orb, I intercepted it and briefly felt an incarnation of pure hate pass through me. P.H.A.N.T.O.M psychics had managed to warp the energy of the Aesir into a kind of metaphysical incarnation of fascism. Unfortunately for them, my powers were fueled by hate.

"Burn, baby, burn!" I said, re-directing the incredible magical power outward in a wave of fire that caused all three of the remaining hover pyramids to explode. They rained shrapnel and ruin, but I was pretty sure it was better than the locals getting exterminated by the assault. Also, it was better than us getting massacred.

Mercury's dome collapsed and she took several deep breaths to recover. "Thanks for that."

"Welcome," I said, shrugging. "Remember, the best part about magic is it's the universe's cheat codes and completely unfair in how it's applied."

"Uh, did you just burn up my powers forever?" Ken asked. He looked terrified that he'd lost the one thing that made him special.

"Let's hope not," I said, having no idea whether I did or not.

"Don't worry, though. If it's a worst-case scenario, I know some aliens who can give you some new ones. Ones without built-in evil."

That seemed to mollify Ken. "That's good to hear. I already get enough crap from my sister for getting worse grades than her. I can't imagine how much worse it would be if she was the only one with superpowers."

"It's terrible," I remember growing up with a sister who could talk to the dead. "They try and tell you that you're every bit as special without powers, but we all know it's bull—"

"Gary!" Gabrielle said. "People with superpowers are not superior beings. We're all equal in our capacity to love."

Mercury, Ken, and I looked at Gabrielle like she was crazy. Which she was. I believed in universal equality and all that jazz, but superpowers were awesome.

Let's be honest.

Cindy was utterly soaked in blood and when she returned to her normal form, she was still covered in carnage like Carrie after her prom night.

She didn't seem to mind. In fact, she looked remarkably chill. "That was awesome. I feel like I've contributed heavily to making America Nazi-free again."

"The Hollow Earth," I corrected her.

"Eh, same difference," Cindy said, smiling. "You know, I think blood is a good look for me."

Ken looked over at me. "Why do her clothes disappear when she becomes a werewolf and then reappear when she's not? How does that work with her being covered in blood?"

"Magic," I explained. "Also, stop trying to figure ways of seeing her naked."

"That may be hard," Ken said. "I *am* a fourteen-year-old boy."

"That is a sound and rational argument," Cindy said, walking over and hugging me. "I feel like I should bite you and make you my mate alongside Gabrielle."

"You couldn't break the skin," Gabrielle said, looking uncomfortable with the transformation Cindy had undergone.

I gently scratched behind Cindy's ears as I tried to figure out a way we could cure her. As much as she seemed to be taking to the whole lycanthropy thing, the simple fact was I didn't think it would work out for her. Let's face it, being a canine was all fun and games until you had to get shots and a flea collar. Plus, you just knew that Cindy would take up the entire bed now that she had lupine instincts.

Gabrielle took a few potshots with her pistols at fleeing P.H.A.N.T.O.M forces but there was little chance any of them were going to get away. The battle had been won and we now had to focus on contacting our loved ones. "Gary, can you tell if our kids are alright?"

"The tracking spell is still active, so they're alive," I said, taking a deep breath. I could always sense it in the back of my head. "Better than a baby monitor."

"Except for that time, you left them alone and they almost wrecked Atlantis," Cindy said, pulling away from me.

"The Henchbots were watching them!" I said, raising my hands. "How was I supposed to know Leia had an override for them? Mistakes were made. New parent problems!"

"She made those robots!" Cindy snapped.

Honestly, I was eager to track the pair down. As much as I wanted to find Diabloman and my niece, the simple fact was that my children dominated my thoughts now that I knew they were down here with me. They had been the real reason I'd retired from supervillainy, as much as I liked to attribute it to Mandy's death.

I had responsibilities to my children that meant playing dress-up wasn't an option anymore. At least, that's what I'd thought. The problem was the Call to Heroism (Villainy?) knew where I lived. If retiring my cloak and villain name didn't protect my family, then what was the point of retiring? Superheroes tried to leave the Great Game all the time, usually having more options to do so than your average supervillain, but they always ended up being drawn back in. That was because when you had the power to make a difference in the world, it was very hard to argue that you shouldn't.

Mandy, the real Mandy, had known the truth and still influenced me. Still influenced Cindy. Hell, it still influenced all the people whose lives she'd saved in her short time as a superhero. While I had been playing around, pretending to be the bad guy like a Super-themed mod for *Grand Theft Auto,* she had been genuinely thinking about how she could use her training to fight evil. The world would have been a very different place if she'd gotten the Reaper's Cloak instead of me.

That was when a giant moth landed on the rooftop with us. I did a double take and wondered if kaiju were just going to be a thing now. The moth was twenty feet long and it had numerous saddles on its back, loaded with people I knew and loved. There was Diabloman, a teenage woman wearing a version of his costume, Mister Inventor, Jane Doe, Agent G, and my children in the latter two's arms.

There was one additional person on the giant moth, though. A person I recognized and made my blood run cold. She was dressed in a crown, jeweled necklaces, a cloak tied around her neck, a black V-neck wrap, and leather pants that contrasted to her royal paraphernalia.

It was Spellbinder.

Maria Gonzales.

Still wearing my wife's corpse.

My fists began to burn with the fire I conjured inside them.

I had one more person to kill.

CHAPTER THIRTEEN

MY LEAST FAVORITE VAMPIRE

I pulled my right hand back to incinerate Spellbinder, only taking a moment to contemplate how large of a fireball it would require to reduce a vampire like her to ashes. Oh, and how not to hit all of my friends who had clearly been brainwashed by the *evil* vampiress.

Cindy grabbed my hand before I could throw the fireball. "No, Gary! You can't do it!"

"Because our kids are so close?" I asked.

"No!" Cindy said. "She came with a bunch of our allies after the big battle. Obviously, this is one of those 'we have to team up with our enemies' scenes. You know, from comics."

I stared at her. "When the hell did I become the sane one in our group?"

"You changed when you became a father," Cindy said, seriously. "We're all very disappointed in you."

I nodded then threw the fireball at Spellbinder anyway. She made a circular gesture with her free hand and the fireball dissipated.

"Aw, no fair!" I said, frowning. "I should be higher level than you."

Gabrielle rushed forward and gave Spellbinder a hug.

"*Et tu*, Gabby?" I asked, frowning.

Both Ken and Reyan ran up to Spellbinder and knelt before her. "Night Empress."

"Am I the only one who still hates her?" I asked.

"I hate her, too, Gary," Cindy said. "Unless she's willing to pay me a large fee in gold, diamonds, and Hollow Earth loot to forgive her."

I grimaced then struck a mock dramatic pose. "Then I am truly alone."

"Is it just me or have we come here with a bunch of lunatics?" John asked.

"You're only noticing that now?" Mercury asked.

I should have been relieved, really. Spellbinder's presence aside, the group was confirmation that Diabloman and my children were alive. G and Jane were people I trusted to keep the latter safe, so I was glad they were there as well. I also felt guilt for keeping them from their home if I had. As much as I had done my best to show them only the best side of my world, it was infinitely more dangerous than they could ever believe and now they were stuck in an underground warzone.

There was something in Spellbinder's eyes that made me think of Mandy and I hated it. I hated it coming from someone who had lied, deceived, tricked, and other synonyms for the exact same thing. I'd spent a couple of months getting psychotherapy from the Trenchcoat Magician to try to cope with it, but he'd ended up overcharging me and ditching me to date the Bronze Medalist. But hey, good for him. Still, I couldn't let go of my anger. I wanted to make her pay for defiling the good memories I had of my wife and confusing the time I'd spent with her with that of my wife.

I didn't hold it against Diabloman for siding with Spellbinder. She was his sister and someone he had horrifically wronged. Indeed, Maria Gonzales had every bit as much reason to hate her brother as I did for hating her if not more so. Gabrielle, though, bothered me by embracing her so closely. The Texas Guardians had been her family about the same time we'd been engaged and she'd chosen to cut me out of her life because I couldn't be part of her superhuman life. Now I felt like she was choosing them again.

That was when a Mexican ninja threw a pair of katana at me. "I'll defend you, Your Majesty!"

"Lucia, no!" Diabloman shouted,

Goddammit, was it so much to ask for a moment to think? I

turned insubstantial and the katanas passed through me.

"No fair!" the ninja, Lucia, I presumed, said.

"Uh, who the hell are you?" I asked, wondering why my reunion with my ARCHNEMESIS was being interrupted.

"I am Diabolique, Scourge of Evildoers and Agent of Order!" Lucia said.

"She's my daughter, Boss," Diabloman said. "She's decided to go the route of the antihero."

"Ah," I said, really not giving a shit. "Well, consider me defeated. You really shouldn't throw katanas since you have to go pick them up, unless you have magnetic gloves to retrieve them."

"Right," Lucia muttered, embarrassed. She then jogged over to the other side of the building to get her swords.

It was like I'd died and gone to amateur-hour hell for D-List supervillains. I fully expected to see the Shadowmaster and the Darden Valley Guardian hanging around.

"Gary, what are you doing here?" Mr. Inventor asked.

"We're here to kick Nazi ass and chew bubblegum," I answered. "And I'm all out of bubblegum. Also, to rescue you guys."

Cindy ran over to Mr. Inventor, preparing to give him a passionate kiss. Another part of polygamy I was going to have to get used to. She stopped approximately a foot away then sniffed the air.

"Uh, Cindy?" Mr. Inventor asked.

"You two-timing bastard!" Cindy said, suddenly. "Nightgirl? You asked me to marry you!"

"Night*woman* now," Amanda Douglas, a.k.a Nightgirl, said. "I even have sidekicks."

Mr. Inventor looked uncomfortable. "Six months ago. You said no."

"I said I'd think about it," Cindy snapped.

"You said you'd have to compare your options and I'd have to increase my earnings two hundred percent," Mr. Inventor said.

"Those are reasonable demands!" Cindy snapped.

Mr. Inventor sighed. "Sorry, Cindy, I think we're done."

"Uh, yeah, you better be," Amanda said, looking at Mr. Inventor with a *very* annoyed expression on her face.

I noticed that Amanda and Mr. Inventor were also wearing matching wedding bands. I wasn't about to point it out since I was "frenemies" with Amanda and didn't want to see Galahad torn to pieces by were-Cindy. Wow, that is a weird and unusual sentence even by my standards. But since I wasn't invited to their wedding, I decided to draw attention to it anyway.

"Congratulations, you two!" I said, waving. "May you not suffer the horrible fate that seems to be befall all superhero marriages."

Gabrielle glared at me.

"Present company exempted," I said.

"Ugh. Now I'm stuck with Gary!" Cindy said, shaking her fist. "The busted toy you have to share with your siblings. Like a Transformer you keep even though all the paint has fallen off and the arm doesn't work right."

"I am both appalled and confused by that answer," I said.

"Gary is the Al Gore of Supervillains," Mr. Inventor said.

"I don't even know what that means," I replied. "Which seems to be a theme in this conversation."

"Don't worry, Cindy, I'm sure you'll find someone else...or fifteen," Amanda said. "For the weekend."

"While true, now is not the time to antagonize her," I said, pointing out Cindy was a mistress of hypocrisy and very volatile in that moment.

Cindy grew claws and a lupine muzzle before growling at them.

"Case in point," I said.

Mr. Inventor looked at me before taking a step back. "Uh, is Cindy a werewolf?"

"Yea, that's new," I said.

"Cindy, please," Gabrielle said, trying to calm her. "We all love you."

"Am I no one's first pick!?" Cindy snapped. "The hot, crazy supervillain scientist who is still entirely in the desirability range despite having a child? Only I should get to cheat on my partners!"

Reyan looked over at Ken. Both were still on their knees, kneeling before Spellbinder like they were in a fantasy novel. "Is it just me or did superheroism become a soap opera when we weren't looking?"

"It's awesome!" Ken said, cheerfully. "I can't wait to post online about all this."

Reyan rolled her eyes.

I looked over at the newcomers, deliberately avoiding Spellbinder. "I don't suppose Lisa is with you?"

Diabloman exchanged a look with Jane Doe. Then he spoke, "The Society of Superheroes was defeated along with the Texas Guardians, but Spellbinder led a group of Nur'Ab'Sal warriors to liberate a small group of us. Lisa was not among the ones rescued, I'm sorry. Your daughters from the future brought G and Jane down about an hour ago to help us prepare for P.H.A.N.T.O.M's attack. I saw no sign of Kerri, though."

Goddammit.

"So, I've managed to save some relatives but not others," I said, wondering how Kerri was handling things.

"You actually didn't save us," Jane said.

"Quiet," I said, raising my hand. "I'm remembering things in a much more favorable light to myself. Listen—"

"We need to talk," Spellbinder said, walking forward and grabbing my hand.

"No, we—" I started to say.

The two of us disappeared into the shadows and reappeared halfway across the city. We were on top of a ziggurat that had a pair of statues in front of it. They were of Odin and Thor, the latter of whom I remembered having his head cut off by Entropicus during the Eternity Tournament.

There was a lot of power radiating from the Temple of the Aesir, all of it magical in nature. It was impressive, too, because the Inner Sun was putting out so much juice that the ability to sense anything other than it meant it had to be incredible. There was no one else on the summit and I could just barely see the building we'd been on a few seconds prior.

I pulled away. "Take me back, Spellbinder."

"You can't even refer to me as Maria? Or—"

"Don't," I said, dangerously. "You may get to look like her, *wearing her corpse and all*, but you don't get to talk about her."

Spellbinder looked at me with her dark vampire eyes, black except for red irises. "I didn't exactly choose this, Gary. I was trapped between worlds, life and death. Your doppelgänger offered me a chance to escape in order to spy on you. I didn't know it would come with merging my memories with those of your wife. I didn't even remember who I was for years."

"Kind of a shitty spy then, weren't you?" I asked.

Honestly, I wasn't sure I could blame her for what happened. Our world had gone through numerous changes and retcons, thanks to time-travelers, meddling gods, and who knew what else. I'd made death permanent as part of my effort to free humanity but there was no way to know what was real. That felt like a cop out, though. Even if there had been forces beyond comprehension manipulating society, manipulating me, we were who we were now. Maybe that was my opinion because I didn't want to think about how Death had used me then abandoned me when I'd done her bidding.

"Are you having another flashback?" Spellbinder asked, waving her hand in front of me.

"People hate when you do that," I said, knocking her hand away. "How long did you know?"

Spellbinder looked at me. "Long enough. When I started being repulsed by Diabloman, Damien, and when I started hating you being with Cindy. When I started having very complicated feelings about you being in love with my best friend."

"Why? I wasn't your husband."

"Mandy's feelings make mine...complicated," Spellbinder said, looking down. "I don't feel for you, Gary. You're not the person I love, and I know that you will never forgive me. Not for the fact I did try to live in your life for months. I wouldn't forgive me either. I'm not your enemy, though. You have enough of those."

It made me angry that she claimed Gabrielle was her best friend. I considered her to be my best friend and it was petty that I held that against Spellbinder. She was right, though. I never would forgive her, and it was just best that we kept things professional. I wanted to find my niece and make sure my sister was alright.

"Gimme a second," I said, pulling out my cellphone from the folds of my cloak's extra-dimensional space.

"You're not going to be able to get cellphone reception in the center—" Spellbinder started to say.

"Hello?" Kerri answered on the other line.

Spellbinder blinked.

"Hey, Kerri, you okay?" I asked before covering the receiver.

"My daughter built this for me. Still, you would not believe how much I have to pay on my plan to make sure it reaches throughout the solar system."

"Oh, yes," Kerri said, cheerfully. "The U.S. government has frozen all of your accounts, Omega Corporation has voted you off the board, and the mansion has been taken over by the Nightwalker's cousin from Sherwood City. The one who is totally not Robin Hood. I'm also being indicted for like a hundred crimes. I'm not sure what half of them are. I don't know who Rico is or what malfeasance is."

"Would my threatening you help?" I asked.

"Oh, my, yes!" Kerri said. "Also, putting me in touch with the Supervillain Lawyer."

"Yule B. Sari? Yeah, her number is 666-EVIL," I said. "Don't worry, I have her paid up in the souls of pedophiles."

"I can never tell when you're kidding," Kerri said.

"Me either," I said, revealing a central truth about my existence. "However, please let the Foundation for World Harmony know that I will destroy you. I will wreak a horrifying revenge on you and your descendants. Oh, and that you have been under my mind-control the entire time. Maniacal laugh. Maniacal laugh."

"I think you're actually supposed to laugh," Kerri said. "That's also a joke stolen from the Muppets movie."

"I've always considered myself sort of an evil Kermit the Frog," I said.

"I have no idea what to say to that," Kerri said. "Just stay safe. Your children kidnapped themselves and I'm not sure how to respond to that either."

"You were always the most normal of us all."

"Elvis says hi," Kerri said.

"Love you," I paused, remembering I was supposed to be threatening her. "Good night, Kerri. Good work. Sleep well. I'll most likely kill you in the morning."

I hung up.

"Is she going to be alright?" Mandy asked.

"Yule is very good at her job," I said, shrugging. "I've also prepared for this day a long time. The government can't be trusted but I'm the one she wants."

"I see," Spellbinder said. "Are you ready to talk?"

"Are you going to teleport me into an exploding volcano if I don't?"

"Yes."

"Then sure, let's talk for five minutes. Whatever passes for time down here when there's no day or night cycle."

Spellbinder nodded. "I'm the one who sent Ken and Reyan to your home."

"I figured," I said, blinking. "So, what, you're the Vampire Queen of the Earth's Center? Because, wow, you need Flash Gordon as your enemy."

"I fled the surface of the Earth for the Kingdoms Below because I remembered them as a place the Texas Guardians once helped. The surface is not a very welcoming place for Supers. There's a war coming."

"There's always a war coming," I said, unimpressed. "In fact, it's being waged every day. P.H.A.N.T.O.M versus the world, extremists versus moderates, superheroes versus villains, aliens versus humans. I'm not going to let people say I need to take a side between humans and Supers."

"Even when they come for your family?" Spellbinder asked.

I stared at her. "I think you know that any side who does is the one that should be pitied."

Spellbinder looked down. "P.H.A.N.T.O.M is working for the U.S. government."

"I'd say with a faction of it," I said. "I'm a little past my angry anarchist days."

"Really?"

"Emphasis on the 'little'," I said. "Tom Terror is the immediate threat here. Eliminate him and take his base then we can deal with all the other problems."

"That may harder than you think. He has the Eye of Odin."

"I have a Primal Orb," I said, confident.

"So does he. The Eye of Odin is the Orb of Chaos. It's what's going to allow him to control all of the world's superpowers."

Ah, crap.

I processed what she was saying. "So, you're telling me there's an honest-to-God tomb to raid beneath my feet?"

I tried not to be excited. Tried and failed. You see, if you've been following my adventures for the past few years then you'll understand that I am enormously immature. Things like going into a trap-filled maze, possibly carrying a torch, is the sort of thing I dream of.

"Yes," Spellbinder said. "I figured I needed the world's greatest crook to crack this case and you are he."

I stared at her. "So, just how many people have you sent in there before me?"

"Sixteen," Spellbinder said without hesitation. "Mr. Inventor got closest but even he had to turn back."

I nodded. "There's only one problem: I'm not sure why, exactly, I am supposed to go in there. If Tom Terror has already made off with the loot, then it's just an exercise in bragging rights. It's kind of like the old Tomb of Horror module. It's the most dangerous *Dungeons and Dragons* adventure of all time. The best way to beat it is when you are about to enter, steal the huge solid gold doors and run the other way."

"Gary, has it ever occurred to you the best way to get people to respect you would be to lose your habit of random, meaningless digressions? Maybe make pop culture references past 1989."

"I'd rather die," I said, all too truthfully. "I mean, it helps that I know there's an afterlife and I'm best friends with the Devil, but the sentiment is still there."

"The temple still contains the Spear of Odin," Spellbinder said. "It's an Ultranian artifact that allows the manipulation of the Inner Sun as the ley lines that give people superpowers. It can also be used to temporarily suppress the Primal Orbs and allow their retrieval without killing their host."

"Versus just killing Tom and ripping it out of his eye," I suggested.

Yeah, Spellbinder was lying to me. I'd been manipulated by the best over the years and could tell when someone was trying to play me. As much as Spellbinder was trying to say she'd only known she wasn't Mandy for a few months, this was just another layer of deception. That just made me feel more inclined to go along with her, though. I was going to turn the tables on her at some point and get my revenge.

"Yes," Spellbinder said. "There is also a grove of Golden Apples. Items that could give you, Cindy, and Diabloman immortality."

This seemed to be way too good of an offer. "So, it's directly beneath us? Right?"

"Yes, in the heart of the temple," Spellbinder said. "I'll give you the—"

I grabbed her wrist and turned us insubstantial as the two of us fell through the top of the temple.

CHAPTER FOURTEEN

GARY KARKOFSKY AND THE UNCHARTED TOMB WITH A MUMMY

This may surprise you. Shock you even. However, it is true. I am not a very good planner.

I know, I know, it's crazy. One look at me and you think that this devastatingly handsome sex machine is also a brilliant Machiavellian schemer. That such intricate social and mental planning is the only way he could survive so many dangerous archvillains, get Luke Skywalker back for his own trilogy, and steal the Crown Jewels three times in a month. Yes, that was all on me. But the truth is I suck at coming up with actual schemes.

So, big surprise, I don't plan my actions ahead of time. The Nightwalker had a hundred plans for every possible contingency from Ultragod going rogue to an attack by giant mole people. Utragod was a swift thinker but made sure to make calm, deliberate, and well-thought-out decisions. Mister Chaos was known to spend months imprisoned in New Bedlam Asylum, just so he could plan his next move.

Me? I just sort of play it by ear.

In this case, I chose to grab Spellbinder and pull her into the Temple of the Aesir. I thought I was being clever by using my insubstantiality powers to skip past all the traps, monsters, and other things inside your typical dungeon to get right to the loot. Basically, the best way to solve an open-air maze is to climb to the top of the wall and skip to the center. I should have realized that if it was that easy then Spellbinder would have done that herself.

Instead of us landing in the middle of a pile of treasure, which I imagined would be a Smaug-like horde that would replace all the wealth I'd lost to the U.S. government, we instead fell for a long time down a seemingly infinite black void.

"Ahhhhhhhhh!" I shouted.

"Gary, what have you done!?" Spellbinder shouted back.

"Ahhhhhhhh!" I shouted some more.

"This isn't helping," Spellbinder said, significantly more subdued.

"Ahhhhhhhh!"

"In another moment down went Alice after it, never once considering how in the world she was to get out again," a deep booming male voice spoke in the void. We weren't alone here and whatever was with us wasn't corporeal.

"Now you're just copying *Alice in Wonderland*," Spellbinder said as we continued to fall.

My response? "Ahhhhhhhh!"

"Shut up, Gary!" Spellbinder shouted.

The two of us then landed in the middle of a long labyrinthine corridor that looked like a stereotypical fantasy dungeon. There were manacles on the wall, a couple of skeletons on the ground, and everything was made of ancient Medieval masonry. Light was provided by strategically placed torches that would have taken an entire team of people to light every day but were probably just magical.

I got up and looked around. I saw a heavy rock on the ground. Lifting it up, I sent it skipping down the hallway and watched darts fly through the air, a couple of swinging pendulums with battle axes attached to the bottom, and a section of wall that opened up before shooting spikes out to impale the opposite wall.

"Huh," I said, blinking. "I guess this is a less racist Temple of Doom."

"Goddammit, Gary!" Spellbinder said, standing up. "I cannot believe you."

"No, seriously, *Indiana Jones and the Temple of Doom* was really racist," I said, shrugging. "I mean, I love the action scenes but there's nothing but slander against Hinduism in that film.

Kali isn't Satan and no one eats baby snakes. That's in addition to the fact Kate Capshaw is no Karen Allen. Oddly enough, I didn't have a problem with Short Round. Everyone wanted to be Indy's adopted kid. Where did he go anyway? Did he get killed in the next adventure or did Indy ditch him?"

Spellbinder got up and felt her face. "You've transported us both into the pocket dimension of the Aesir temple."

"Pocket dimension?" I asked.

"Yes," Spellbinder said. "The Chaos Orb was put in one when the temple was constructed six months ago."

"Only six months?" I asked, looking around. "Damn, I was hoping this was an ancient temple, but I suppose the Chaos Orb was on Hell Island a year ago. Continuity nod!"

"Argh!" Spellbinder said, shaking with rage. "You are such a fucking child. No wonder Mandy thought you were going to abandon her for this goofy supervillain B.S."

All amusement left my face. "You don't get to tell me that, Spellbinder."

I was trying to be polite here. I'd been summoned to the center of the Earth by Spellbinder to fight Nazis, which was the kind of thing you put aside personal issues for. However, I really wanted to just blast her again with my fire powers and hoped they worked in incinerating her. I felt soiled around her and the fact people seemed to be missing we didn't have an *affair* was pissing me off. I wasn't seduced into being in a relationship with Spellbinder, I'd been tricked. Emotionally and physically violated.

"Call me Maria," Maria said. "I left behind Spellbinder when I died saving the world and went to an empty void."

Well boo freaking hoo. I'd died like twice myself and it was no picnic for me either. Friends with Death or not.

"Yeah, that's not going to happen," I said. "I'm barely avoiding blasting you."

"Says the man who treated his wife like crap and preferred to hang around a bunch of homicidal psychopaths," Maria replied, somehow putting me on the defensive. Wasn't she aware she was the bad guy here? Not the fun kind either.

"Listen, I love being in the center of the Earth fighting Nazis and riding dinosaurs," I said, my voice low and cold. "However, I would give it all up to be with my wife again."

"Would you?" Maria asked. "Because from where I'm standing it's your pathological need to be a supervillain that got her killed."

Mandy had wanted to be a superhero. She'd refused to evacuate Falconcrest City during a frigging zombie apocalypse, but I wasn't going to argue that with Maria. She didn't deserve to speak about my wife—having her memories or not.

I decided to let her have it. Figuratively, at least. "You know what? Screw this. We're done. I'm going to abandon you here and go get the Chaos Stone for myself. Good luck figuring a way out. Hopefully there's a minotaur in here you can drain for his blood."

I turned insubstantial and levitated up to leave but found myself blocked by the ceiling. Apparently, I couldn't pass through the magical barriers around me. That made a perfectly dramatic exit look silly. After almost a minute of banging up against the ceiling and walls, I levitated back down.

"Are you finished?" Maria asked.

"Okay, but I'm still not helping you," I said, deciding we were stuck together. "We're officially the Gaullist and Communist Resistance of France against the Nazis. Same enemy. Different goals. No friendship."

"You sound like a really lazy genius," Maria muttered. "Either that or the world's most educated idiot."

"Thank you," I said. "But save your compliments. They're not going to help you."

"Please, Gary, *you owe me*," Maria said. She put her hands on her hips and smiled at me in a condescending way.

I did a double take. "Owe *you*? What *the hell* do I owe *you*?"

Stretching out with my powers, I blasted each of the mechanisms along the wall one after another. I froze over the dart cannons, destroyed the swinging pendulums, and filled up the pit trap with ice. I felt like an old-school Rogue searching for traps. Well, Wizard-Rogue hybrid. Man, I was a geek. Like, to "I am unhealthily obsessed and need therapy" levels.

"I tolerated your antics better than your real wife would

have while we were married," Maria said, making air quotes. "Mandy never would have encouraged your worst and most selfish impulses the way I did or ignored your adultery."

"Mandy was *dead* when I hooked up with Cindy."

"And Gabrielle?" Maria asked. "I encouraged you to be with her to increase your position in the superhero community."

"You're sick."

"If Mandy had her way, your little menagerie of weirdos and lost toys would have all gone away and you would have gone back to your normal life. A life you hated."

I somehow resisted incinerating her. At this point, I wasn't even sure why since we were in the perfect place for a murder. "Mandy *died* for Cindy."

"Because she was a hero, Gary," Maria said, her voice dripping with contempt. "But one ill-suited for you. She never wanted children and I let you have those, too. Cindy and Gabrielle were just all too willing to provide. Not that you're anything resembling a father to either. Pathetic."

I turned around and glowed with an aura of barely suppressed magical power. "I remind you this is coming from a woman who made a pact with my evil(er) doppelgänger to spy on me, stuck with me through prison, and stayed with me for years after the guy who hired her was *dead*. You're not really much of a superheroine yourself."

Maria looked down. "I tried to be a heroine before, Gary. To do the right thing and fight against my demonic parentage, the cult that raised me, and my insane brother. Do you know what it got me?"

"What's that?" I asked.

"Killed," Maria said, the bitterness in her voice audible. "Worse, I was damned by whatever gods ruled the afterlife since I didn't move on but just had to wait to be resurrected like so many other heroes or villains. When I was returned, it was as a bloodsucking creature from hell. One *you* created because you couldn't live a normal life for your wife, so you made her a monster."

I took a deep breath. She was coming at me with all my insecurities, but the simple fact was I didn't believe any of it. "And yet you still stuck around. Pretended to love me, Cindy, and our child. So how pathetic are you?"

"Don't hide behind your kids, Gary. Its contemptible. As for why I stayed with you and your mistress—well, where else was I supposed to go?" Maria asked. "I'd been poor, hated, and unloved before. I prefer being rich."

"You know, I could argue with you or point out I know the answers to a lot of those questions, but I think we're past the point of words now." I conjured the Primal Orb. Then I whispered a short spell. "skcus msiripmav."

That was *vampirism sucks* spelled backwards, by the way. A lot of wizard incantations are just gobbledygook like Pig Latin or twin speak. The magic was in the man not the words. That was one of the things I was really annoyed about learning after studying Enochian for six months.

Maria chuckled and said, "You were always a crap wizard, Gary. I knew more magic when I was four than you'll ever—"

That was when Maria started throwing up blood. I don't mean little spurts of it either. I'm talking a massive, disgusting gusher of it that sprayed the walls, sprayed me, and kept coming long after it would have emptied the contents of a normal person's stomach. Maria thrashed on the ground for several minutes until I saw her stop.

I checked my cellphone and took a picture of her covered in blood for my InstaPic page. "Wow, that took a while. I sure hope no monsters are attracted by blood."

It was a small vengeance but one I was glad I took. Somehow, I couldn't bring myself to attack her again, but this felt good.

"What...what did you do?" Maria said, coughing.

"Just a reminder that my magic is *explicitly control of death and dead things* like vampires. Antagonizing me is not a good idea. I'm cutting you a lot of slack because I'm insane enough to believe there's something worth saving in Diabloman's sister."

"He murdered me!" Maria snarled. "He murdered my lover, Rico."

Oddly, the more Maria lashed out, the less angry I was at her. I hated her for what she'd done but the personal anger was diminishing. I could tell she hated herself for what she'd done.

Slinking into someone else's life and pretending to be Mandy was the only way she'd been able to find some sort of happiness. The fact we'd been forced to be together by Merciful for years while imprisoned by him had also probably induced a kind of mutual Stockholm Syndrome. Or maybe I was just trying to cut her some slack because she looked identical to my wife. It was easier to believe she was a victim, too, rather than trying to maintain my outrage.

"Yeah, Rico Chavez, a.k.a. the Guitarist. Diabloman killed him and then he killed you. You were left alone and abandoned by people who mourned your death but didn't realize you were all dead. Other Gary took advantage of that. Then you sought people who could love you. Now that you've been rejected, you're lashing out in order to feel like you have some control over your life. That includes trying to get me to hate you."

"Which is more believable than I hated you but stayed with you because it was easier."

"Well, I know that's not true."

"Why's that?" I said, squeezing my cloak to get the blood out of it.

I looked at her and raised an eyebrow. "Do either of our lives look particularly easy right now?"

Maria shrugged. "Well, I'm an underground queen and you're a former billionaire in a relationship with the world's greatest superheroine."

Okay, maybe not my best argument. "Listen, let's just clear the air. I don't like you; you don't like me. However, we're both stuck in this temple right now."

"Because of you," Maria said.

"Let's not quibble over details. The fact is you planned to send me here to get some magic doohickeys and then steal them from me."

"You don't know that," Maria said.

I snorted. "Lady, please, I knew your game the moment I saw you. Does Diabloman know you're eventually going to kill him?"

Maria looked away. "He believes he can atone for what he's done."

"He's tried for years," I said. "That's why he joined my

organization. What he did to you destroyed him emotionally and physically. He never recovered."

"World's smallest violin playing."

I shrugged. "Maybe we've all done unforgivable things."

I was thinking about the fact I'd let Mandy die.

"That's the thing about unforgivable actions, Gary," Maria said, softening her voice for the first time since we came here. "They can't be forgiven. I'll use Diabloman until I have no use for him and then turn on him. I hope you're there to help him pick up the pieces."

I shrugged. "D and I are best friends. Nothing could break us up."

Maria shook her head. "It's a shame we didn't meet under any other circumstances."

"Let's not go that far," I said, cutting her off. "I was a mark and I can respect you conning me. I just can't forgive you using my wife's identity to do it."

Maria shouted down the hall. "We're ready to find the artifacts! Show us what we have to do!"

"Who are you talking to?" I asked, confused.

"The Guardian of the Temple," Maria said, simply.

"You must pass three trials to find the antechamber. Tests of Courage, Wisdom, and Strength." The big booming voice we'd heard earlier spoke. "Only those who pass all three tests will be judged worthy of the final challenge. Those who slay one of the monsters guarding the Three Great Treasures will be allowed to take one."

"Three great treasures?" I asked.

"The Eye of Odin, the Spear of Odin, and the Golden Apples," Maria explained.

"I was being rhetorical. Besides, it's technically two great treasures since Tom Terror took the Eye. I feel like any test of wisdom that doesn't weed out Nazis is also a poorly designed one."

"I said wisdom, not being a scumbag."

I blinked. "Wait, you're not just a generic spooky voice?"

The voice didn't take the time to answer. "Time for the Trial of Courage! Unleash the draugr!"

That was when a bunch of screaming undead Vikings ran at

us from the other side. They were mummified corpses dressed in armor and wielding Medieval weapons. All of them had glowing eyes and reeked of powerful necromantic energy. Not even the monsters during the zombie apocalypse in Falconcrest City had felt as powerful or as deadly.

"Huh, Viking mummies," I said, before turning around to blast them. "That's new."

CHAPTER FIFTEEN

RIDDLE ME THIS, CLOAKMAN

"Murder, murder, murder," I said, blasting mummified Viking after mummified Viking. They charged at me like zombies and didn't have much intelligence. In fact, the actual zombies I'd fought in Falconcrest City had been much more cunning.

These bastards just charged at me with battle axes, swords, hatchets, and clawed hands. A few of them could shout magic spells in the language of dragons, which I believed was straight up copyright infringement. There were two more for every one I struck down and soon I ended up flanked from behind by another group of endless undead Northmen. Though, assuming these were Vikings from the Hollow Earth, that would actually make them *Centermen*. Weird what kind of things you think about in the middle of combat.

Maria wasn't standing still, though, as she blasted mummy after mummy with her own significant magical powers. I regretted the fact that I'd turned her back into a human since a vampire Spellbinder would have been a lot more helpful. On the other hand, I wasn't sure her falling would be a bad thing. It would spare me having to tell Diabloman I'd killed his sister when it came down to one of us betraying the other.

"We're being overwhelmed!" Maria said, throwing up a magical shield to give us a few seconds of breathing room.

"No kidding!" I said, stretching my neck out. "You know I'm a bit out of practice fighting hordes of the undead. There was a time when I could have just blasted all of these guys to pieces."

Maria stared at me. "Then why don't you?"

"I'm saving all of my nasty Dark Side Sith powers for you."

"We need to work together if we're going to survive this."

"Oh?" I asked. "Is that how you convinced all of the other heroes to ignore what a frigging monster you are?"

"Gary, you have a body count in four figures and yet somehow people still think you're a harmless goof. Don't talk to me about being a monster. As for how I got everyone to work with me, it was a combination of the fact we were facing a bigger threat and the fact I can control people's minds."

"You're just admitting that, huh?"

"I figure the more I make you angry, the more likely you'll be able to unleash some of that sweet-sweet unholy death magic. We need a demigod to fight against the Nazis down here and unfortunately you only get your juices flowing when pissed off."

"Yeah, well, you never got my juices flowing because something-something, you're not attractive. Insult, insult." I paused. Not because I'd run out of snark to throw at her, though I obviously had. "Wait, hold on. Something you said."

A huge Draugr with a glowing war hammer began smashing the energy shield, causing Maria to fall to her knees and cracks to form on it. "Could our argument wait a bit?"

"Nope," I said, cracking my knuckles. "I just remembered that I control the Orb of Death!"

"For something other than making me nauseous?" Mandy asked as her shield dissipated.

"That I can resolve all of this with a snap," I said, snapping my fingers.

I then drained all the necromantic energy from the draugr surrounding us and used that power to draw still more energy from them until they turned to powdery dust. There were close to a thousand of them destroyed by the end. It left me feeling like I was close to full power and capable of working incredible miracles. Then it slowly ebbed away because I wasn't strong enough to hold onto it.

Maria looked at me. "Unbelievable."

"Thank you," I said proudly, as I saw the hundreds of piles

of dust and pieces of armor scattered down both ends of the hall.

"No, I mean that you can do advanced complicated magic like that but completely screw up the simplest things."

I shrugged. "I actually have no idea how magic is supposed to work so I make it up as I go along. I call it *Better Living through Ignorance.*"

"Uh-huh," Maria said, shaking her head.

"Like the fact Neil Peart became the world's greatest drummer by choosing to do an amazing set of fast triplets on timbales during the song 'Time Stands Still'. He got the idea from a Genesis song that did the same. However, they had done it by slowing the tape down during recording."

Maria blinked. "Are you really taking the time to discuss Rush's drummer during our quest for a mythical spear?"

"It appears I am," I said, pausing. "It's like the old saying goes: you're either a Beatles fan or a Rolling Stones fan. Given it took me thirty years to figure out the former was a pun and not a misspelling, I'm the latter."

Maria threw up her hands and walked down the hall. "You're going to be the first one against the wall when the revolution comes, Gary."

"Speaking of revolutions, how the hell did you get to be queen of the Norztec people down here? That was a pun on Norse and Aztec, by the way."

"Yeah, I got that," Maria said, walking to the end of the hall from where I'd managed to clear out all the traps. "As for how I became queen of Nur'Ab'Sal, it's fairly simple—I killed the previous queen."

"In single combat?" I asked. "Are we really in one of those 'you keep what you kill' societies? Because, honestly, I really think they'd do better with elections."

"No, I turned her into a vampire then revealed it to the public after she fed on a few members of her court. I slew them all and was proclaimed a hero for it."

I blinked. "Wow, you aren't even trying to be a hero anymore, are you?"

"Says the guy with the idiotic codename of Merciless: The Supervillain without Mercy."

I paused. "It's less stupid than yours."

"Excuse me? What's wrong with Spellbinder?"

"Not Spellbinder; Night Empress."

"Night Empress is an awesome codename," Maria snapped.

I rolled my eyes. "They don't have night in the Hollow Earth. Does anyone here even know what night means?"

Mandy blinked then cursed. "Godsdammit."

"Oh will you two just screw and get it over with," the mysterious voice intoned.

"Thank you, I'm good," I said, looking up at the ceiling.

"Who are you?" Maria looked up.

"My name is not important," the voice said.

"It's Odin," I said. "It's the Temple of the Aesir. It's Odin's spear. Mysterious voice making enigmatic proclamations. It's Odin."

There was a pause. "Not necessarily."

"Come on, really?" I asked. "I mean, what was your next move? Show up as a one-eyed old man in a cloak and give us the next challenge before dramatically revealing yourself after we've solved it?"

"You're not getting into the spirit of things, Gary."

I shrugged. "You're not my god, either, so that makes us even."

"What is the next challenge!?" Maria shouted, shaking her fists at the darkened hallway before us. It had no twists or turns but led straight into an empty void. Looking back, I also saw that the previous hallway had vanished.

"No, Gary has ruined it," Odin said, sighing. "If you're not going to take this seriously, you're not going to be able to get my magic items."

"I'm taking this seriously!" Maria shouted. "What kind of sexist bull is this?"

"Hey, I had Valkyrie! I was progressive by ancient deity standards!" Odin snapped. "But fine, if you want the second test then we'll do a standard riddle contest."

"Just don't make it a riddle where the answer is time, mountains, or something similarly easy," I asked. "Let's step up our game a bit here."

Maria slapped my chest.

"Fine!" Odin growled, clearly having planned to use one of the classics. "Why is a raven like a writing desk?"

Maria looked appalled. "That's cheating! There's no answer to that riddle! That was the point. Also, what does *Alice in Wonderland* have to do with the Norse gods? This is the second time you've referenced them!"

Odin didn't answer her question. Instead, he bellowed, "Answer or stay imprisoned for all time in my labyrinth!"

"They were both written on by Edgar Allan Poe," I said.

"Wait, what?" Odin asked.

"People have had literally century to come up with an answer," I said.

"What's in my pocket?" Odin asked again.

"Whatever has been put inside it," I said. "I'm better at this than Gollum. Better looking, too. My wife used to call me a dorky Legolas."

"What is the average air speed velocity of a laden swallow?" Odin asked.

"African or European?" I asked.

"African," Odin said, cheating in our *Monty Python and the Holy Grail* one-off.

"Twenty-four miles per hour," I said, simply. "Wikipedia."

That was when the door at the end of the hall opened. "Very well. You truly are one of Earth's most knowledgeable mortals. Well, mortal-ish."

"In the Socrates sense of knowing I know nothing at all? Yes," I said. "Well, nothing and endless amounts of pop culture."

Maria just stared. It was clear that my winning a riddle challenge with the gods had broken her brain. "I will never believe the universe makes sense again."

"The real question is why you ever bothered believing it in the first place," I said, walking down the hallway and turning insubstantial to avoid the columns of flame triggered by the traps Odin had put in the wall.

Because if you ever trusted a god specifically identified as a Trickster then you weren't long for the world. The only divine being anyone had a consistent track record in defeating was the Devil and that was only if you were good with a fiddle, court challenges, or a clever peasant.

Maria followed me, protecting herself with a defensive shield. "I wonder what the next challenge will be. It's supposed to be a test of strength."

"I hope it's karaoke."

Maria felt the bridge of her nose. "Gary, why the hell would it be karaoke?"

"I didn't say it was," I replied, heading through the door. "I just am hoping it is karaoke. I'm fully capable of singing both halves of Toto's 'Africa' despite the fact it was designed to be sung by two people with different vocal ranges."

"Jesus," Maria said, making me uncomfortable since she still looked like Mandy. Mandy had been a Wiccan and never would have sworn by him. I tried not to let it bother me but that wasn't going to happen.

"If we do sing karaoke, we can do Paula Abdul's 'Opposites Attract'. I'll let you sing the cat," I said, regretting it instantly as it was a song I'd loved singing with Mandy. Mind you, she was a former professional singer and I was autotuned all to hell when I was a member of the Black Eyed Peas (long story).

The room on the other side of the door led to a fabulous treasure room. I'd mentioned earlier that I wanted to find a Smaug-sized treasure hoard in hopes of recuperating my losses and this certainly fit the bill. It was easily three or four football stadiums in size and at least fifty feet in height. There were piles and piles of gold coins in every direction, jewels thrown about haphazardly, and spears spread throughout.

I mean, *thousands* of spears made of gold or silver that were richly decorated. They were prominently displayed in the grip of bejeweled Odin statues or in display cases sticking out of the horde around us. At the center of the chamber was an enormous bronze brazier that burned with a fire the size of a two-story building.

"So, yeah, this just screams trap doesn't it?" I asked.

"Ya think?" Mandy asked, looking around.

"Yeah, if we touch any of the treasure, then a monster will appear, or we'll be cursed, or the entire place will collapse around us."

Mandy nodded. "Wanna bet the spear is the only one that looks beat up and covered in blood?"

"I don't take sucker's bets," I said. "It's almost certainly the only spear that looks like it was made for killing people instead of decorating someone's wall."

It was then a bolt of lightning descended from the ceiling like the ones that turned Ken and Reyan into superheroes. This one, however, turned into an old man dressed as a fisherman with one eye. He had a long thick beard but was dressed pretty modern for an ancient Norse God.

"Can I get some petitioners who are not quite as genre savvy as you two?" Odin asked. His voice was every bit as booming as when it had emanated from the walls around us.

I raised my hands. "Listen, it's not my fault that this genre has been played out. I'm just glad you didn't have an enormous ball rolling down the tunnel. Also, I do want to know what's with all the pop culture references. That's normally my sort of thing."

Odin shrugged. "After Ragnarök, there wasn't much to do but watch television as the world left us behind."

"Wait, *after* Ragnarök? Didn't you guys die in that?" Maria asked.

Odin frowned. "We did. It was at the end of the universe when Diabloman brought an end to all things."

I grimaced. "He's never going to live that down, is he?"

"No!" Maria snapped. "No, he is not!"

Odin shrugged. "The Society of Superheroes brought us back with the Great Cosmic Reboot and we returned along with the new universe, rather than being left to enjoy our afterlives. Baldur was very disappointed. It left us free of our fate but without any purpose to our lives. Thor, at least, tried to be a hero. He ended up dying in the Eternity Tournament."

I grimaced. I remembered the Eternity Tournament opening with Entropicus tossing Thor's head down the steps of his palace on Hell Island. I hadn't given it much thought at the time, Thor just being another mythological figure to me, but hundreds of heroes had been killed there. It had meant many worlds were deprived of their champions and were now suffering from that loss. Worse, many families were stripped of their loved ones with semi-omniscient beings like Odin being the only ones to know the reasons why.

"I'm sorry," I said.

Odin closed his one good eye. The other was an empty socket. "Don't be. He died fighting evil, and while I'd love to see Entropicus destroyed for good, that is not my fate. It might be yours, though."

"I don't believe in fate," I said.

Odin just laughed at me.

"So how do we get the spear?" Maria asked. "What's the final test?"

Odin opened his good eye and looked between us. "One of you must defeat the other."

"We're not going to—" I started to say.

Only to be blasted in the back by Maria.

CHAPTER SIXTEEN

CURSE YOUR SUDDEN BUT INEVITABLE BETRAYAL

I woke up about half an hour later, which meant I'd gotten both barrels of Spellbinder's power. I felt like I'd had to regenerate an entire back full of third-degree burns and it was a miracle I wasn't dead. Actually, I wasn't sure what could kill me. I decided to avoid the old standbys of decapitation, fire, holy items, and erotic asphyxiation.

"Man, I wish I'd betrayed her first," I said, slowly sitting up. "I was planning on doing it, too. This just makes her look like the cleverer villain."

"Sorry, Gary," Odin said, standing over me. His voice was far less intimidating and more conversational with none of the previous echo. "The truth is some people are just naturally trustworthy. It's why I didn't lock up Loki to be horrifically tortured for centuries until after the whole murdering Baldur thing."

I got up and dusted myself off. My cloak had fixed itself from where Maria had blasted me. "Yeah, I've got to say that was the second worst breakup of all time. The original Paul and John."

"I thought you weren't a Beatles fan."

"Well, I was just making that up. You can like...hey, wait, where did your reverb go?" I asked.

"Err," Odin immediately deepened his voice. "I don't know what you mean."

"No, no," I corrected the All-Father. "You can't just go back to that. Besides, I'm pretty sure we've all figured out it was an act anyway."

Odin smirked. "Eh, you fake it until you make it in this business."

"Which business is that?"

"Godhood," Odin said, simply. "I was once a typical Viking warrior until I found the Orb of Chaos and the Ultranian control spear. Then I worshiped Odin so hard that both allowed me to become him. I became his avatar and retroactively always was."

"That makes no sense," I said.

Odin shrugged. "Neither does the majority of how the universe works."

I looked around for Maria and saw no sign of her. "So, I take it that Maria got away with the spear?"

"She got away with *a* spear," Odin said. "I gave her a fake."

I blinked. "Why? She passed your tests."

"Yes, accent on *my* tests," Odin said. "I'm the one who determines who gets what from them."

I stared at him. "Then why did you let Tom Terror, *Nazi Mad Scientist*, get away with the Chaos Orb?"

"You're really hung up on this Nazi thing," Odin said, sounding like he thought it was akin to smoking or body odor.

"Yeah, I kinda am!"

Odin muttered. "I lost it in a dice game."

"Wait, what?" I asked.

"I lost it in a Surtur-damned dice game!" Odin snapped. "Tom Terror was supposed to die in my labyrinth's traps, but he plowed through all of them. I was going to fight him in the final challenge so he couldn't take off with the orb but then he mentioned dice and well, I kind of lost control of myself. I'll twist my word to the point of incomprehensibility, look what I did to the dwarves who made Mjölnir, but I never vanir on a debt."

"Vanir on a debt?" I asked.

"Vanir are a bunch of dirty-dirty lying cheats," Odin said. "Sexy as hell, though. I used to have a marriage like yours and the wife would often invite a few of those—"

I rubbed the bridge of my nose. "Listen, Santa, I need that spear."

Odin frowned. "I am *not* Santa. Why do people keep confusing us?"

"You live up north, you're magical, the beard—"

"That describes Ned Stark, but you don't see him delivering toys."

It didn't describe Ned Stark, but I wasn't going to belabor the point. "Listen, are you going to give me the spear or not?"

"What do you need it for?" Odin asked. "This spear and I have been through a lot together."

"I'll give it back," I said, lying to the deity. "Maria said that it could be used to suppress the powers of the Primal Orbs, which I think is a very good idea if I don't want to die. It is also necessary to turn the doohickey that Tom Terror is going to, uh, and the McGuffin."

"You have no idea what it's for, do you?" Odin asked, crossing his arms.

"Some of what I said was accurate!" I snapped back. "Probably."

Odin let loose a hearty laugh that made his stomach roll like a bowl full of jelly. Being as Hanukah is a religion about victory over pagans occupying your homeland, I didn't have any dog in this Santa vs. Odin fight. Still, Odin really did have a strong resemblance to Old Saint Nick.

Odin sighed. "One hundred thousand years ago, the Ultranians were Ultra-Force based beings who came to this world to examine proto-humanity. They created this pocket-dimension in the center of the Earth and set up all sorts of monitoring stations. They performed a lot of experiments on the still-evolving race and put the Super-gene in the most explosive breeders. From there, they took sample *homo sapiens idaltu* across the universe to populate their worlds. That's why most of the universe's other species resemble humans."

"In a world of jetpacks and talking monkeys, I really have never bothered speculating on that," I said. "As far as I'm concerned, that's like worrying about why people spontaneously break into song during musicals."

I mean, really, sometimes you just had to go with it.

"Nevertheless, it's true," Odin said, looking at me with his one good eye. "The spear is the key to regulating the development of your race. Tom Terror has access to all the machinery but is still figuring out how to turn it on or off. With the spear, he or you could accelerate humanity's evolution by millions of years."

I blinked. "Evolution actually doesn't go in a straight line. People aren't always getting smarter, stronger, or better. It's just improvements in medicine—"

Odin looked annoyed, which surprised me as I'd thought the conversation would have irritated him long before that point. "In other words, giving you the spear means there's a bigger likelihood of Tom Terror or Maria getting control over humanity's future."

I blinked. "What, you don't think I can take both of them out?"

Odin didn't answer. It was as clear a statement of his lack of faith in me as could be made. Honestly, it was starting to annoy me that the only people who had any belief I could kick ass were the fascists.

I sighed. "Let's gamble for it. My orb for your spear."

Odin's eye twinkled. It was the look of a compulsive gambler who had just been given an unlimited line of credit at the craps table. "Haha. Now you're talking. What game?"

"Rock, paper, scissors," I said, dryly.

Odin visibly deflated but nodded. "Fine."

"One, two, three," I said, holding out my hand flat.

Odin stared, having made a fist. "Son of a…. How?"

I sighed. "Really? Was there any doubt that you, the god of badass burly dudes, was going to do rock?"

Odin grumbled something about being the god of wisdom. "It's a stupid game. Rock should break paper."

"It's magic paper. Pony up with the spear," I said, holding out my hand.

"My pony has eight legs," Odin said, conjuring Gungnir and handing it over. "I want this back."

"Sure, sure," I said, again lying.

I took it and gazed at it. Much to my annoyance, the spear didn't look anything like one used to kill things. Instead, it looked like something out of the future or a cartoon. It was only vaguely spear-like and more like a tuning fork made from alien metal. It glowed with a large number of Kirby dots that appeared in and out of time while resonating with a strange unearthly music. I felt the power within in it, and while I didn't put it past Odin to cheat me, I believed it was the real deal.

"Thanks," I said, staring at it.

"You have no idea how to use this thing, do you?" Odin asked.

"Not a clue," I said. "That's never stopped me before, though."

"Well, don't get yourself killed," Odin said. "Wait until you're in battle to die."

I nodded then turned around to depart, stopping midstep. "Can I ask you a question?"

"If you don't expect me to answer," Odin said. "Nothing is free in this life, Gary."

"Yeah, but talk is cheap."

Odin seemed to consider that. "Alright, you can ask."

"Is there anything of Mandy in Maria or am I only just getting my wires crossed?" I asked. "I hate her, but I want to think there's something redeemable in her. Maybe just because she's all that's left of my wife."

Odin didn't respond for a moment.

"So, I guess you're not answering," I said, starting to walk again.

Odin grumbled then looked to the ceiling. "When the old universe was destroyed in the Great Retcon, a flaw was introduced into the universe. One that inevitably resulted in all of the victories of heroes becoming ash. Evil always rising to fight again. Entropicus was the embodiment of that flaw and has had many incarnations over the millennia. Cain, Emperor Titus, Caligula, Nero, Tom Terror, President Omega, and Gorthax the Tyrant of 10,000 Galaxies. All predecessors to the evil god he becomes at the end of time."

I was confused. "I'm not sure what this has to do with Mandy."

"He is the evil at the heart of this four-color comic book world that Destruction and Death have tried to keep imprisoned. Ultragod was their weapon against it and Merciful was tricked into killing him in the belief he could get his world back. He tried to make the world perfect to make sure he could never rise to power. When you needed your wife at your side, desperately, he contacted Mandy's soul and asked for her help against him. Merciful showed her the hellish future that could be delayed but not averted. She refused."

"She refused?" I asked, remembering that Mandy (secretly Maria in her body) had claimed to have spent two hundred years in a hellish dystopian future.

"Yes," Odin said. "She would never be a pawn to evil— even if that evil wore her husband's face. So, Merciful found another heroine and showed her the same horror. Spellbinder was broken by what she saw. She'll do anything to take over the world now to prevent Entropicus from conquering reality."

I sighed. "Do we really need a dictator to stop another dictator?"

"No," Odin said, surprising me. "We need a hero. Someone who can inspire people to remember that while evil can't be defeated, good can't either. You know, bullshit like that."

"So Maria is a fallen hero," I said. "Full on Annie Skywalker."

"Just like you're a really irresponsible Luke Skywalker," Odin said. "Or Rey, but she's a Mary Sue."

"Hey, I like Rey," I said. "I just hate the movies she's in."

"Kylo Ren?" Odin suggested.

"Okay, you're now just being insulting," I said. "The only thing we have in common is we're both devastatingly handsome supervillain fanboys."

Odin waved goodbye. "Good luck, Gary. You're going to need it. Remember, some evils need to be fought with good and some evils need to be fought with evil."

"I think that's quoting a Vin Diesel movie."

"Yeah, yeah, there's not much for gods to do in the afterlife except watch television and screw with the living. You'll figure that out soon enough."

"I'm not a god," I said, simply. "No matter what the kooky magic test says."

"You are. Just like the lamer kid brother of a better god, like me. Donnie Wahlberg to Mark Wahlberg. John Wilkes Booth to Edwin Booth. Cain to Abel."

"I'm beginning to see why Loki betrayed you guys."

Odin's expression turned grave. "For a thousand years, Loki and I searched for a way to avert Ragnarök. He was desperate to avoid betraying his brothers in blood. In the end, he discovered that if he didn't lead the forces of the enemy then they'd end up being led by an undead Baldur resurrected by Hel. We'd lose and no new world would rise from the ashes. So he took one for the team and murdered my son. He became the monster that we'd slay."

"Yeah, I don't recall that from my *Bulfinch's Mythology*."

"Maybe because I'm making it up. Maybe Loki was just a jackass. It's also possible he was like you and being the bad guy was just what he was meant to be."

I didn't answer. Instead, I stuck out my thumb. "So, how do I get out of here?"

Odin gestured and a doorway opened to the labyrinth. He reached into his pocket and tossed me a golden apple.

I caught it. "What's this for?"

"A gift," Odin said. "Just in case you need a power boost or a cure for any horrible condition. It's the last of them."

"What will the rest of the Aesir eat?" I asked.

"What rest of the Aesir?" Odin said, slowly vanishing from sight.

I was kind of disappointed I didn't get to fight a giant snake or spider as the climax to my big treasure hunt, but I was glad I'd managed to acquire the weapon I was looking for. Putting away the Golden Apple, I walked out the door and was surprised to find myself surrounded by thousands of Nur'Ab'Sal citizens. They were every color of the rainbow, dressed in togas and exotic dress that combined traditions from all the world's people. They were just the kind of people that P.H.A.N.T.O.M wanted to wipe from the face of the Earth. It probably was the second-most abominable country in the world to them after Brazil.

Standing among the crowd of onlookers were my associates: Cindy, Mr. Inventor, Diabloman, his daughter, Reyan, Ken, and others. There was no sign of Maria, though, and I suspected she'd gone directly after Tom Terror. Good for her. I wasn't concerned about that now, though. Right now, I was only interested in the people before me.

Whether they were heroes or villains on the surface, they were all here united in the protection of the locals. It was, for the first time, perhaps the only time, I'd ever done anything just for the sake of being the good guy. It felt good and I was sad I couldn't be the hero that they needed. Not because I wasn't able to try. It was the fact that I was a murderer and didn't regret the lives I'd taken. There was too much hatred in my heart.

But that didn't matter that day.

"Yeah, none of you guys have to fear P.H.A.N.T.O.M anymore. We're going to get rid of them," I said.

It wasn't the Saint Crispin's Day Speech.

It would do, though.

CHAPTER SEVENTEEN

TAKING A MOMENT TO FIGURE OUT MY NEXT MOVE

So, I was made King of Nur'Ab'Sal.

Apparently, they had some strange leadership traditions down in the Hollow Earth. Things like watery tarts throwing swords at you being the basis for their system of government, except it was Norse gods and spears. Maria had abandoned the place and left us to clean up the aftermath of P.H.A.N.T.O.M's attack. I understood her logic. Organizing people getting pulled from wreckage and being healed of injuries would slow us down and prevent us from following her.

I had to admit I was torn between my desire to go after her and my niece immediately and taking care of a lot of suffering people. I was really screwing up this supervillain thing. In the end, I decided to do the unthinkable and plan ahead. The city's workers were caring for everyone; I was going to sit down and find out everything I could about P.H.A.N.T.O.M's defenses and plot my next move. You know, after being distracted by something completely stupid.

"You enter into the Tomb of Vecna and see that the walls are lined with granite statues of the one-eyed Lich God. All of them hold braziers burning with a sickly green fire and there is a sense of all-consuming evil about the place."

"I search for traps," Jane said, shaking the twenty-sider in her hand a few times before tossing it on the stone table to the side of the throne room.

The throne room was at the top of a ziggurat with a pair of

stone thrones prominently displayed at the end. It looked a bit like a smaller version of the one at the end of Star Wars. I know, I use that for every one of my pop culture references, but it really did. There also wasn't any sign of Princess Leia passing out medals to Han and Luke. Have you ever wondered why Chewie didn't get a medal? I'll tell you why. Racism. Think about that every time you watch that movie. The fact droids are slaves, too.

Where was I? Oh yes, Diabloman, Jane, Case, John, and I were sitting around a stone table with a map in front of us of the Hollow Earth. We were supposed to be planning our attack on the Nazis, but it had somehow descended into a game of *Dungeons and Dragons*. Being criminals, we were playing for cash and stacks of gold coins were lined up on the edges of the table.

Case, being the sanest one in the group, of course was the only one to question this activity while playing. "Gary, have you ever been diagnosed with ADD?"

"My inability to concentrate on one task for more than a minute is a choice rather than a... wait, what was I talking about? That die is really shiny!"

Jane pulled out a laser pointer and moved it around the table.

"Ah!" I said, covering my eyes. "No more."

"I use this to taunt the werecats in Bright Falls," Jane said, cheerfully.

Case sniggered before his expression turned serious. "I'm not going to be able to stay here, Gary."

"Well, of course we're going to have to leave," I said, simply. "As nice as Viking Atlantis is, it's not a place I see myself staying for long. I mean, they don't have the Internet, except on my phone, and that's just no substitute when you're a dedicated multiplayer—"

"I mean back to my Earth," Case said, frowning.

I blinked. "I thought you hated it there."

"I do," Case said, blinking. "I also got a call from my daughter."

"You have a daughter?" Jane asked, sounding more than a little offended. Clearly, Case hadn't bothered to fill her in on all of the details of his pre-tournament life.

"Technically, the daughter of the psychotic paramilitary

force leader I was cloned from," Case said.

"Only here does that make perfect sense," Jane said. "Well here and *Metal Gear Solid.*"

"How did you get a call?" I asked. "I mean, I thought my cellphone coverage was good but not interdimensional."

"There's a lot of remote viewing devices here. Things that can look between parallel realities," Case replied. "I decided to check in on the people I left behind. They think I'm in a coma since I'm being astrally projected here. I don't want her standing over me forever."

Jane looked down. "Yeah, I kind of have to go as well. Time is passing differently there but my family is worried, too. It's been about three days for me and they're about ready to call an exorcist."

They both looked at each other, clearly more upset about leaving the other behind than this world.

I looked between them. "There's more, isn't there?"

Jane looked down. "I love your daughters, Gary. I want to have a little deer herd just like them someday. That's not going to happen if I don't return to my body. Also, they're in danger because of all this. One minute in a cute mansion, the next a war zone. You need to find a safe place for them."

"I don't think either of your worlds are safe for them," I said, getting the implication of what they thought I should do.

"It might keep them alive," Jane said. "Listen, we can arrange—"

I raised my hands up in the air like I just didn't care. "BEGONE!"

Jane and Case didn't have a moment to react before both blinked out of existence, returned to their bodies back on their respective Earths. Disrupting divine magic was surprisingly easy when you were the Chosen of the God who cast the spell.

Diabloman looked up. "That was ill-advised."

I took a deep breath. "I've been encountering a lot of really nasty stuff, lately. Maybe it's time that I start figuring out how to keep the people I love from it."

"The people you love who include a dedicated cyborg super-soldier and a weredeer shamaness who would have been very helpful during the upcoming fight against P.H.A.N.T.O.M," John said, simply. "Smart."

I glared at him. "Says the guy who can sleep in a bucket."

John casually slid Case and Jane's gold coins into his pile. "Now that's just mean. I don't sleep in a bucket unless it's a full moon."

"I'll try and contact them afterward," I said, pausing. "Apologize. Otherwise, Leia will be so furious that I sent away her bestie."

"Mindy, too," Diabloman said. "Jane helped her pick out her supervillain name. Ms. Teri."

"Mindy is a *newborn*," I pointed out. "She should not be worried about codenames. Potty training should be the height of her current ambitions."

I already had one super-smart child that had inherited hyper-cognition from some alien abductee ancestor or exposure to arcane magical energies, I didn't need another one. F.I.T (The Falconcrest Institute of Technology) was already throwing grant money at Leia and it was interfering with my attempts to raise her to be unlike Cindy.

And myself.

"Your family is strange," Diabloman said, before falling silent. There was clearly something weighing on my luchador friend. "Still, I don't know why you would send away two of your best friends."

"It's complicated," I said.

The truth was I was just sick of losing people. Cloak, Mandy, Ultragod, my brother after his resurrection, and then Mandy again. I didn't have the strength to keep losing the people I cared for. Maybe it would have been possible to endure if everyone who died came back after a few years. But the thing was I needed to get over that. This was bigger than me, bigger than all of us, and I'd made my choice—I now had to live with it. Or die with it.

"So, am I next to be sent home?" John asked, shaking me out of my fugue. He didn't look particularly upset at the prospect, but John had about three facial expressions: angry, angrier, and really pissed-off stoic. He was kind of like John Wayne in that respect.

"Well, you aren't astrally projected but physically here," I said, frowning. "Also, I thought you'd want to stay here permanently."

Truth be told, I was already regretting sending away Case and Jane. The fact was that I couldn't risk them against a bunch of Nazis. Tom Terror had supervillain teams with him down here and could remove powers at will. If he could also bestow them, we were potentially facing an army of fascist super freaks following their Führer. Which meant we were fucked. I still hadn't figured out a way to help Ken and he was a ticking time bomb of superpowered fury.

"Super Freaks," John said, singing. "They're super-freaky."

I stared at him.

"Rick James?" John asked.

"Sorry, my pop culture references begin at the Eighties," I said, pretending I didn't get it. "Wait, they have disco in the wasteland you come from?

"I knew a ghoul who had some records." John frowned. "Though, honestly, it's starting to look like this universe isn't any safer than my own."

"We'll deal with the Nazis," I said, sounding more confident than I felt.

"That's not the only thing that worries me," John replied. "Your world is like an acrobat someone is firing a hundred bullets at. It's possible you might jump out of the way of a few but at least some of those are going to hit."

"You actually can't jump out of the way of bullets," I said, pointing out a fact. "I mean, unless you have superspeed. I tried and I still have scars from it. Thank God for healing factors, am I right?"

"Which god?" John asked, dryly.

"There's something else we need to talk about," Diabloman said, probably referring to the undead elephant in the room that was his sister.

"Like why you should vote Merciless for 20XX?" I asked. "Why settle for the lesser evil?"

"No," Diabloman said. "Also, that's Cthulhu's tagline."

"I stole it," I said.

"Cthulhu ran for office?" John asked. "That seems a bit out of character for him."

I chuckled, knowing the eldritch abomination playing cowboy was joking.

"I mean my sister," Diabloman said, pausing. "I hope you understand why I abandoned you to go work for her."

"Because you have a history of poor life choices?" I asked. "Obviously, including working for me."

Diabloman snorted. "I did so because family is the most important thing. It should trump everything else in a person's life."

"Except your Satanist family who ordered you to kill Maria in the first place," I said, pointing out an uncomfortable fact.

"*Sí*," Diabloman muttered, looking down. "Ever since I died and was reborn for the second time, I have felt a great weight lifted off my shoulders. I realized I wanted to make atonement for my sins. That started with my trying to seek out my sister and offering my service to her."

I grimaced, realizing that what Diabloman wanted to do was impossible. He'd killed Maria's true love, and that wasn't something you could ever be forgiven for. Forget the whole "destroying the universe" thing, he'd personally wronged her in a way that was beyond the pale. She'd forgive her own murder before what he'd done to the Guitarist. Actually, now that I thought about it, he had murdered her, too.

Yeesh.

"You realize Maria's kind of evil now, right?" I said, disgusted. "What with the whole 'rape by deception' thing." Yeah, there I'd said it. It couldn't be taken back now. Sorry for everyone who was hoping I'd backpedal on that.

Diabloman didn't respond for a while. "*Sí*. I am the person who corrupted her, though. I am the one who will have to redeem her."

I didn't have a response to that. "Right."

I didn't know if redemption was a real thing outside of *Star Wars* and *Angel*. I used to be a big believer in it, but the simple fact was that once you took a life, that was permanent. There were no do-overs for that. I mean, I'd learned that lesson the hard way. There was no making it up to Mr. and Mrs. Goon for the fact I'd killed a few hundred of their relatives. That government agent I'd liquefied this morning had a family somewhere. I mean, yeah, they were probably scumbags like him, but they'd miss him.

Maybe.

Okay, I wasn't helping my case.

"Maybe you should focus on trying to look after your daughter," I said, diverting the subject. "If she's going to become a superhero or supervillain then she's going to need a lot of training. The Super lifestyle has never been more dangerous."

Diabloman seemed to think about that. "I agree."

"Good," I said. "Now let's get back to the game. Rocks fall and kill Jane's and Case's characters."

Diabloman wasn't finished, though. "My daughter is but seventeen. I ask you not to sleep with her."

"Wait, what!?" I blinked, then got furious. "What the hell is wrong with you?"

Diabloman misinterpreted my reaction. "It is not that long a wait."

"I like women!" I snapped. "*Adult* women! Specifically, ones I am in love with. Gabrielle can bench-press a tanker truck. I am not interested in cheating on her."

"You regularly sleep with Cindy. Which is like sleeping with all of Falconcrest City."

"I heard that!" Cindy called from the other side of the throne room where she was modeling a bunch of Nur'Ab'Sal fashion in front of quicksilver mirrors. "I am a doctor, goddammit, and very safe!"

"My apologies," Diabloman called out. "You are a very clean harlot."

"Thank you!" Cindy called back.

"Are you spying on us?" I called over to Cindy.

"Obviously!" Cindy answered back. "I can't believe you banned me for life from your tabletop games."

"You cheated!" I snapped.

"Those dice came up twenties on their own," Cindy said.

"The fact that they had metal interiors and I had a magnet was just coincidence."

"Fair enough," I said, not really wanting to get into it. "I swear, it's like people don't understand that some people prefer to be with one person."

Which is totally how I felt. I mean, yes, I'd been with other people than Cindy and Gabrielle over the past year while mourning Mandy, but that was business. Sometimes you need to seduce the queen of a country, a supervillainess or superheroine, to get at something like your Okmarian Death Ray or the crown jewels of Londonium. Okay, wow, I had problems. Gabrielle and I needed to establish where we stood. Because, honestly, I wasn't all that sure these days. I'd tried to offer being exclusive with her, but she'd backed away faster than a speeding bullet.

"It's just, well—" Diabloman looked embarrassed.

"What?" I asked.

"I thought you and Ultragoddess were having problems," Diabloman said.

John raised an eyebrow.

"What makes you think that?" I asked, defensively.

"The fact she spends half her time in space and another half flying around the world punching things. The rest of the time, which is nonexistent if you can do basic math, is short dates with you and leaving you to watch the kids. That's not a healthy relationship. That's a regular booty call and free babysitting."

I looked over at Cindy. "You can have the decency to be here when having a conversation with me."

Cindy walked in, dressed in a large array of jewelry and a strategically placed white wrap that substituted for clothes. "I'm just saying if she likes it, she should put a ring on it. Also, we need to loot this place like there's no tomorrow."

I rolled my eyes. "We're not imperialists, Cindy."

"Well, why the hell not!" Cindy said. "It's not racist if we're doing it just because want their stuff, is it?"

John laughed at that one, which bothered me.

"They have polygamy down here in the Hollow Earth," Diabloman said, before slamming his fist on the stone table.

"You could marry both and they could marry their loved ones. *Then you could conquer this land and rule as one large family of intertwined nobility.*"

"Pass," Cindy said, shrugging. "I prefer being the mistress. I'm in Gary's will anyway. Wait, I am in your will, right?"

"I'm immortal," I said, remembering what Mercury said about godhood. "Probably. So, I don't have a will."

"Dammit," Cindy said, before realizing what she said. "I mean, good. By the way, if you want more kids, you need to get someone else to birth them. I put on a whole inch because of Leia and while I love her, she's going to have to pay that back by inventing me a suit of armor or something. I suggest you go seduce Nightgirl and let Galahad find you two in bed. Then I will point and laugh."

"No," I said.

"Diabloman?" Cindy asked.

"Marriages are sacrosanct," Diabloman said. "Or should be."

"Oh come on!" Cindy said. "That's not been true since Henry the Eighth."

I pinched the bridge of my nose to stave off a migraine coming on. "I am *not* sleeping with anyone else. Gabrielle and I are *fine.*"

Gabrielle then walked into the room, wearing a toga that stopped before her knees and a little crown. "Gary, we need to talk."

I knew what that meant. "Goddammit."

CHAPTER EIGHTEEN

POOLS, POLYAMORY, AND PROPOSALS

It turned out I was very wrong. Gabrielle wanted to spend some private time with me alone in the Room of Pools, which was apparently a Medieval set of hot tubs that were fed by pipes and aqueducts. We were in one of the dozen or so heated baths that had curtains cordoning them off and it was sinfully decadent. Well, that and the fact we were enjoying the two-person pool party the media had celebrated for decades in college-age movies.

"You know, the ancient Romans considered communal bathing to be hedonistic," I said, relaxing next to Gabrielle as she rested her shoulder on mine. Neither of us were wearing any clothes but if this were a comic book, the steam around us would have covered up any naughty bits. You know, assuming someone was reading a comic about us now. I'm talking to you, Jane.

"I can't imagine why," Gabrielle asked. "Mind you, these were the people who considered leaving an infant on trash piles a perfectly good way of reducing family size."

"Were I a supervillain two thousand years ago, I'd go by the Masadan Manhunter and be terrorizing them. In fact, once I run out of Hitlers to kill, I'm going to target Emperor Titus."

Gabrielle laughed, assuming I was joking. "You have no idea how much I've missed you."

I frowned. "Well, nothing was keeping you from coming around more often."

Gabrielle sat up. "It's a hard world to leave without a heroine to protect it. The loss of so many champions to permanent death has left it extra-vulnerable. There's just not enough new heroes to replace the ones we've lost."

Way to twist the knife, Gabby. "Yeah, especially not with mad scientists turning young black superheroes into young white supervillains."

"Yeah, what the hell is up with that?" Gabrielle asked, disgusted. "It's just *weird.*"

Gabrielle was the world's most prominent hero right now and, like itor not, both she and her father had been political figures simply by being indestructible flying black Americans. Gabrielle might not be especially beloved because of her outspokenness but that was a quality I loved about her. It made her disgust over the treatment of a new hero with a similar background and powers all the more visceral.

"I'll ask Tom Terror's ghost."

Gabrielle frowned. "You need to be careful with Doctor Terror, Gary. He's the worst foe my father ever faced."

"Even worse than Entropicus?" I asked, semi-ironically.

"Yes," Gabrielle said, frowning. "He was the only person my father was ever tempted to kill outright after WWII."

"The world would be a better place if he had," I said.

"Maybe," Gabrielle said, looking concerned. "He was always an irredeemable monster but my father believed once you opened that Pandora's Box then you couldn't close it."

"Technically, you could close Pandora's Box, but if you did then you sealed in hope."

"Gary, don't be a know-it-all."

"I don't know if that's possible," I said.

Gabrielle gave a light snort. "I always wanted to live up to his ideals, but I could never believe the law was on our side. Whenever we put on our wigs and glasses, we were just ordinary Americans and that was a constant stream of harassment and suspicion. People cheered Ultragod as the Second Coming then arrested my father for loitering in the Eighties."

I didn't know how to respond to that, so I decided to switch subjects. "No shame in being Neutral Good instead of Lawful Good. I think you need to know what Leia and Mindy told me about the future—"

"That I'm not inspiring enough to prevent the apocalypse?" Gabrielle asked.

"Oh, you heard that."

"Ultra-hearing," Gabrielle said, tapping her ears.

"I'm sorry," I said.

Gabrielle blinked. "I don't believe the future is written. I could change my ways and become the perfect little princess they remember me as in my teenage years, then light the way for them. But that would mean making even more sacrifices involving my family. You're my only family now, Gary, and I refuse to do that."

I frowned. "Even though I'm a shameless lothario who doesn't deserve you and has a child by another woman?"

I didn't know if I wanted Gabrielle putting off her destiny, or non-destiny, since it'd be going against what people said about her future, because of me. I wasn't worth it. Leia and Mindy were but I'd lived down to my worst expectations as a super-villain. Killing a federal agent was going to cause all sorts of problems for Gabrielle and I didn't want that. She could save the world if she wanted to and be a torch for the next century.

Gabrielle, to my surprise, took what I said completely differently. "Gary, I don't care about who else you love."

I blinked. "Wait, what?"

"We got together while you were with Mandy and Cindy. Not being an idiot, I kind of knew what I was getting into. Just like you did with me."

I stiffened. "That wasn't Mandy."

Maria had shown her true colors and I wasn't going to back down in our next encounter. Only one of us could rule the world and I was determined to make sure that wasn't her. Even if I wasn't sure I wanted to rule the world anymore. Tears for Fears would be so disappointed in me.

"I'm sorry, Gary," Gabrielle said. "I want to ignore all of the terrible things she's done, but I can't—not when I see how much Maria's name makes you sick."

It really did.

"So, back to what in the hell now?" I asked, deciding to divert the subject back to my second-favorite topic: sex with beautiful superhumans. The first being *Star Wars*. Err, I mean my family. They were totally not three. "You're *not* bothered by me sleeping with other women?"

"Loving, not sleeping with," Gabrielle pointed out. "There's a difference. At least in romantic relationships."

Yes, if you were twelve. "We should probably be very specific here."

I also noted she was talking about who else *she* was with.

"Not Cindy," Gabrielle said, looking embarrassed. "For multiple reasons. You do realize I've been with other people, right?"

I didn't want names. "Yeah. You're a woman with a lot of love to give, Gabby. Any man (or woman) would be stupid not to realize that."

"There's Rory Macleod, a.k.a Water Horse," Gabrielle said, not realizing I *really* didn't want names.

"Wait, the guy who becomes a flying stallion?" I asked. "What do you even need with a flying horse? You fly!"

I mean, I could think of a few reasons, but I hoped that wasn't what she meant. Goddammit, that was a mental image that wasn't going away.

"He's the immortal protector of Scotland. He hunts Unseelie Fae," Gabrielle said. "Plus, there's Ultramind X in the fortieth century."

"Talk about a long-distance romance," I muttered. "Do they know about me?"

"It wouldn't be fair if they didn't," Gabrielle said.

"Yeah," I said, sucking up my jealousy.

"My father was with Polly Perkins, Penelope Porter, and a mermaid," Gabrielle said. "Guinevere and him—"

"Ah, Moses. Really?" I interrupted, having had that told to me by Cloak. "I mean, I thought the shippers and fanfic writers were just making that up."

"Guinevere had a thing with the Nightwalker, too, and Aquarius."

"I am very weirded out. This changes a lot of my opinion of the Society of Superheroes headquarters or as I now will mentally refer to it: The Love Shack."

Gabrielle looked amused. "When you're immortal and in a

nonstop conflict with evil, I suppose you seek what comfort you can."

"Is that what I am? Comfort?" I asked.

Now wasn't the time to bring up the fact I didn't want to be with anyone but Gabrielle...and Cindy. Also, Eliza Dushku. Not that I'd made any moves toward her but if we met at a party and hit it off then that would be okay. Okay, I lost whatever point I was trying to make there.

Oh, right, when you were a supervillain and a superhero with hundreds of adventures then you were bound to develop unconventional relationships. Like Case and Jane, who I pretended were not just straight up cheating on their partners. Okay, bad example.

Gabrielle turned to me. "You're the father of my child, Gary. My children. I love you. I will always love you."

"Then marry me."

I wasn't just throwing it out there. I was fully prepared to commit my entire life to her and never look at anyone else ever again. I wanted to be with Gabrielle and Gabrielle alone if she wanted it that way or part of a weird trapezoid if that was what it took to have her in my life. I just wanted people to know how much I loved her, and marriage was a symbol of that. Nothing said true love like the willingness to shell out a small fortune for jewelry, weddings, and the legal fees to make sure they could strip you dry if you didn't make them happy. And yes, that was my father's description of the institution after one of his fights with my mom.

Gabrielle paused and looked down into the water.

"Not the reaction I was expecting," I said, softly. "Mind you, I can't crush coal into diamonds to get a ring."

Gabrielle shook her head. "Gary, it's not you, it's my enemies."

"We've had this conversation before, Gabrielle. I was hoping you'd maybe have figured out that I'm not the same helpless college student I was before. Also, the whole mind-wiping me thing? Dick move."

Gabrielle blinked but didn't meet my gaze. Instead, she just stared forward. "It's not you I'm worried about. You've more than proven capable of handling yourself against the worst scum of the Multiverse. No, it's Mindy and Leia."

"The children you've been deliberately avoiding." That came out much harsher than intended.

Gabrielle looked like she'd been punched in the gut. "Gary, do you know what happened to Aquarius' daughter?"

That killed the mood quickly. "Yeah, I do."

Aquarius the King of Atlantis had married an alien woman and had a child with her named Neptina. The family had been controversial from the start because of being an alien-Atlantean hybrid as well as a superhero's daughter. My brother Keith had been in jail at the time but he'd had a partner named Doug Calistos, a.k.a Whipray.

Whipray was one of those supervillains that didn't have my charming personality or a code of ethics. He was a homophobic, misogynist, racist piece of garbage who eventually turned on Keith, turning state's evidence, so he was a rat, too. Whipray's most infamous act was the one that had permanently soured superhuman-supervillain relations. I mean, not that they'd ever been good, but he'd crossed the line that led to antiheroes like Shoot-Em-Up and the Extreme! He'd snuck into the royal palace and killed the infant girl.

"I hear Aquarius fed him to a dozen sharks," I said. "One piece at a time."

Honestly, I thought he was too soft on Whipray. I would have done much worse to someone who laid a hand on my child, but I think we've already established that. Capital punishment is the least thing you can do to anyone who harms a child.

"Smaller fish I believe," Gabrielle said. "He was never the same afterward."

"I don't blame him," I said.

"He does you," Gabrielle said.

"Excuse me?" I asked.

"You're the brother of Whipray's partner," Gabrielle said. "Stingray taught Whipray everything he knew."

"Which, in the words of Dark Helmet, makes us absolutely nothing," I pointed out.

"He won't care, and neither will others," Gabrielle said. "If we get married, Gary, it's putting a target on not just you but our family."

"So, you want me to be your dirty little secret," I said, moving away.

Gabrielle sighed. "My mother got kidnapped, attacked, and cursed on a regular basis. Hell, she even got turned into a goat once."

Polly Perkins was the gold standard for damsels in distress. This wasn't because she wasn't a tough old broad. Several supervillains found out to their lasting regret that she was a lot more willing to use lethal force than her nigh-omnipotent husband. However, she'd probably been kidnapped over a hundred times over the years. It was only a miracle she'd ended up with nothing more than the occasional broken bone or bloody nose. Other superhero boyfriends and girlfriends weren't so lucky.

I'd noticed a lot of bad guys who targeted the few superheroes with public identities' loved ones tended to die in tragic accidents while being arrested. A little more subtle than what Aquarius did to his son's murderer but no less effective. Most crooks got the message and the rest were quickly sorted out by Darwin. World's Smallest Violin here.

"Your mother spent like a decade trying to prove Moses Anders was Ultragod," I pointed out, remembering some of the silly reality comics I'd read as a child. "My guess is your father made some stupid argument about his secret identity keeping her safe but missing that people still knew she was important to him."

"Yeah," Gabrielle said, wistfully. "My mother knew what she wanted and took it. No matter the cost."

"Also, I think the ship has sailed on the supervillain community knowing we're together. They were all there when I rescued you from Merciful."

Gabrielle sighed. "Yeah."

"And the fact that I have a mixed-race indestructible child," I pointed out, "who glows when she flies. You don't have to be Tom Terror to do the math on that one."

Gabrielle didn't have an answer for that. "I suppose we

could brainwash the entire world or I could spin around the planet—"

"No spinning around the planet," I interrupted. "It never works, and everyone gets a headache."

Gabrielle smirked then frowned. "I just don't want my children living in fear."

A nasty part of me wanted to point out that if she wanted to claim Leia as her child, too, then she should marry me. Otherwise, it was just her occasionally showing up to give gifts for the holidays and spending time with them. Of course, I didn't say that because I wasn't an idiot. The greatest superpower of all was one I was still struggling with: keeping my big mouth shut. "We all live in fear. It's part of knowing life is trying to kill you."

Gabrielle smiled. "Then you're right. We should get married. Down here."

"What?"

"People suspecting you're the father of Ultragoddess's daughter isn't the same as knowing it," Gabrielle said, softly. "Besides, a lot of criminals are deeply stupid."

"Speaking as an evil genius, you are correct. Mind you, I have an Honorary Doctorate in Superpowered Thievery from the Crooked Isles."

"Gary—"

"Which means people have to call me Doctor Merciless: The Doctor without Mercy."

"Gary—"

"Man, did that piss off Cindy. She hates whenever supervillains use a doctorate in their names without a PHD. Even the Brothel Madame with her Pimps and Hookers Degree."

"Gary!"

"Right, you want to get married here? It will be for ourselves, our friends, and our loved ones. But it will be official."

In that moment, I didn't care about either of our reputations. Whether superheroes would come after me for corrupting their idol or whether supervillains would come after her because, well, she was Ultragoddess. People would hate her for loving me and maybe it was dangerous for us to be together.

But I loved her. Like the Nightwalker and Larceny Lass, the Nightwalker and Ms. Demeanor, the Nightwalker—okay, that guy had a problem.

Gabrielle looked uncertain about my proposal. "I don't know. Who would even perform the ceremony?"

"I'm sure there's a sun-worshiping weirdo around here we can hire for some shiny beads—which sounded a LOT more racist out loud than in my head. Listen, I'm not sure my rabbi will agree our marriage down here is valid, it would mean a lot to me. We can figure out how this affects our other relationships later."

I was certain Cindy would demand a prenuptial agreement that would guarantee her three mansions and a small island off the coast of Hawaii. One of the good ones, not the leper ones as Homer Simpson would say. That is if she didn't try to invite herself on the honeymoon to get her next reality TV show off the ground. Cindy in Paradise. Sounded like a porno.

"I've always wanted to be your wife, Gary," Gabrielle said. "But—"

"But what?"

"It didn't feel right when you were mourning your wife. Both times."

I blinked. "Yeah. Well, I'll always be mourning her. That doesn't mean I'll love you less."

"Or Cindy." It seemed to bother her that I left her off, which was not usually how these things went.

"Or Cindy," I said, pausing. "Is that a yes?"

"Yes, Gary."

CHAPTER NINETEEN

TOM TERROR TERRIFIES THE TRIO (MINUS ONE)

So, of course, that's when we get attacked. Superior Boy was back and the superpowered Aryan form of poor Ken Masterson was followed by him grabbing both me and Gabrielle by our throats. He could have killed both of us in an instant but instead just gloated.

"You didn't think P.H.A.N.T.O.M had installed a chip to force Ken to transform at will!" Superior Boy said, laughing. "Once more the Master Race triumphs over—"

I aimed my hand at his groin then froze it over.

"Son of a—" Superior Boy started to say.

Gabrielle then gave him a knee to it, making a painful crunching sound as if something had broken to pieces.

"Ahhhh!" Superior Boy said, falling to his knees.

I summoned my cloak around me and the Spear of Odin and aimed it at him. "Sorry, Ken."

Superior Boy hissed at me and then disappeared with a zip behind Gabrielle, holding her in a headlock. "Strike at me and I shall snap her pretty neck!"

A part of me wondered why people with superspeed didn't automatically win every single encounter they had. Was it because the brain couldn't keep up with their speed, time-dilation, or were people just not capable of properly harnessing the full extent of their abilities? I mean, if I had superspeed not only would I have taken over the world by now, but I would have had time to fix the *Star Wars* sequels and get Daisy Ridley the role of Lara Croft in the next *Tomb Raider*.

"Right," I said, aiming the spear at him and pushing a button that resulted in a blast of Ultra-Force energy striking them both.

Superior Boy laughed it off. "You fool! Do you really think that Ultranian weaponry can harm a being empowered by the gods?!"

Gabrielle's eyes glowed. Her uniform appeared over her as she crackled with the power of the immortals.

"Oh, crap," Superior Boy said.

Gabrielle proceeded to smash him out the side of the temple before starting to deliver the mother of all beatdowns.

"Have fun, ya dickless Nazi freak," I said, waving bye. "Also, take note that I'm insulting the weird demonic second personality possessing you, Ken. No offense to you. My sympathies go out to you. Just not your brainwashed self."

"That's just silly," Tom Terror's voice spoke behind me. "We simply brought out his true self. At least, how he should have been."

I spun around and blasted him. Instead, the energy blast passed through a hologram of the overweight, sweaty bald man in a khaki shirt and camouflage pants. His right eye was missing and replaced by a clear purple crystal with a lightning bolt scar etched into it. The Chaos Orb I presumed. He looked a lot like Marlon Brando's Colonel Kurtz but there was something vile in his presence that exceeded that role. Standing behind him, one foot in height was a little mechanical spider with a red eye. It was projecting the hologram I was looking at.

"Oh, look, it's the Godfather of Suck," I said, trying and failing to come up with a decent insult.

Tom Terror just smiled. "I'm surprised to see you down here, Gary. Usually, supervillains end their lives one of three ways: in jail, dead, or retiring on a pile of money. I thought you'd picked option three."

"Yes, well, I found myself coming out of retirement for one last fight."

"That never ends well outside of movies. The older fighters almost inevitably lose and embarrass themselves," Tom said, his voice lowering. "You should have quit while you were ahead. Killing Ultragod, seducing his daughter, taking over Falconcrest City, and preventing superheroes from being resurrected is a career I almost envy."

Some of that was my evil(er) doppelganger. The rest was, uh, well, sadly accurate. "Afraid I'll show you up, you Nazi jackass?"

Tom Terror chuckled. "I'm not a Nazi."

Okay, that took me by surprise. "What?"

"I have long since exceeded the ambitions of that failed painter. There are planets named after me, conquered in Earth's name. Alien races I've exterminated or enslaved. The technology I've created will form the basis of the First Great Interstellar Human Empire. Plus, I'm not racist."

I stared at him. "Really, that's what you're ending on?"

"Not that racism isn't useful," Tom Terror said. "Gerald Ford said that if you can convince a man he is fundamentally better than another man and it is his best interest to keep them down, then he won't notice when you pick his pocket. White supremacists are an easy source of recruits for P.H.A.N.T.O.M. Lonely, bitter, isolated, and misogynist young fools with no prospects are as common now as they ever were. The difference is now we have the Internet to contact them."

I stared at him. "What? You're the leader of the Alt-Reich?"

Tom Terror actually laughed. "Oh, that's a good one. We need branding like that. It's why I'm here to offer you a job."

My disgust was so great I wanted to vomit on him, but he wasn't here, and I really liked this bathhouse's tile. "Yeah, I don't think so."

"If it's the Jewish thing, we can work around that," Tom Terror said, cheerfully. "One of our chief spokesmen is a fundamentalist pedophile."

"Oh you charmer, you." I clutched the Spear of Odin tightly. "How about we just settle this personally? I come to you, kill you, and then end this whole 'take over the world' business."

Tom Terror snorted. "There you go again, underestimating my ambitions. Gary, with the sorry state of the Society of Superheroes, taking over the world is child's play. It's really mostly a question of which archvillain will be in charge and I've been ignoring the fight between them to focus on larger matters."

"Larger matters?" I asked.

"Superhuman trafficking," Tom Terror said, as if it was the cleverest idea in the world.

"Superhuman trafficking?" I repeated his word, wondering what I was missing. "That's more important than taking over the world? Frigging slavery?"

"Earth is a backwater shithole I'm ashamed of being from," Tom Terror said, wrinkling his nose in disgust. "The Ultranian colonies of humans are far more advanced than us and that's not counting the thousands of other species in Galaxy Prime. We're centuries behind the technological curve and it will require a vast amount of resources to shift our economy to a galactic-level one, let alone make us a superpower. But we do have one resource no one else in the universe has an abundance of."

"Superhumans," I said, starting to appreciate the shape of his plan. "That's what you're doing. You're kidnapping super-humans in preparation for brainwashing them like Superior Boy. Once you have control of the Inner Sun, you'll be able to use it to turn regular people into living weapons. From there sell them to every tinpot dictator or corporation in the galaxy."

"Precisely," Tom Terror replied. "How very observant. Part of why I wish you would join me. Where else would I find some-one so close to my level?"

"Try the local..." I paused. "Nope. Not going to waste a *Raiders of the Lost Ark* quote on you. Here's the question, though, how would that benefit you? I mean, aside from you making trillions in Venusian dollars."

"I will trade our 'human resources' in exchange for the technology and materials to up humanity's potential. To make us a galactic player."

"Sounds reasonable except for the whole slavery part," I said, sarcastically. "But there's going to be a really evil part to go with the evil part."

"Oh, yes," Tom Terror said, his smile becoming somewhere between Emperor Palpatine while torturing Luke with force lightning and Satan's during a baby barbeque. "There is a very evil twist."

"Which is?"

"Why would I tell you?" Tom Terror said. "We've long since passed the point where I'm compelled to reveal vital information that could be used against me."

"Yes, but gloating is a pleasure everyone should be able to enjoy. Besides, why do you think I care about a bunch of dead aliens? Even if most of them are human."

I'd read him correctly because he nodded. "Very well. When the time is right, when the Supers on a thousand worlds are ready, then I will activate their Xenocide code. They will exterminate the populations of every human habitable world they have been sold to along with dozens of others. Humanity will become the center of an all-encompassing Imperium with my army of cloned Ultra-Force Space Marines as the basis for an unstoppable—"

I sniggered.

"What?"

"For the Emperor!" I shouted. "Death to the Xeno and Heretic!"

"You are doing that thing where everything someone tells you relates to a child's game, aren't you?"

"Pretty much."

"Is it *Star Wars*?" Tom Terror asked, confused. "*Star Trek*?"

"No," I said, annoyed I had to explain myself. Then again, it was unlikely Tom Terror did much tabletop gaming.

Tom Terror shook his head. "Well I don't care. Whatever the case, I will rule over the entire galaxy as its God-Emperor."

I frowned. "Okay, you're doing this deliberately now."

"Not all of us are addicted to television and the Internet, Gary," Tom said. "But since I'm not a twelve-year-old boy, I'm going to give you my demands."

"Tom, this has been the most fun I've had talking to a fascist since I used to troll Supechan, but I'm going to go now," I said, turned around. "I have to get prepared to finish off the rest of your army of tin soldiers before one rides away."

"Your niece," Tom Terror said.

I stopped dead in my tracks.

"What?" I asked.

"Lisa Karkofsky," Tom Terror said, chuckling. "The only remnant of your idiot brother's legacy. You know I don't understand human attachments. I've never held the kind of emotional investment in others. However, I'm able to use that weakness when it's convenient. It would be a terrible shame if something untoward were to happen to her."

I looked at him with fire in my eyes. "You Nazi son of a bitch."

"Ex-Nazi," Tom said, chuckling. "But I can assure there are many elements in my army that would like to get to know a young Jewish—"

"Don't go there," I interrupted.

"What?" Tom asked.

"Don't threaten to kill her or anything else. You've got me. I'll do what you say," I said, softly. "But you will regret it if you finish that sentence."

I could feel the Death Orb reach maximum power. I considered just reaching into that hologram and eradicating him, but if I did there was no guarantee Lisa wouldn't suffer the consequences. I had to play this cool and that wasn't something I was good at. I'd do it anyway, for Lisa's sake.

"So quickly you fold? Such a shame," Tom said. "I hadn't even gotten to the other members of your family."

"Yeah, lucky for us both," I said, not joking. "What do you want?"

"The Spear of Odin," Tom said, plainly. "What else? Deliver to me and I'll let you and your little family of freaks leave."

"You and I both know you can't allow that."

"Why not?" Tom asked, laughing. "You've already cowardly fled from the field of battle multiple times because of suffering losses. You've hidden in your mentor's mansion and watched the world pass you by for a year, no matter how much your Ultranian lover needed you. What's one more betrayal? I'll wipe your children's memories and brainwash dear Gabrielle into being the deeply devoted slave you deserve. From there, we'll part ways. All you have to do is what you've always been best at: nothing."

Tom didn't understand love. Big surprise. He didn't realize

what he proposed was worse than murdering my family. Taking away the beautiful spark that made them who they were. I wasn't stupid enough to believe any of his promises either. This was, after all, the guy Churchill feared most. Any agreement between the two of us wasn't going to be worth the air it was breathed into. So be it.

"Sure," I said, staring at him. "Just tell me when and where."

"Then bring it to the Blood of Loge," Tom Terror said. "It is an active volcano that I'm using as P.H.A.N.T.O.M's base. You'll find me, my armies, and all the wonderful Society of Superhero members still remaining waiting for you there."

I blinked. "As impressive as I find the idea of a volcano lair, isn't it horrendously impractical to build in an active volcano? I mean, Blofeld at least used an inactive volcano. I mean, there's such a thing as convection and getting anywhere near lava will sear your face off. Look what happened to Anakin Skywalker in *Revenge of the Sith* and that was a downplayed example. Presumably because he had the Force to reduce the heat."

I was trying to distract Tom Terror with a speech of pure nonsense because I needed to figure a way out of this that didn't involve me betraying my few remaining principles (like: "never give in to Nazis" and "never betray a family member"). Unfortunately, I was coming up blank. He had me boxed in. The only thing I cared more about than hurting the Third Reich and their fanboys was my loved ones. A monster like Tom Terror couldn't understand that and would kill his own dog if it meant he had an advantage over his foes. It was doubly terrible since at least some of his antecedents in World War II had liked animals. "Worse than Hitler" was not a phrase I used lightly.

Tom Terror frowned. Ironically, as I pondered matters of real important, he was thinking about his volcano lair's architecture. "I use a combination of energy shields, heat distributors, and non-malleable metals to construct it."

"But still—"

"It looks like hell when I stare out a window, so shut up," Tom Terror growled. "Now bring the damn spear or your superhero niece gets it."

"Right, right," I nodded. I heard Gabrielle flying back, and

I aimed the Spear of Odin at the little mechanical spider and blew it to pieces. Tom Terror's hologram disappeared and left me alone to ponder my options.

Gabrielle was holding the unconscious and beaten form of Superior Boy, which she threw on the ground. "I think I've figured out a way to restore him to his original form. I'm going to need the Spear of Odin, though."

I believed in Gabrielle. I believed she was perfectly capable of making sure that we took down Tom Terror, rescued the Society of Superheroes, and saved the day. I also was of the mind that if we did it her way then it was very possible Lisa would die. Worse, that Tom Terror would come back knowing who my family members were. The people I cared about most. Cindy and Gabrielle could take care of themselves but what about Kerri?

Leia?

Mindy?

I'd stupidly sent Jane and Case home in the middle of the war we were fighting because I didn't want them endangered, but I needed someone who was capable of defending my children in order to feel comfortable leaving them alone. In that moment, I realized I could take over the world. It was the only way I'd ever be able to make sure my children were safe.

"Gabrielle, you'd forgive me just about anything, right?" I asked.

"Gary, that's usually the kind of statement someone who is about to do something unforgivable makes."

"Sorry," I said, turning the Spear of Odin on her. "Sudden but inevitable betrayal."

The Ultra-Force that hit her caused her eyes to glow bright as her powers overloaded and she fell to the ground unconscious.

"Oh, yeah," I said, looking down. "I am in deep shit."

CHAPTER TWENTY

THE WORLD'S GREATEST CRIMINAL MIND

"This is a really ridiculous idea," John said, as he had transformed into an identical copy of my cloak and was presently resting on top of me.

I was flying a Doom Bubble, which was a grossly impractical flying motorcycle with an egg-shell like dome around it. It was one of the P.H.A.N.T.O.M vehicles recovered from the downed hover pyramids and my ride toward their home base.

"Believe me, I'm not happy about it either," I said, sighing. "I feel like I'm covered in a manta ray."

"Just be glad you're wearing your regular cloak underneath it," John said. "Otherwise this would be weird."

"That would be where this gets weird?" Mercury's tiny doll-sized form asked from my pocket. We'd shrunk her down with local magic. The Norsetecs had some weird powers. After shrinking the scientist witch, I was able to tuck her inside my cloak. She wasn't inside John because that would be even weirder.

Allegedly.

"Listen, it's a simple enough plan," I said, preparing to explain my horrifically complicated plan. "Tom Terror knows most of my associates, but he doesn't know you. So, I'm going to sneak you into their base, and we'll kill everybody there. What do you think?"

"That's not a plan," John said. "That's an objective."

"What, you think you could do better?"

"Given the fact I was a highly trained commando? Yes!"

John said, somehow speaking despite having no lungs.

"I should point out that I'm a genius," Mercury said. "The magic in our world is alien geometry, algebra, and sanity-shredding Jungian psychology. Your magic is something any idiot can learn. Case in point."

I paused. "You know, I'm beginning to wonder if I should have chosen you guys to come with me over Diabloman and Cindy."

"Yes, why did you?" Mercury squeaked. "Ugh. When did you last wash this cloak? It smells like a cemetery and a locker room in here."

"That's John," I said. "I just took a bath."

"I will eat you," John said.

"Listen, I know exactly what I'm doing," I said, dodging out of the way of an enormous eagle that had never existed in the natural world. The Doom Bubble, I swear, made noises like the Jetsons' flying car from the old Hanna-Barbera cartoon. I had to wonder who had decided that feature was worth adding and why he'd decided to join an international terrorist organization devoted to white supremacy.

"Is that why you're going the wrong way?" John asked.

I blinked and paused. "Uh, I'm taking the scenic route."

"We're on the side of the Hollow Earth," Mercury said. "You've literally been going in the wrong direction since the beginning."

"And you're just telling me now?" I asked, making a *tsk-tsk* noise. "Clearly, you've failed my test to determine whether or not you are worthy allies."

"Just hit the autopilot and it'll take you back to the P.H.A.N.T.O.M base," John said.

"And how would you know that?" I asked.

"I read the instruction manual in the glove compartment," John replied.

I blinked. "So, my next test is to ask you which button is the—"

John interrupted by shooting a black gooey tentacle out of my cloak and tapping a blue button on the dashboard. The Doom Bubble turned and started past the Inner Sun (from a safe distance). We were rushing toward a valley far above us. The Hollow Earth looked a lot bigger from the Doom Bubble. It wasn't just jungles and the Norsetecs. I saw beautiful amphibious civilizations sculpted of coral, a series of Medieval castles straight out of Westeros, and many other long-dead civilizations that had survived down there. I was tempted to take pot shots at the Romans descended from the Lost Legion but figured it wasn't kosher to blame people for the sins of their father. Either way, this was a magical place in the Hogwarts sense, and I wished I could explore it as a tourist rather than a revolutionary.

"I meant to do that," I said, sounding insincere even to myself. "Just letting you know you're still dealing with the World's Greatest Criminal Mind. I even have it on my playlist."

I pulled out my cellphone and tapped it. Vincent Price's rendition of the song from *The Great Mouse Detective* started playing. It was amazing how many Disney songs suddenly became awesome when you had a pair of young daughters.

"I'd make fun of you, Gary, but I don't think there's any point," Mercury said, popping her head out of my pocket and looking around like a mouse or a purse dog. "Also, I'm the one following you, so clearly I'm the bigger fool here."

"So sayeth Obi-Wan," I said, nodding. "Listen, do you want to hear my plan or not?"

"Do you actually have a plan?" John asked. "Or is this one of those things where you claim to have one and that everything is going exactly as you have foreseen."

"Listen, that's a supervillain staple," I said, offended. "It makes you look like an omniscient badass always one step ahead versus a guy who is constantly screwing up. You just claim all of your horrible defeats and losses are part of some grander stratagem."

"And that works?" Mercury asked, unimpressed.

"Yes, Barbie, it does. Because there's one constant across the multiverse and that's the fact that most criminals are deeply stupid."

"You realize what that means about you," John said, clearly starting to be more amused by my ridiculousness than offended.

"I am not a majority," I said, simply. "I am unique. I am a devious, diabolical, debonair desperado that will dare to defy the dark and—"

My cellphone rang.

"Oh, crap, it's Gabrielle," I said, immediately throwing my cellphone out the side of the Doom Bubble.

John caught it with a tentacle and pulled it back into the Doom Bubble. "You shouldn't ignore your girlfriend."

"Fiancée, again," I corrected. "For the second time, I mean. Mind you, I'm pretty sure she's rethinking accepting that offer."

"Why? What did you do?" Mercury asked, climbing out of my pocket and sitting beside me. I regretted making the Barbie joke too early since she really did look like a doll. Well, an action figure.

"I kind of blasted her with the Spear of Odin," I said, listening to the ringing.

"Yeah, that will do it," John said.

"I left her a note," I said, taking a deep breath and hitting the receive button. "I'm sure she'll—"

"WHAT THE FUCK, GARY!?" Gabrielle asked on the other side.

"Or not," I said. "He has Lisa. I couldn't allow him to see you coming."

"How about you tell me this instead of SHOOTING ME IN THE FACE!?" Gabrielle asked.

"Err—"

"In the face!" Gabrielle repeated. "Oh, and maybe you remember that I lead a superhero team called the Shadow Seven. You know, a team of superhero infiltrators with experience in breaking into highly secure military facilities like P.H.A.N.T.O.M runs."

"There is that," I said, increasingly aware of how bad an idea this was.

"Maybe it would be a good idea to have someone with superspeed or invulnerability to call in when Tom Terror inevitably betrays you? Because nothing says trustworthy like Nazi scientist!" Gabrielle continued to lay into me.

"Technically, he's not a Nazi," Mercury said.

"There's no such thing as an ex-Nazi," I replied. "It's why I got in trouble when I time traveled to NASA during the Sixties in order to meet Miss Luna and the Space Cadets."

"What happened there?" Mercury asked.

"I kicked Wernher von Braun in the junk," I said, sheepishly. The one thing that rivaled my hatred of Nazis was my love of space travel. The former won out.

"Do not ignore me, Gary!" Gabrielle shouted.

I spoke into the phone. "Bzzzt....bszzztt. Oh no, the static interference from solar flares is...bzzzzt...breaking up!"

"You're just making static noises in the phone!" Gabrielle said.

"I just...bzzzt...love you!" Then I froze over the phone before tossing it out of the Doom Bubble again and blowing it up with a blast of flame before John could catch it.

"We could have used that phone to contact the others and coordinate our attacks," John said, dryly. "You know, instead of wasting a valuable resource because you can't talk to your girlfriend."

"Fiancée," I corrected. "I prefer to think of her as that if I'm horribly killed trying to liberate Poland."

Mercury felt her head as if having a tiny headache. "Poland?"

"Yes, I'm naming all territory occupied by P.H.A.N.T.O.M as part of that country. Mostly because I'm going to need a new country to live in since I've been kicked out of the United States. I have relatives there and they make awesome video games."

"I'd say that's in exceptionally bad taste, but we've crossed that line long ago," John said.

"Well then let's sit here in complete silence," I said, stoically. "Because I just realized my music collection was on that phone and some would be really awesome right now. Some Blind Guardian, maybe some Sabaton—"

That was when alarms went off inside the Doom Bubble and I saw a rocket heading our way. I immediately turned insubstantial and Mercury fell through the bottom of the machine with me. I hadn't been touching her when I turned, and it made me think my powers had grown. Mind you, the fact I was falling from an exploding vehicle should have worried me more.

Especially since we weren't falling to the ground. No, we were falling toward the Inner Sun.

"Oh, shit!" I said, grabbing Mercury in midair.

"Hey, watch where you put your fingers!" Mercury shouted.

"We're about to be incinerated! The gravity here does not make any sense!" I snapped.

"It actually makes perfect sense if you—" Mercury said as we came closer and closer to the blinding orange inferno beneath us.

I was prepared to die before I remembered, oh, right, I could levitate and immediately drew a serious boost of energy from the Inner Sun and zipped down to the valley above my head. I had to readjust my perception of gravity but soon found myself on two feet again.

I also found myself in Mordor.

It was easy to figure out this was the Blood of Loge since it was a massive land of ash, lava streams, and spikey black outcroppings of rock. The place looked like a little slice of hell on Earth and was decorated in Tom Terror's style.

There were numerous scattered fortresses visible as well as a number of prison camps spread throughout the region. The Blood of Loge was built around a central volcano that had a sinister-but-ridiculous-looking giant metal skull with bone-shaped pipes pouring out black smoke into the air. It was something straight out of a cartoon and would have been hilarious if not for the fact I saw a parade of beaten, battered, and abused slaves being led by Exterminator-robots into the first floor of Tom Terror's base. People who were going to be experimented on as part of his insane human trafficking plan.

Checking my surroundings, I saw several white hills that it took me a second to realize were piles of bones. There were thousands of corpses that had been left to rot out in the open, their skin bleached white by the eternal sun. Demonic rat-bat scavengers feasted on them before my eyes. At one point, I saw a bunch of corpses being pushed up against that wall of death by bulldozers. I couldn't tell if they were victims of Tom Terror's experiments, former heroes, or just the dead from his war against the rest of the Hollow Earth.

"It's a rare occasion that I encounter something simultaneously so ridiculous and horrifying," I said.

"Seems pretty normal to me," Mercury said. "Also, if I'm not supposed to be hidden, then why am I tiny?"

"Oh, right," I said, putting her in my pocket. "Better?"

"No, not in the slightest," Mercury said.

"Listen, my plan is brilliant," I said, lying through my teeth. "You just don't know the details because I've psychically purged myself of the real plan and hypnotized myself into believing the real plan is the stupid one that I told you earlier."

"I literally don't know if you're being serious or not," John said.

"Shut up, people aren't supposed to know you can talk," I said, pausing. "Actually, my having a talking cloak is something I'm famous for. Never mind. In fact, do you want a job?"

"No!" John said. "Gods and Old Ones, I may return to my world to get back to people properly terrified of monsters."

I was about to agree that was a good idea when a beautiful woman with blonde hair tied in dual pigtails and a form-fitting blue jumpsuit used a jetpack to fly over to my side and pull out a clipboard. I blinked. She was identical to Cindy except for hair color.

"What the hell?" I asked.

The Not-Cindy pulled out a clipboard. "Hiya! I'm Tina Terror, Assistant to Professor Terror! I'm here for your orientation into your defeat, capture, and brainwashing."

"What now?"

"Defeat, capture, and brainwashing," Tina said. "You are Merciless: The Supervillain without Mercy™, correct?"

"Uh, yes," I said, confused. "Why do you look like Cindy?"

"Because I am a Cindy-model bioroid! Cindy Wachkowski is widely believed to be the best henchwoman who ever lived and I'm the prototype for an entire line of executive supervillain assistants based on her. When you need a perky female minion, shop P.H.A.N.T.O.M's quality selection of merchandise."

I stared at her, outweirded by someone else for possibly the first time in my life. "I fully believe Cindy will be less upset by the fact she's been copied by P.H.A.N.T.O.M than the fact she's not getting paid for the use of her likeness."

She leaned in and gave an exaggerated wink. "We're fully equipped, you know. Feel free to make use of our services before your horrific death of personality."

"I think I saw this bit in *Austin Powers*," Mercury said.

"It bothers me that movie survived the apocalypse," I said. "Listen, Lisa, the only fascist I have ever been attracted to was Alison Doody's character in *The Last Crusade*. That caused me a lot of confusion and forced me to do a lot of soul-searching before I remembered there are a lot more fish in the sea. I am immune to your robotic charms."

"Mmm hmm," Tina said, writing on her clipboard. "Do you have anything to declare before your capture?"

"Uh, I'm not going to be captured?" I asked.

"Tinaisabombsayswhat?" Tina said.

"What?" I replied.

That was when Tina exploded, releasing a torrent of anti-magical energy that caused me to scream and fall to the ground thrashing.

CHAPTER TWENTY-ONE

THE SUPERVILLAIN IN THE IRON MASK

I was buried alive. I was surrounded by empty darkness with a thick metal membrane weighing down on all my body. I'd never been in a suit of armor before, let alone one that felt like I was inside a tank but that's how I felt now.

"Khan!" I shouted at the top of my lungs, uncertain anyone could hear me.

No one did.

There are some fundamental truths to the universe. Don't eat yellow snow. Don't date your ex's sister, there's no way it will work, and you will look like a monster. Sorry, Keith, but you shouldn't have done that. Also, don't trust guys who peddle easy answers. These you and others can buy in my book *Merciless' Book of Universal Truths* for $29.99 in eBook format. Another truth, not in the book, was if you weren't killed by a supervillain attack, you were probably going to wake up in a deathtrap of some kind.

I tried to use my powers, even though I was pretty sure Tom Terror had disabled them. Much to my surprise that resulted in machinery activating inside the suit of armor. I could suddenly see in 360 degrees (that was awkward), feel the weight around me lift, and a sense of tremendous power emanated from the suit. Then I tried to move, only to find myself still restrained to a table akin to the one Doctor Frankenstein used to keep down the Creature.

I was inside a laboratory that nicely combined Gothic Mad Scientist with 24th-century futurism. The place had globes full of electricity like those science toys in the Eighties, tubes full of iridescent green fluid with bodies floating in them, chemistry sets, and weird half-completed electrical projects. It was terrible if you were a serious scientist since they had the biology, engineering, and physics projects all pushed up against one another. It was also just a sign of how brilliant a polymath Tom Terror was since his personal workshop was a place that he could advance disciplines of science alone in his spare time. Either that or he was just reverse-engineering alien and Ultranian tech so he could claim it as his own. The Nazis did that in *Wolfenstein* because they couldn't invent shit.

Jewish Super-Science 4 Ever.

Tom Terror walked into the room wearing a blood-splattered smock and carrying a tray with a brain on it. Following him was another Tina Terror that looked eerily like Cindy. "Ah, good to see you've finally awakened, Merciless."

"You expect me to talk?" I asked, doing my best Connery impersonation.

"Nothing you could say would be of interest to me," the mad scientist said, cheerfully.

"Dammit, you ruined it," I said, sighing. "But what could I expect from the World's Second Greatest Criminal Mind?"

"Oh, you flatter me," Tom said, seemingly genuinely amused by my efforts rather than insulted. "Unfortunately, no, I do expect you to die."

"Thank you, I appreciate a little *Goldfinger*," I said.

"As do we all," Tom Terror said. "I prefer the original Fleming novels, though, in all their misogynist, racist glory. Written back in a time when you could get away with curing a lesbian with masculinity."

I grimaced at the "cure" line and would have blasted him if I could turn insubstantial. The metal suit I was in was sucking up all my powers, though. "I thought you said you weren't a racist."

"I lied," Tom Terror said. "Mind you, I consider all beings my inferior. I just consider some more inferior than others."

"It was nice knowing you," Tina Terror said, smiling cheerfully. "Want a handjob before you die?"

I blinked. "Well, you got some of Cindy's mannerisms down at least."

I had a feeling Cindy had heard that somehow and was going to kick my ass for it the next time we met. Well, either that or insist on tummy rubs and snacks. I had no idea what were-Cindy would want now.

Tom Terror grimaced. "Ugh. Time compression. I hate that. Always trying to find out what you've done, who you've done it to, and who still exists in your reality."

"Yeah, it's terrible," I said, not really caring about what Tom Terror thought about how reality had been altered repeatedly.

"I've been a mad scientist, Nazi, businessman, gangster, powered armored conqueror, and redheaded Australian clone at various points in my career. Sorting through all the memories is a royal pain in the ass. One of the high costs of time travel and traveling the multiverse. The exposure to unusual tachyons can have quite the effect on one's sanity."

He proceeded to go over to the side of the table I was tied to and pull out a power drill, which caused my eyes to widen. "What are you going to do with that?"

Tom pulled the trigger on the power drill and held it in front of my face. "I'm going to hold it up in front of you menacingly for a few seconds."

"Oh," I said.

"Bet you wish you'd taken that handjob now, right?" Tina asked, grinning.

Tom reached over and shut her off, apparently having built-in a switch on the base of her neck.

I did my best to avoid a mental joke about wishing Cindy had one of those. Dammit, failed that one. This wasn't good, he was being more entertaining than me. I didn't know if there were laws of universal narrative progression, but I did know that if you weren't the one making the jokes then you were screwed. The brain had only so much power and when you were trying to make sense of comedy, that meant you were only using about thirty percent of your brain on whatever task you were trying to do. I fully attributed this to fifty percent of why I'd managed to survive as long as I had. The other fifty percent being a combination of dumb luck and the fact the Reaper's Cloak combined with the Orb of Death were a surprisingly versatile set of powers.

"What is this thing?" I finally asked, unable to think of anything witty. The worst sign of my predicament yet.

"You are presently in the Overlord suit," Tom Terror said. "It is a magi-tech suit of battle armor that absorbs all of your powers while redirecting them to P.H.A.N.T.O.M's robot army. It's also completely under my control as you might imagine. I've stuffed numerous would-be rivals into it over the years."

Overlord was yet another villain I was familiar with. I know, surprise-surprise, I know everything about everyone as the major supervillain geek that I am. Well you're wrong, as seventy-five years of superheroism is a lot of information to process. There are quite a few heroes and villains I haven't memorized the adventures of completely. Like Canada's superhero team? Nada. The Iron Age independent guys? Stayed away from them like a once-burned infant to a hot stove. But the Overlord? The Overlord I knew.

He was the "modern" leader of P.H.A.N.T.O.M and generally considered the lesser evil due to the fact he ruled his own country and mostly just bothered various science teams. Yes, he'd tried to take over the world a few times, but he'd done it with style. He also had denounced the organization's racial supremacist roots, which was part of why you could occasionally find toys of the group despite their being a fascist organization devoted to evil. A lot of people thought he was based on Darth Vader or vice versa.

"Wait, the Overlord is a fake?" I asked, horrified.

"Yes," Tom Terror said, amused. "One of my ways of leaving behind a mouse for the various superhero cats to play with. I've faked my death many times with robots, clones, and explosions that would incinerate my body but that doesn't give people the closure for me to operate in peace. So, on occasion, I send out the Overlord to be beaten up then die in my place. There have been a number of Overlords, and there are all manner of Internet theories as to whether they were the real Overlord or a catspaw."

"And how does this deal with me?" I asked, wondering how

badly I'd screwed up.

"Well, you'll be the last," Tom Terror said. "It will be a great tragedy when you kill the Society of Superheroes along with every single Hollow Earth citizen with a devastating plague. One that will shock and horrify the Earth. Sadly, a heroic Superior Boy will destroy you, and then the United States will move in to claim the suddenly empty Earth. I drew from history and the fate of the Native Americans for this plan."

God, he was a racist old fuck. "I don't think Ken will be too happy about this plan."

"Don't worry," Tom said, his right eye glowing. "I plan to replace my consciousness with his and vice versa. From then on, I shall be known as the Superior Man."

"I think that title is taken," I said. "Like, outside of our planet, there's this whole media empire about him. He seems nice enough, and was created by two Jewish guys, according to Jane."

"Silence!" Tom Terror said, looking down on me. "You robbed me of the chance to eliminate my greatest enemy and I will make your death more painful for it. You will be there when you kill your niece, your children, your brides, and all your friends. You will go down in infamy. People will spit your name for centuries."

"Yeah, I'm not up for that," I said.

"You will be," Tom Terror said. "But first, a random bit of cruelty."

That was when Lisa walked into the room and I felt like someone stabbed me in the gut. She was wearing a P.H.A.N.T.O.M officer's uniform, which was kind of a gray S.S. Officer's with a miniskirt (yes, Tom was sexist as well as racist—who could have guessed?). She looked a great deal like my sister except she had fiery-red orange hair and glowing eyes that sparked. You know, because her powers were based on generating tiny explosions like fireworks.

Lisa gave the P.H.A.N.T.O.M salute. "Schreck Heil!"

"Mother puss bucket," I said. "I am never going to be able to look at her the same way again. This is what ruined my friendship with Prince Harry."

Tom Terror looked confused before shaking it off, showing that I hadn't completely lost my control. "Your niece will
supervise your brainwashing. I've almost completed turning
the Society of Superheroes into mindless obedient servants."

"Versus killing them outright or selling them into inter-
galactic slavery?" I asked, immediately regretting what I just
said. Tom Terror was a narcissistic sadist according to the talk
show psychologists of the time (many of whom ended up mysteriously dead soon after). That meant he was addicted to the,
"slowly lower a superhero into a death trap while I'm away" sort
of villainy.

That might have been subtly due to Destruction's influence,
but it was also possible he was just a super-genius serial killer of
the kind that mostly exist in pop culture (since actual serial killers tended to be dumber than a post-Hannibal Lecter aside). He
got off on the fear, which made his name apropos. By the way,
his birth name was Tomas Schreck, which means Tom Terror.
Crazy, huh?

Damn, my undiagnosed ADD or just general easily
distractedness!

Tom Terror looked down and chuckled. "When you have
hated as long and deeply as I have, Merciless, you'll find that
mere death is the least of the things you can deal with. Besides,
I don't believe your wish that death should be final worked."

"I'm...what?" I asked.

Tom Terror smiled. "Alternate reality doppelgangers, clones,
brain uploads, time-plucked past selves, and more. There are so
many ways to get around literal resurrection. Besides, we both
know you didn't really mean it."

I had no answer for that. "Maybe you just want to make sure
you'll get the hero next time. Because in this new world there
won't be a next time."

Tom Terror chuckled and walked away as if he was amused
by a private joke. "Begin the process to strip him of his memories. I want him pledging allegiance to the battle flag of Ruritania
by the end of the hour."

"Yes, *mein führer*," Lisa said, sickening me.

Tom Terror turned around and walked away. "There's

something you should know before you die."

"Your evil plan?" I asked.

Tom Terror laughed, which was not a pleasant thing to hear. "Oh, that's good."

"What do you mean?"

"I already told you my evil plan," Tom Terror said.

"Oh, right," I said. "Actually, that was more like your evil objective."

Thank you, John, for that.

Tom Terror shook his head. "The thing you should know is why I'm doing this."

"Oh, the other thing that supervillains always tell people they're planning to kill," I said. "Sure, Tom, go ahead."

"It's fun," Tom replied. "Something you've hinted on but never quite fully embraced. You hated your drab, boring, and eventless life. You hated your wife, the children you never got to have because of her, and all the little peons you weren't murdering. It's why you secretly rejoiced when you were freed of it."

"I'd give anything to go back to that boring life," I said, only partially lying. I couldn't give up Leia and Mindy.

But I'd die to get back Mandy.

"Sure," Tom said, entering an elevator. "You just keep telling yourself that."

The elevator doors shut on him and I heard it moving up out of the room as I was left alone with Lisa.

"Do your worst, you evil Nazi bitch inhabiting my niece's corpse!" I said, growling. "I will never betray the Good Old United States of America and Old Glory, except for all the times I have, but not to you! Torture is an ineffective means of interrogation, anyway, even though you're doing it just to torture me. May God strike you down in the name of the Ark of the Covenant that I really hope the U.S. government eventually gave to Israel after Indiana Jones recovered it. Oh, say can you see, by the dawn—"

"Gary, I'm not a Nazi," Lisa said. "I'm just pretending to be brainwashed."

I paused. "Oh, well, I knew that."

Lisa made a strangling gesture. "I swear, you are so bad at this!"

I turned my metal faceplate to her. "Ah, but wait, how do I know you're not actually brainwashed into pretending not to be brainwashed?"

"Because Tom Terror isn't as crazy and/or stupid as you."

"I think you mean crazy awesome."

"No, I don't," Lisa said, making a finger gun and zapping my restraints. She then blasted the Overlord suit's joints and side. That allowed me to move but didn't free me from the suit.

"Can you get me out of this thing?" I asked.

Lisa nodded and conjured a glowing candle-like flame on the end of her forefinger. "Sure, just don't move."

She started using it as a blowtorch as I stood there motionless.

"How is everyone?" I asked. "Are you the only one not brainwashed? How are you not brainwashed?"

"All of the Society of Superheroes, Texas Guardians, and other heroes belonging to the Foundation for Harmony Emergency Team have been psionically conditioned to be able to resist brainwashing over time. Your mind resets after a few hours. We're all playing it cool."

Aside from wondering why Tom Terror missed that, I was quite impressed. "Wow, that's a great idea. Who came up with that?"

"Merciful," Lisa said, citing my insane alternate universe doppelganger. "He made an incredible number of improvements to superhuman security during his time as a Society of Superheroes member. The Nightwalker had pointed out they needed better mind-control defenses before but didn't push the issue in case they needed to subdue a powerful hero with it at some point."

"But you'd mostly need to subdue a powerful hero if they were mind-contr..." I trailed off, ignoring what she was saying. "Do you know what happened to Mercury and John?"

Lisa shook her head. "I'm sorry, I don't. Unfortunately, the power in the prison cells is still working despite Tom thinking we're all brainwashed. I've used a camouflage spell to cloak myself, given to me by the Trenchcoat Magician while he was hitting on me, but it won't work indefinitely. It can only keep the Skull Castle's A.I. fooled for so long."

"Skull Castle?" I asked. "Dammit, I should have come up with that."

I'd really screwed up here. I needed to rescue as many people as I could. Thanks to Lisa, I probably could.

Lisa's efforts allowed me to push the Overlord armor open like a coffin lid, exposing me to the light. I also made a mental note to beat the crap out of the Trenchcoat Magician for hitting on my barely legal niece.

"Free!" I said, jumping out.

"Oh, Merciful Moses, Gary!" Lisa said, turning around and looking disgusted. "That's going to be a nightmare for my therapist and me to discuss."

I looked down. "Right, better conjure a cloak."

I snapped my fingers.

Nothing happened.

"Ah, crap."

CHAPTER TWENTY-TWO

THE RULES OF SUPERVILLAINY ARE BROKEN!

"Oh, that isn't good," I said, staring at my hand. I'd lost my superpowers. That meant Tom Terror had the Death Orb.

Yeah, that wasn't good. He already had one of the Primal Orbs and they had turned a semi-competent mid-tier supervillain (not naming names, but me) into one of the most powerful wizards on Earth. What could it do for someone who was widely acknowledged as the most dangerous mortal in the multiverse?

"Yeah," Lisa said, looking away. "I haven't been this traumatized since I went looking for superhero slash and ended up finding an entire archive about you and Stingray."

I wrinkled my brow, disgusted. "They do know we're brothers, right?"

"I think that was the point!" Lisa said, looking nauseous. I didn't envy her making that discovery while looking for some quiet-time fiction.

"The Internet is dark and full of terrors. Also, really disturbing porn." I sighed and walked over to one of the surgical tables, grabbed a sheet and wrapped it around me as a toga before putting another sheet over my head as a makeshift hooded cloak. "Okay, you can open your eyes."

"You replicated your costume in bedsheets? Really?" Lisa asked, turning around and looking confused.

"You're dressed as a Nazi," I pointed out. "You don't get to give me fashion advice."

Lisa rolled her eyes. "It's always Nazis with you."

"P.H.A.N.T.O.M is *run* by a bunch of Na..." I started to choke out angrily before calming myself. "You know, screw it, we're just going to stop the bad guys and forget this entire incident ever happened. Like Kentucky is trying to forget that Nazi paraphernalia was something that could be sold at their state fair until 2018."

Yes, I know that was an oddly specific example, but I learned that fact while talking to C.T. Phipps about being the ghostwriter for my autobiography. Yeesh. Some things you could just do without knowing.

"You did it again," Lisa said. "Stop bringing attention to the bad guys' ideology."

"What? Your plan is to *ignore* white supremacy into submission?" I asked, processing that. I could have looked for a doctor's outfit or coveralls in the laboratory but didn't want to accidentally put on Tom Terror's underwear. Maybe that was a weird thing to worry about right now, but it was something in the back of my head. Who knew what kind of weird diseases or rashes he'd picked up on other worlds? That and we weren't anywhere near the same size.

"Yes, we should ignore them!" Lisa said, sounding oddly interested in the subject for a woman trapped in a base surrounded by fascist minions. "There's no such thing as bad publicity. The best thing to do is just ban them from all social media until they shrivel up and die from no Internet."

"Your generation confounds me," I said, checking for anything I could use for a weapon. In the end, there were just devices I couldn't figure out the use of and left alone. I didn't want to grab what I thought was a death ray and end up firing the invincibility ray. There was one time I took something from Cindy's room that turned out to be most definitely not a weapon. Very embarrassing. "I swear, Lisa, it's the music you kids listen to. All your Lorde and Cardi B. Tsk-tsk."

"Uncle Gary—" Lisa groaned.

I continued, finding nothing useful but a personal energy shield belt I wrapped around my toga. "In fact, your whole media. Clearly you can't trust anyone who doesn't know what

ALF or *Full House* is. Where did I go wrong raising you?"

"You didn't." Lisa said. "I lived with my grandparents until a few years ago and you spent most of that time in prison."

I paused. "Oh, right. Mind you, I'm still hashing out my timeline. I'm not sure how much time I've spent doing things like raising my family versus team-ups and crossovers. My history is twisted like a pretzel dipped in sauce, eaten, then replaced with another pretzel."

"Uncle Gary—"

"It's like Theseus' ship. If you replace the entirety of a Medieval Greek tourist attraction with no wood paneling after the termites and weather destroy the original but do it one board at a time, is it still the same ship? I have some cyborg friends who have wondered about that. It also applies to brain cells."

I wasn't exaggerating either. Time travel, alternate realities, and the acts of all-powerful gods had left me confused as to what the hell was going on in my life. It was part of the reason why I'd retired from supervillainy and had tried to live as normal a life as a billionaire with two Super daughters could. It hadn't worked out well as anyone reading this book could probably pick up on. I was terrified that, one day, I would wake up and my family would be missing, and I wouldn't even remember they were gone. That worry kept me up at night and was infinitely more terrifying than the idea some enemy of mine from the past (living or dead) might come to kill me. Wow, that got depressing quickly.

Lisa looked at me like I'd wandered off mentally. Which I had. At least it wasn't a flashback. "Uncle Gary, you didn't used to be this scatter-brained. Have all the times you've had the crap beaten out of you caused brain damage?"

"That's impossible. I regenerate all damage," I said, before pausing. "Though that would mean I'd remember everything from the time I gained my powers and I don't. Huh. Maybe I should contact a neurologist."

"Uncle Gary, we've got like a minute left on my spell keeping us from being found and we started with a lot of spare time."

"Oh, right," I said. "So, uh, where are we going again?"

I was doing my very best not to think about the fact that my niece was no closer to being out of danger than she had been when I had concocted this stupid plan. Indeed, I'd actually made things worse by bringing John and Mercury with me. I'd given Tom Terror the weapons he'd looked for, an all-powerful magical artifact, and forced Lisa to rescue me. I was going to have to give her something awesome for Hanukah. Like Australia.

"We need to free all the other superheroes and shut down the activation of Tom Terror's superweapon," Lisa explained our current goals. "Plus get the Spear of Odin and the two Primal Orbs from him. Once Tom Terror is stripped of his power and the heroes are free, we should be able to overthrow the last of P.H.A.N.T.O.M."

I was skeptical of this being the last of P.H.A.N.T.O.M. People had decided the legacy of World War II was dealt many times before. Every time, the (tiki) torch-wielding jackboots had shown up again and again. Still, I was willing to give it a shot and nodded. "Gotcha. Pretty basic video game logic. Go to place one, do the thing, move onto the next one."

"If you say so," Lisa said, turning around to walk out the door.

That was when it occurred to me this could all be another one of Tom Terror's twisted mind games. I'd failed miserably in this mission so far because I couldn't think ahead. I was so used to relying on my mastery of how things were supposed to work, in comics and movies, that I was failing because those were no longer the rules. Destruction's love of the genre and forcing it onto reality was no longer the case and now anything could happen. I needed to be smarter and more cunning than ever before. That started with anticipating the twists before they happened.

I immediately grabbed her and checked Lisa's neck. "Ho-ho! I have found your off-switch, Robo-Lisa, and know that you are actually part of a plot by Tom Terror to..."

She didn't have an off-switch.

"Oh," I said. "Well, isn't that embarrassing."

Yeah, this was going to be a long-long period of adjustment.

Lisa glared at me and pulled away. "You actually thought

this was all a complicated plot by Tom Terror?"

"Err, sort of?" I asked.

"And you didn't think I could actually escape on my own?" Lisa asked, frowning. "After all the training and working with superheroes I've done? Gee, thanks, Uncle Gary."

I felt guilty for underestimating her. "You will always be my brother's little girl, Lisa. My brother's little girl who I am vaguely condescending to."

"Vaguely?" Lisa pushed me away and the two of us departed from the room, leaving behind Tina Terror. A part of me was reluctant to do that since she bore such a resemblance to Cindy. That and I was always hesitant about leaving an enemy behind me. It was proof positive, somewhere along the way, I'd become a "real" supervillain since I lived in a constant state of paranoia and battle readiness. It was just another price I'd paid for living the way I did. You know, to go along with all the excitement and ridiculous rock-star excess.

What was my point again?

Either way, we headed down the halls and it seemed that the Trenchcoat Magician's spell was still holding. We were passed by many armored P.H.A.N.T.O.M Skull Troopers, Elite Guardsmen, and officers dressed like Lisa.

"You should have me in binders until we reach the Detention Level," I said, walking behind Lisa.

"Does every sentence out of your mouth have to be a pop culture reference?" Lisa said, sighing.

"No," I said, pausing. Then I grimaced and gritted my teeth before sucking in a breath. "Chewbacca. Dammit!"

Lisa muttered a series of obscenities. "I'd say I wish I'd gone to live with my mother, but I still remember how she tried to sell me to Omega Corps' media division."

"Now, now, it's not that your mother didn't love you. It's just that she loved money more."

Lisa chuckled at that. It was a bitter chuckle but that was something we all shared.

"Thanks," Lisa said. "We'll get through this or die trying."

"It's the second part that worries me."

Somehow, we managed to get into an elevator down to the

basement. I felt the magic around us shiver, and then die.

"Yeah, the spell has gone away," I said, upset I'd used so much of its time getting my head straight. I had the beginnings of a plan forming as well as the sense I had come up with a plan earlier but just...forgotten it. That wasn't going to do me any good right then, though.

"I don't suppose you have any magic that could help," Lisa muttered. "Because I don't know how much magic is your own and how much belonged to the Reaper's Cloak and Primal Orb."

"Everyone in the world can do magic if they recite the proper number of invocations, make use of spiritual deals, or know the right chants. The big difference between science and magic is that it's less like building a generator to get electricity than it is signing up with a power company. The gods, spirits, and demons you invoke can shut off your source of oomph whenever they want. They may also not have enough for what you want to do or charge more than it's worth."

"That was a surprisingly concise metaphor," Lisa said.

"Thank you," I said, crackling lightning between my two palms. "The Ultranians left the Inner Sun here as a sort of open-source magical power line to tap. At least, that's how I'm choosing to view it. I can tap that but—"

Someone, probably me, had said I was a fitth-level wizard without the Reaper's Cloak and that felt like an accurate summation. Mind you, I had an additional ten levels of Thief and probably a couple extra of the Wiseass Prestige Class but that didn't help me do cosmic alterations to the universe. If you weren't familiar with *Dungeons and Dragons* then, the short answer was I wasn't very good at magic even if I was a very good crook. The Inner Sun might boost my powers significantly, but if I ran into someone else with magic down here then I was probably screwed.

"There's a but coming, isn't there?" Lisa asked. "A big but."

Yeah, there was a but coming. I did not like big buts, I could not lie.

"Well, I have to build my own power line to it and I'm not that great of an engineer," I said, sighing. "Death claimed she bred hundreds of generations to create our family, but none

of us have particularly shown that much in the way of necromantic talent. I mean, Kerri sees ghosts but I'm thinking more
Voldemort than Luna Lovegood."

"I never read Harry Potter or saw the movies, so I have no
idea who those people are," Lisa said.

I pointed at her. "And yet you knew who they are."

The elevator kept going.

"How deep is this going?" I asked.

"Up," Lisa corrected. "It's going up. Remember, we're in the
center of the Earth."

"Ah," I said, shaking my head. "We're still going with that,
huh. So, want to tell me if you're seeing someone. When are you
going to be bringing someone back to the mansion? You know,
as soon as we get an exact replica built on some island with no
extradition tre—"

That was when the elevator flipped over and the two of us
fell on our faces.

"What the hell!" I said, lying on the bottom of the elevator.

The elevator doors then pinged.

"Sorry, that's a thing with gravity around here," Lisa said.

"Why not put chairs with straps in them?" I shouted.

"A mad scientist invented it!" Lisa snapped, getting up.
"How should I know!?"

Thankfully, no P.H.A.N.T.O.M troops came to investigate
our shouts and we were left alone. I climbed to my feet and
walked out into the central computer core of Skull Castle. It was
a massive weird three-story circular computer core rising out
of the ground with hundreds of servers operating simultaneously around it. Computer cables ran in and out of it, looking
like snakes, or tentacles in the dim illumination.

Large floating holographic screens showed various parts
of the Hollow Earth, surface world, alien planets, and even a
few alternate realities. I actually got a glimpse of Earth-B on the
other side of Earth's orbit. There, the League of Superheroes was
punching a giant robot and I saw an alternate version of Mandy
fighting alongside an arrow-shooting Cindy.

I sucked in my breath. "The fact we could just enter down
here and there's no one to meet us is really ominous."

"That's because I wanted you to be down here," a deep, ominous voice spoke.

I turned around and saw a balding middle-aged man in a button-down blue shirt, brown pants, and an ugly red tie. He had tiny glasses resting on the bridge of his nose and the body of someone who had probably once played football but had long since lost the war against doughnuts. In his right hand was an alien pistol that had three spikes at the end exchanging an arc of lightning.

"Uh-huh," I said, looking back.

"You don't know how long I've waited for this day," the man said, softly. "How I've schemed, plotted, and accumulated power. Years turned to decades. Each night, I went to bed knowing I was one step closer to bringing about your end and that was the only thing that—"

Lisa blasted him in the face with her sparkler powers, throwing him back. She ran over, grabbed his gun, and shot him in the face. The man disintegrated and all that was left was a fine white powder.

"Hey," I shouted. "Not cool."

"What?" Lisa asked, turning around. "He was planning on killing you!"

"Yeah, but he was mid-monologue!" I said, appalled. "There's rules against these kinds of things! It's killing someone in the Continental! That was a John Wick reference by the way."

"I *know*. It's something from this century," Lisa said. "That was Steve Duck, though. The President's Chief of Staff. He seemed to know you."

"And now we'll never know what his beef with me was!" I said, shaking my head. "This is going to bug me for the rest of the day!"

That was when the computer core spoke. "Gary, is that you?"

Oh, hell, I recognized the voice.

CHAPTER TWENTY-THREE

AN OLD(ISH) FRIEND RETURNS (IF YOU REMEMBER HER)

Iturned around and looked up at the holograms above us. All of them had been replaced with the image of a brunette, thirty-something woman with thick glasses and slightly more weight than you tended to find in the superhero community.

The digital woman was wearing a white lab coat over a button-down shirt. Oh, and she had six metal arms sticking out of her back. One of them was fetching her a digital cup of coffee "off-camera" and handing it to one of her regular arms.

"Niki Tesla?" I asked, blinking. "You're alive?"

Niki Tesla was a German-American henchwoman I briefly employed as part of my gang, back when I was trying to bring back Mandy and become a full-on criminal mastermind. She was a mad scientist, albeit not quite as mad or science-y as my daughter, and someone I had a great deal of fondness for. Unfortunately, being a supervillain was not a healthy lifestyle and she ended up having her throat slit along with my newest recruit at the time, the Fruitbat.

"Alive is a matter of definition," Niki Tesla said, her voice echoing from all the screens speaking at once like a kind of techno-choir. "I was dead at the hands of Merciful. Thanks for warning me about him by the way—"

"I didn't know!" I snapped.

"But I had my brain backed up every day on the Internet via my Thinking Cap," Niki said. "Brain uploading is the Diet Coke of immortality, I admit, but I didn't believe in an afterlife and brain cells are constantly dying before being replaced, so consciousness as we define it is an illusion anyway."

I cocked my head sideways. "You realize that you literally worked for a necromancer, right?"

Niki frowned. "Well, obviously I felt stupid when I met you! That doesn't change the point I was an active A.I. postmortem."

I frowned and shook my head. "And now you're working for P.H.A.N.T.O.M."

"Not willingly!" Niki protested. "Believe me, Germans hate fascists more than any other people on the planet now."

Both Lisa and I stared up at her skeptically.

"Excepting Jewish people," Niki said. "Romani, Slavs, gays...listen, just accept we really don't like fascists, okay!"

"And yet you're working for them," I said, thinking about the possibilities for why she might be doing such. Blackmail, intimidation, captured family members, boredom, and a really good paycheck all were possibilities. "Just how powerful is your A.I.?"

"Unlimited," Niki said, grimacing. "I thought breaking the rules would be within my supervillain rights. Tom Terror trapped me while I was trying to take down P.H.A.N.T.O.M during President Omega's takeover."

"So, almost immediately after you died," Lisa said, frowning. She'd been at ground zero for all that.

"Yes," Niki said. "I screwed up and gave the worst people in the world access to a Cognition A.I."

"Yeah," I said, shaking my head. "You really did."

Cognition A.I., a.k.a sentient programs that could infinitely expand their processing power, was outlawed by international treaty, and I don't mean those laws that everyone ignores like not invade sovereign nations without U.N. approval. No, it was one of those laws that people actually paid attention to. With the exception of Android John, the only robot President and the only robot President ever brought down by a sex scandal, no one trusted super-powerful intelligences that could hack through anything. There was a "dismantle on sight" order for them and rightfully so. All of them inevitably went crazy from the crap on the Internet or their lack of physical bodies.

P.H.A.N.T.O.M having access to a Cognition A.I. explained a great deal about why the Earth was so screwed up right now. Even if you were a genius like me and stole their big fortune in gold (see *The Mercurial Merciless* #117 for that exciting adventure), they could just digitally create however much money they needed. It was also a terrifying realization that the hatred for superheroes and public opinion also sliding against Supers could have been influenced by their datamining and campaigns of disinformation.

"I'm sorry, Gary," Niki said.

"For, what?" I asked. "This isn't your fault."

Maybe I was being a bit too forgiving, but having lost so many friends over the years it was good to have one come back. The implications of it, that maybe other people had come back from the dead before the deadline (ouch! Incredibly lame non-intentional pun), also gave me hope rather than anger. It also made me wonder about what Tom Terror had said earlier, that no sooner had I made a law in the fabric of the multiverse than people started to find loopholes.

"For this," Niki said, sadly as her holograms all glitched simultaneously.

That was when dozens of metallic tentacles popped out of the ground, each of them holding a ray gun with a built-in laser sight. All the laser sights zoomed in on me and Lisa, making us the subject of hundreds of individual dots. Alarms blared all over the chamber and, presumably, over the rest of the fortress. Yeah, this was not good.

"Man, if only there were a few hundred cats in this room," Lisa said, trying to make a quip and failing. "You know, because, uh, there's a lot of red dots."

"Really, that's what you're going with?" I said, looking to my niece.

"I don't know! I don't quip!" Lisa said. "That's what the third Nightgirl does! I just look serious and blow stuff up!"

"There's a third Nightgirl? I didn't know there was a second," I said, surprised. "Man, I need to renew my *Teen Superhero* magazine subscription, but the mailwoman looks at me weird when she hands it to me."

"Please be silent," Niki said, her voice sounding more afraid for my wellbeing than intimidating. If she'd been reprogrammed to serve P.H.A.N.T.O.M but not to be loyal to it, then this was pretty close to mind control. "I'm ordered to alert Tom Terror in these sorts of situations and try to disable you."

"See! I knew she was evil!" Lisa snapped. "Come on, let's blast all of these. You can turn insubstantial!"

"These use unusual dimensional energies," Niki said, pleading. "You can turn insubstantial and they'll still kill you."

"Why are you warning us?" I asked, wanting to be sure my hypothesis was correct.

"Tom Terror is a sadist who gets off on all manner of suffering," Niki said, disgusted. "He couldn't change all of my programming without destroying me, but he could install commands that override all my other priorities. Like the Robot's First Laws. All my self-preservation is secondary to serving P.H.A.N.T.O.M and Tom Terror specifically."

"I'm sorry," I meant that. I couldn't imagine what it would be like to have something you absolutely did not want to do but had to do every single second of the day. It would warp the strongest of minds and drive weaker ones insane.

"I can't do anything against them. I can only resist in small ways and only if I feel like I can justify it like Tom Terror wanting you alive to torture personally. Which is why you have to kill me."

"Wait, what?" I asked, doing a double take. I had the beginnings of a cunning plan, but like Blackadder at the end of most seasons, it would probably get me killed.

Screw it. If I was going to get killed, then I might as well try to do something to save my niece and a good friend. Well, henchwoman. Niki was the second-best one I ever had that meant something despite having only ever had two.

"I'm prepared to die if it means no longer serving these goose-stepping disgraces to my country. Destroy me and allow me to heroically sacrifice myself again… Gary, what are you doing?"

"Hold on," I said, casting a spell to reach into a portal in the air. All it required was for me to draw a circle in the air with my finger. "This is like second-level magic. I need to see if I can access my Reaper's Cloak's pocket dimension. Car keys, magic golden apple, and oh, cool, my Boba Fett flash drive containing one hundred terabytes of blackmail material on all the world's leaders!"

There was also a bunch of stuff I wasn't mentioning like my porn collection, my secret weapon against Tom Terror, and seventy-three cents in change. Have you noticed credit cards have eliminated any need for change in society? Even soda machines take them these days so, really, what was the point? We should get rid of coins the same way we got rid of the half-penny.

"Gary—" Niki said, sounding concerned. "This isn't funny. My urge to kill is rising and not in a good or sexual way."

"There's a sexual way?" Lisa asked.

"Oh, you sweet summer child," Niki said. "The things that went on in that mansion during Gary's depressed period were amazing. Wild parties don't even begin to describe it. I slept with Dracula and the new Prismatic Commando. The former Black Eagle. Oh, how I miss sex. Even touching myself—"

Lisa plugged her ears. "Uncle Gary, please hurry up."

"Ah ha!" I said, pulling out a spiral paper notebook of the kind that cost about a dollar at your local grocery store. I opened the notebook and recited three words in a long-dead language. I mispronounced it badly but repeated it several times. That wasn't my fault, though, since I'd written out my incantations phonetically. I may have had the world's cheapest spell book, but it was top-notch for ease of use.

"Uh, Gary, what did you just do?" Lisa asked. It was the kind of question that was accompanied by an acute sense of horror mixed with disbelief. In other words, the reaction people generally had to my cunning plans.

"Magic!" I said, cheerfully. "I figured that brainwashing was essentially a form of programming and *Suggestion* is a third-level spell. So, I'm suggesting Niki no longer be loyal to Tom Terror and P.H.A.N.T.O.M."

Lisa stared at me in horror and grabbed my makeshift cloak before shaking me. "Your entire plan for us not dying relies on *Dungeons and Dragons*? Is this the real world, Gary!"

"The real world is infinitely stranger than your philosophy something, something Horatio," I said, flubbing the overused line from *Hamlet*.

That was when Niki's laser guns lowered. The expression on the holographic Niki's face was confused, pained, and tired. It was like she was waking up from a dream but hadn't quite managed it yet.

"Are you goddamn kidding me?" Lisa stared in disbelief. "That did not just work!"

"Don't look a gift horse in the mouth," I said, solemnly. "We should be grateful to our God that he rewards stupidity."

Lisa felt her face.

Niki's glitching got much more severe. "I feel calmer, more me, now. It's...painful. Like two voices competing for attention in my head. I can't—"

The guns raised at us again then turned against one another before starting to fire. The entire place became a shooting gallery.

"Crap!" I shouted, seeking shelter behind some of the servers.

Lisa unloaded with her fireworks powers, causing numerous guns to explode as we fled from the laser blasts firing at us. One of the blasts nicked the top of my shoulder and stung like hell, sending me to the ground.

"Ow!" I shouted, hiding behind a now non-functioning server. "This is totally not like the movies! Ow! Intense pain!"

A laser blast passed through the server above me.

"These machines aren't laser proof, Gary!" Lisa said. "They don't make good cover!"

"Video games didn't teach me that!" I snapped.

Niki Tesla screamed and clutched the side of her head. "Gary! Run!"

"No!" I shouted. Then I drew on the Inner Sun even though we were separated from it by a lot of solid rock. I'd established a connection with it and still had my SECRET PLAN that included a SECRET WEAPON. Channeling that power, I cast the spell one more time. "Get that crap out of your head and be free, computer lady!"

The power surged through me and it was the second most powerful spell I'd ever cast in my life. Because magic was *not* like *Dungeons and Dragons* and you could spend more power doing something simple than you could ever doing something special. Also, you didn't forget spells after you cast them—which was bizarre and only for game balance anyway. Either way, I felt my power wash over the computer room, and it was good. Then nothing. No gunfire, no noise, no explosions.

"Ow!" I said, grimacing. "Still shot! Not healing!"

"Oh, don't be a baby, Gary," Niki said, only one hologram remaining above our heads. "That laser blast cauterized the wound almost instantly."

"That is not how healing works!" I snapped. "Ponda Baba probably went into shock after his arm was cut off in the cantina!"

"Should I even ask?" Lisa asked, looking up. "I mean, I'm just assuming it's a *Star Wars* thing."

"It's always a *Star Wars* thing with Gary," Niki said, sounding more bored than grateful that I'd just saved her from enslavement to fascists. "On Earth-B, his good guy doppelgänger is called Star Knight and he has a lightsaber."

"You're kidding," Lisa said, blinking.

"I have a lightsaber, too," I said, painfully clutching the wound on my shoulder. God, it stung. "I just don't use it because it's a hilariously impractical weapon in real life. Unlike a bow and arrow which is the most practical weapon any superhero could use aside from a boomerang or lasso. Don't ask me how that works."

Pieces of the ceiling fell around us. There were numerous echoes of distant explosions and other less-distinct noises. "Is that good ominous noise or not?"

"Good-ish," Niki said, glitching again. "Hopefully. I've turned off all the power suppressors, incinerated the biological weapons to be used on the Hollow Earth, and released the Society of Superheroes."

"Oh, yay!" I said, pausing. "Why is that not completely good news?"

"It is going to be a bloody battle," Niki said. "There are no restraints."

I stared up at her. "There never were. We just pretended there were. That's what makes them heroes. The fact they do what they can knowing they can die and probably will. Also, I may be ready to pass out, so I'm starting to mutter. Is this what shock feels like?"

Lisa slapped me across the face.

Hard.

"That doesn't help shock!" I snapped. "God, now it does seem like I raised you."

"You did," Lisa said, smirking. "Much to my disgust. You are my role model. My role model in how to change the world by bumbling through life."

"I'd hug you but I've been frigging shot!" I snapped before smiling.

"This is touching but I'm fleeing now because Tom Terror is coming right this way," Niki said, fading away. "Look me up if you survive."

"Yeah, well, I can take—"

I was interrupted in my badass boast by the entirety of the floor exploding, revealing a twelve-foot-tall green and purple mecha with a bubbleheaded dome. It had huge arms that stretched out like a gorilla and a pair of giant legs with shoulder-based rocket-launchers. There were numerous other cannons built on the side, some of which I recognized as belonging to other supervillains that had been welded on. Tom Terror was driving it, both his eyes replaced with Primal Orbs. Arguably even worse, in his right hand I saw the Spear of Odin. I felt the power radiating outward from him, and knew that it dwarfed the entire Society of Superheroes combined.

He looked *pissed*.

"Dammit," I muttered.

CHAPTER TWENTY-FOUR

GODS AND MONSTERS (I'M BOTH)

"Lisa, are you pondering what I'm pondering?" I asked, looking upon Tom Terror's mammoth weapons-covered mecha.

"That we're going to die horribly?" Lisa said, backing away.

"That this might very well be the missing link to proving Tom Terror was the inspiration for such classic video game characters as Dr. Wily and Doctor Robotnik, or Doctor Eggman as he's known in Japan."

"Oh my God, I'm going to die with my idiot uncle," Lisa said, covering her face.

"Idiot *savant*," I corrected.

And yeah, we were screwed. I had a habit of being able to pull a rabbit out of my hat to keep my audience mesmerized and the villains screwed. By the way, this was my first and perhaps only acknowledgement that I fought more bad guys than I did good guys, but I was officially out of ideas. I'd done my best to outthink, outfight, or outdo my opponents, but right now I was a normal guy in a bedsheet with a horribly burned shoulder. I was also in a world that didn't necessarily reward heroism. Good, bad, or indifferent—we all ended up in the grave now.

It was kind of like the prayer to Crom in the 1982 *Conan the Barbarian* movie with Arnold Schwarzenegger where he asks his god to intervene on his behalf just because he's the underdog. I admit the only thing I remember from that film is the nudity, the prayer, the music, and Arnold punching a camel. But right now, it was relevant to my situation because I intended to go into my final battle against impossible odds with dignity.

Maybe I could distract Tom Terror long enough for Lisa to get away and join the rest of the heroes. They could have a big punch-up where they all team up and give him an epic beatdown before he died dramatically. As ends went, it was still a heroic one and I would embrace it like a man.

I lifted my fist into the air and charged forth. "FREEEDOM!"

Yeah, it didn't go over well. You see, clothes are things that need to be fitted to you unless you have a tight belt and I was wandering around in a bedsheet. So, in true physical comedy fashion, I ended up tripping on my own sheet and slamming face first into the floor. This would have been hilarious if not for the fact I broke my nose on the floor when I landed and it started spilling copious amounts of blood.

Lisa looked down, embarrassed. "Please tell me that was deliberate, Uncle Gary."

I looked forward at Tom Terror as his mecha stomped toward us. "Tell them I died the way I lived: half naked and confused."

"Eww," Lisa said, scrunching up her nose.

Tom Terror's voice spoke from his mecha's speakers. "I confess, Merciless, I am going to enjoy killing you much more than I thought I would. When your doppelgänger killed Ultragod, a light went out in my heart. The inspiration for countless inventions, schemes, and plots was no more. None of the other heroes or even villains were worth my time or effort. It was almost too easy to plot and plan around their feeble brains. It was like Lucifer invading Heaven with the hosts of Hell only to find God had committed suicide."

"You know, most people don't usually compare themselves to Satan," I said, slowly standing and adjusting my toga.

"Most people are sheep," Tom Terror said, looming above me. He then scooped me up in his left clawed hand. "I will grant you a few last words before I kill you, your niece, your children, and your whores. What do you have to say?"

Tom Terror lifted the Spear of Odin to my face and I suspected he wanted it to glow. It didn't, though.

"Well, I actually did have a cunning plan," I said, smiling. "I just made sure I didn't remember it until now. *Hypnosis* is a first-level spell!"

That was when the Spear of Odin transformed into a disgusting blob with hundreds of tentacles that slithered all over Tom Terror's arm, ripping apart his weapons. John had been masquerading as the trident from the beginning. I'd just had him covering up my cloak. It was a really stupid plan but it worked out pretty well. Oh, and there was a second part of my plan, too! Glad I remembered that. I reached into the portable hole I'd conjured, grabbed Mercury and hurled her out of it. "Attack, my flying monkey!"

"What the hell! You left me in there for hours!" Mercury said, flying through the air like a tiny doll. Somehow she managed to do a backflip and land. Then she blasted Tom Terror with two blasts of glowing mystical energy.

Lisa fired her miniature explosions, aiming at the same points Mercury had attacked. Her blasts penetrated the energy shield of the mecha, blasting him back.

"Ha-ha!" I said.

That was when Tom Terror swatted Mercury out of the air with a backhand, ran an electrical current through his interior that shocked John and me, and kicked Lisa across the room. I had no idea whether they were alive or dead. Tom Terror squeezed his fist and I felt ribs break. One of the fingers buried itself in my leg. I t was a miracle I was still alive.

"Not a very good plan," Tom Terror said, shaking his head before turning his suit back to me. "Goodbye."

I used my last remaining spell, telekinesis, to pull the golden apple Odin had given me into my mouth and bite into it. Then I swallowed. I didn't even chew. Supposedly, these things were the source of the Aesir's immortality. I was very interested in how it would affect someone who was already a god—albeit a really iddy biddy diddy god.

Tom Terror looked confused then horrified. All of my injuries healed over, my bedsheet was replaced with a black Reaper's Cloak, and I felt back to my previous strength. Then I burned away the arm holding me and blasted his mecha with enough heat to match the surface of the sun.

"God mode!" I shouted, immediately regretting I hadn't

gone with something less likely to be dated. "Iddy biddy diddy god is now all powerful!"

I blasted Tom Terror with every bit of power the apple gave me. The mecha was powerful but it folded underneath my assault and I soon felt Terror himself being incinerated. It took a lot more juice than I expected. Nevertheless, I felt the moment he disappeared in the flames. Only the Primal Orbs were left. So, of course, it didn't go right.

All of the flame I was using to destroy Tom Terror vanished, drained away by another force. I was knocked down from the sky where I was hovering and sent skidding across the floor. Despite my supposed godhood, I was every bit as weakened as I had been before. The force that struck me was like an enormous fist landing on a cockroach, with me as the cockroach.

Tom Terror reconstituted with the two Primal Orbs replacing his eyes. He wore a white body suit and glowed with the power of both orbs. "Now I am reborn! I should have realized that it would require the power of Chaos and Death to reach my full potential. I should thank you, Mercil—"

I threw ice at him. It melted off him. I threw more fire at him. It was absorbed by him. I even picked up one of the laser guns and threw it at him, only for it to bounce off his head.

"Okay, now you're just embarrassing yourself," Tom Terror said, approaching. He conjured a glowing ball of energy then threw it at me. It exploded and burned against my flesh, sending me to the ground. I would have died if not for the fact I was still overcharged as a god. Unfortunately, not charged enough to beat Tom Terror as long as he had those two artifacts.

"F..." I tried to say. "errk...mmmph."

"Yes, not quite the defiant proclamation of resistance you hoped," Tom Terror said, moving at superspeed to start pounding his superpowered fists into me. He threw me against the wreckage of a computer server, and then smashed my face against it. Following that, he threw me on the ground and crushed both my hands with two stomps. I couldn't even feel it. My body had given out on me. Tom wasn't done with me, though. "No more games. No more taunts. No more hesitation. All I want to know from you is where the Spear of Odin is. Tell me and I'll spare one of your children. You can flip a coin for which one lives. Personally, I recommend the white one. Oh, wait, she's Jewish. Never mind."

That was when I blinked with my one remaining good eye. I wasn't looking at Tom Terror, I was looking behind him.

"Was that your answer?" Tom Terror asked.

That was when he looked down past me, perhaps seeing the shadow on the ground of a flying woman holding a spear.

"Hi, Tom," Gabrielle said, clutching the item, which surrounded her in an unearthly glow. "Goodbye, Tom."

Tom Terror spun around and turned his hands towards her, only to have the spear impale him right between the eyes. The glow from the spear caused his entire body to shimmer then turn into a golden skeleton then to powder. The Primal Orbs in his eye sockets fell to the ground on the powder and I could only stare at them. I was dying from the beatings I'd received and not even godhood could save me.

"Luv….lurv…." I tried to say my last words.

Gabrielle set the spear to one side and lifted both Primal Orbs. She placed them in my ruined hands. "Gary, the world still needs your kind of villainy."

But did it?

This mission had been a big eye-opener for just how silly and selfish all the terrible things I'd done had been. I'd thought superheroism was lame and stupid while being a rebel was what was cool. Well, I still believed the latter. However, the former I didn't believe in the slightest. A year ago, I'd considered becoming a good guy but had ended up retiring instead. My daughters needed me to try to conquer the world, to give the uneducated angry masses someone to hate. To basically do the musical *Wicked* except with me instead of Idina Menzel.

Random factoid: That was Gabrielle's favorite musical and if I had to hear the song "Defying Gravity" one more time before I died then it would be one too many. She was also a huge *Frozen* fan, which made me think she had a thing for misunderstood villainess types, possibly misunderstood bad people in general, and if so—well, that would explain a lot.

The simple fact was I didn't want to be the bad guy anymore

and wasn't going to be. If I did manage to survive this, chose to absorb the power of the Primal Orbs, then I would do so in order to make the world a better place. To be the hero the world needed me to be, rather than the villain I'd selfishly wanted to be. I'd do it for Gabrielle, Cindy, Leia, and Mindy. I'd do it for Mandy, too, because she deserved someone better than the man she'd married. The person who'd failed to protect her after she'd protected and supported me. I'd be—

"Fixed," Gabrielle said.

I blinked. Both of my eyes were good now. "Huh?"

I didn't feel any pain, but I'd assumed that was because my body was too injured to. In fact, it looked like I was completely healed. The big difference was both orbs had disappeared into my palms and I felt their energy coursing through my body. My black cloak turned a deep crimson shade of red and I felt new magic developing in the back of my mind. I was stronger, harder, and probably no longer in need of a checkup for brain damage. I remembered embarrassing incidents from grade school I'd been glad to forget. I also remembered all the retcons and faded memories I'd lost due to President Omega screwing with the timeline.

"I am healed," I said, not believing it. "I also have a second Primal Orb! Yes, nothing can stop me now! The world will tremble at the mere mention of the name Merciless! Doctor Merciless! No, King Merciless! Fools, they thought they could stop me and—"

Gabrielle gave me a light slap on the cheek.

"Err, sorry," I said, blinking. "Just was briefly overwhelmed by my godlike powers."

"You don't have godlike powers," Gabrielle said. "You still have the exact same amount of gas you had before. Now you just have a second car to divide it between."

I blinked rapidly. "Wait, you mean I'm not all powerful?"

"No, Gary," Gabrielle said.

"Well that sucks," I said, rolling my head around. "Is that why you gave me the Primal Orbs?"

"Well, it was to save your life, but I figure my dad would think you're the safest hands in the universe to put them in since you can't use them to their full capacity," Gabrielle said, smiling. "I agree with him. It's kind of like giving the One Ring to Gollum or Tom Bombadil. It's a temporary solution but better than giving them to Sauron."

"Did you compare the father of your children to Gollum?" I asked, raising an eyebrow.

"The metaphor gets weird if I said Legolas." Gabrielle said, kissing me on the lips before pulling away. "Come on, let's go check the others and make sure they're not dead."

Surprisingly enough, they weren't.

CHAPTER TWENTY-FIVE

THIS IS SUSPICIOUSLY NOT THE EPILOGUE

What followed was a little too good to be true. Call me para-noid, it's the natural result of living in Falconcrest City where the average reaction to a man dying in the street was to take his wallet, but everything seemed to have worked out. Tom Terror was dead, the Primal Orbs and Spear of Odin were recovered, and the Hollow Earth had been liberated from the forces of P.H.A.N.T.O.M. That made me suspicious. There was always another shoe to drop and they usually landed on my head.

Despite this, everything looked on the up and up. An hour after Tom Terror's death, the central computer room was full of all the surviving heroes. They'd made short work of the remain-ing P.H.A.N.T.O.M troops once their powers had been restored (thanks, Niki) and were celebrating their victory by breaking out Tom Terror's classy German beer stores. There had been casualties among the heroes, but it seemed like the majority had made it through unscathed. Indeed, I didn't even recognize the dead superheroes and they seemed like the kind of usual C-List fodder that died during events to make things seem serious. Sorry, Rat-man, I'm sure you had a mother.

The deaths weren't dampening the party spirit either. Guinevere, who was conspicuously ignoring my presence, was a veteran of World War II and seemed to have that kind of will-ingness to let go while not dishonoring their sacrifice. It was ironic, or perhaps apropos, that I was the Champion of Death and had never learned to deal with loss.

Even so, I wasn't the kind of guy who wanted to enjoy a cold beer with a bunch of superheroes after having been tortured and almost killed. I was healed of all my injuries, but the pain's aftermath was a reminder of how close I'd come to being killed. So, instead, I sat in the back of the room and tried to avoid socializing with anyone who wasn't part of my team. Even that was a reminder this had been a nasty fight that had come very close to a complete loss.

"So, anyone trying to arrest you?" Mercury said, her head bandaged and one of her eyes covered. One benefit of our world's technology and magic meant she'd be fine in a few hours.

John was recovering in the back. He was dressed in a long trench coat, black and white, and had a featureless mask on that I was pretty sure was his face. Plus, he wore a cute little fedora. He was really getting into the spirit of things. Albeit, he was a bit more Pulp than Silver Age. More Shadow and Doc Savage than Ultragod. I blamed the fact he was a creation of H.P. Lovecraft's world. Well, H.P. Lovecraft-ish world.

"They haven't arrested me yet," I said, sipping from my mug of hot cocoa. It turned out, like Saruman was of tobacco, Tom Terror was a connoisseur of fine chocolates. Because Germans like chocolate. Really, that guy had a serious foreign culture fetish. "Everyone knows that I'm the guy who helped save them. I think they're fully ready to let bygones be bygones—especially since I'm not feeling terribly supervillainy lately."

It was a hard admission, but the simple fact was I was maybe not the villain I'd always thought I wanted to be.

"Do they know you killed a Federal agent this morning?" Mercury asked.

Or maybe I was just still a murderer and would never be anything more. Either way.

"Was it really just this morning?" I said, sipping the cocoa. "I don't know. Probably not. I imagine that's something that will cause no end of hell for me when I get back."

"Why do you want to?" Mercury asked.

"Hmm?" I asked, looking to her.

"Well, you're a king here, kind of," Mercury said. "I think they're more impressed with Gabrielle than you."

"As well they should be," I said.

Mercury continued. "You saved the entire Hollow Earth from Nazis. You're a wizard and they're fond of those guys as well. Why not set up shop here and say to hell with dealing with the surface?"

"Tempting, but no," I said, sighing. "I'm going to stick around long enough to help these guys leverage the orichalcum trade into something that can keep them from getting invaded every other week. Which, ugh, sounds like responsibility. I can't live without streaming video and genetically-modified food, though."

"Well, with great power comes great—"

"Don't finish that sentence," I said. "There's just something about it that bothers me to no end."

Mercury chuckled. "I'll bring you our old comic book collection from the ruins of Boston when we bring the survivors here."

I looked at her, surprised. "I thought you guys were reconsidering your whole cross-planar Oregon Trail."

I was glad at least someone had benefited from all this. The world was rid of P.H.A.N.T.O.M, but that was a statement that had a ring of falsehood like, "Mission Accomplished", "The economy is just about to recover", and "We have always been at war with East Asia."

"Your world isn't so bad," John grumbled from behind me. "Ridiculous people in costumes murdering each other for petty reasons and wielding the power of great sorcerers aside, your planet still isn't a burnt-out radioactive wasteland."

"Give it time," I said, more bitterly than I'd expected. I wasn't sure why I was so angry about how things had ended. I should have been happy that Tom Terror was dead, and I was, but there was something in the back of my mind I was forgetting. Spellbinder was still missing, we had to treat Viking Lad, and I needed to have a long talk with Diabloman about helping his evil sister, but those didn't seem like pressing concerns. No, there was something else and it was killing me that I couldn't figure out what.

"Got your new real estate picked out?" I asked. "Word of

advice: don't make any treaties where they promise to respect your sovereignty. Not even if they offer you shiny beads. It's always a trap."

John frowned, clearly getting this reference and finding it not particularly respectful of American history. Tough. I wasn't respectful of anything. Not even myself. "The people of Nub'Ab'Sul are giving us the territory around Skull Castle. It's a formerly inhabited kingdom Tom Terror wiped clean off the map."

Yikes.

"It's also a volcanic wasteland," I pointed out. "I mean, yeah, that works if you're an orc or demon but it's not my pick."

I also wouldn't want to live in a place that was a mass grave, but I supposed all of Cthulhu Earth was that for these two.

Mercury smirked, amused by my statement of revulsion. "Volcanos are good. They mean it will be a fertile tropical jungle in a few years. A good environment for building a new civilization for refugees."

"Huh, now I'm thinking of investing," I said, finishing my cocoa. "Visit Mercuryland and John City. It's like Hawaii except formerly owned by Nazis."

"Do you think anyone on the surface would be willing to accept us?" John asked, raising an eyebrow. "Imagine if we asked if they could take in a few million displaced citizens from our world. That sort of thing didn't fly where I was from."

I grimaced. "Yeah, refugees aren't really welcome right now. Or ever. It seems to be the one thing every country on the planet agrees on. Well, actually, there's a few people but they have to deal with—"

"We'll take the volcanic rock," Mercury interrupted. "Skull Castle has a bunch of built-in infrastructure and replicators. We can use those to arm ourselves and sow the seeds of an autonomous city-state. I pity anyone who tries to take our territory."

Yeah, suddenly this didn't sound like such a great idea anymore. Much like every other idea I've had in my life. "Well, you guys enjoy crushing your enemies and hearing the lamentations of their women."

I was unironically happy for them. A bunch of *Mad Max*

monster-hunting badasses and survivalists wasn't the sort of group that you wanted to screw with. Adding them to the population of the Hollow Earth might deter any other would-be invaders from the surface. Mind you, the locals might not get along with them, but hopefully they could sort that out. I got the impression John and Mercury really wanted to establish peaceful relations rather than act as conquerors. I also trusted John to eat whoever disagreed, assuming Mercury didn't blast them first. If not? Well, I'd keep returning until we made it work. It wasn't like I had anything else better to do.

"Have you considered speaking real English? Half of what you say is complete gibberish," Mercury said, apparently not being a fan of Frank Herbert. John's smile indicated he had read the book, however.

"Only half? I actually am like ten IQ points beneath the minimum threshold to be a super scientist," I said, simply.

Mercury crossed her arms. "Uh huh."

"No, seriously," I said, smiling. I used to have a very high IQ before they raised it to 500 maxima because of all the people making nuclear reactors in their basement. Not naming names, but my daughter. I'm hoping Mindy is a genius like her mom, but I worry about being able to handle two super-genius children. I'm already in debt up to my eyeballs for the time she made a toy Godzilla robot and figured out how to make it life-size. It turns out my villain insurance doesn't cover acts of childhood whimsy. Quantaman and Quantawoman shouldn't have published their discoveries online."

"Size-control is a lot more dangerous power than people think," John said.

"That's what she said," Mercury said, grinning.

John gave her a sideways glance.

"What?" Mercury asked. "It's both dirty and true."

I was going to miss these guys. I also made a mental note that after they got everyone through the portal to this world, that we had to shut it down and lock the door behind us. The last thing this world needed was Cthulhu in anything but plushie form. We had local eldritch abominations, thank you very much.

"Yeah, well, I'm going to go talk to Gabrielle and see about getting my kids back," I said. "There's plenty of countries with no extradition treaties on the surface I can hide out in. Maybe I can buy myself a castle in Translovakia."

"Take care, Merciless," Mercury said, smiling. "You're not the worst person I ever met."

"I hope I never have to kill you," John said, giving me a thumbs up.

I took that as high praise.

Gabrielle walked over to me, still holding the Spear of Odin and smiling brightly. "Good to see you're enjoying the victory celebration, Gary. Some of the Society of Superheroes want to give you a medal."

"Not until Chewbacca gets his," I said, solemnly before pounding my chest with a fist. "Solidarity with my Wookie brothers."

"Not this again." Gabrielle rolled her eyes. "Gary, we have something to talk about when this is all done."

"Good sexy-time talk or breaking-up talk because you need to learn to open with something else if it's the former."

Gabrielle smirked. "The former. Mostly I wanted to know how you were holding up. You took a pretty bad beating back there."

"The only thing injured was my everything," I said, dissipating my empty cup of cocoa. "How are you holding up?"

"It was a big win and we needed one of those," Gabrielle said. "Yet it was a win that came after coming perilously close to disaster."

"A lot of people got very used to your father and the other old guard taking the biggest threats themselves," I said. "You showed them you can do the same."

"Thanks." Gabrielle took a deep breath. "Do you think he's gone this time? For good I mean?"

I thought about what Odin had said. That Tom Terror was just a fragment of a much greater evil intrinsic to the universe. Somewhere, across reality, he was probably reincarnating as someone who would grow up to be the next monster that threatened the universe. Monstro the Conqueror, Astro the Mind-Star, or Zing the Horrifying.

Knowing this, I decided to lie. "Yes, I absolutely believe he's gone forever and will never trouble anyone ever again."

"Good." Gabrielle took my hand. "Come on."

Gabrielle brought me to a group of heroes in the center of the room that I recognized as the Society of Superheroes High Council. Which, honestly, was surprisingly pretentious for a group of normally humble heroes. Then again, even Moses Anders referred to himself by the incredibly unsettling title of Ultragod, so maybe every superhero had a bit of the megalomaniac in them.

In this case, the seven members of the High Council were the new Prismatic Commando, Captain Ultra, Guinevere, Aquarius the King of Atlantis, Nightwoman, the Silver Medalist, and Queen Isis the Incredible. They were a garishly dressed collection of heroes and at least one of them (*cough* Captain Ultra *cough*) should have been replaced with Gabrielle. Nevertheless, I was actually grateful to be in front of them as something other than a prisoner.

"Wait, I'm not being arrested again, am I?" I asked.

"Why would they arrest you?" Gabrielle asked.

"Murder, theft, making bad jokes," Nightwoman said, looking surprisingly comfortable among the gods of Earth's superheroic Olympus. You know, as opposed to the actual Olympians who the Society of Superheroes had kicked out of this dimension.

I sniffed the air. "My jokes are never bad, except when they are."

"Are you sure she's not brainwashed?" Captain Ultra asked, looking at Gabrielle.

Captain Ultra, who was a tall man who looked like Will Smith with a shaved head and beard, kept his arms crossed and looked at me in disapproval. He had the look of a man who had spent twenty-plus years as a sidekick with all the repressed anger that implied. I didn't like Captain Ultra for a lot of reasons, not the least that he had phased Gabrielle out of the Society of Superheroes. and had called for Supers to be subject to registration. Which, contrary to the O-Men comic books, isn't bad by itself but is when the government has vocal members wanting to lobotomize or murder Supers.

"Only by love," Guinevere said.

"The worst kind of brainwashing," Aquarius said, softly. He looked like a speedo-wearing Conan the Barbarian with gills. Not exactly the best kind of swimmer's body but the dude moved at Mach 9 so who was I to judge.

"The spirits have a powerful influence over Merciless," Queen Isis said. She was a woman of mixed African and Egyptian descent. "They swirl around him and protect him even as he sends many of them to their greater destiny. The future is obscure but—"

I raised my hand. "You know that I know you're from New Jersey, right?"

Queen Isis frowned and dropped the accent. "Do I interrupt your shtick?"

"Fair enough," I said. "My bad."

"Thank you," Isis muttered.

"So, what is it that you wanted to talk about?" I asked, hoping it wasn't something stupid like whether I was willing to surrender.

"We're here to offer you membership in the Society of Superheroes," Guinevere said, looking into my eyes. "It's time for you to become a superhero."

CHAPTER TWENTY-SIX

AN OFFER I REALLY SHOULD REFUSE

The Society of Superheroes' offer hung in the air like someone giving a high five, only to be left hanging.

I couldn't figure out what to say as I looked at the most powerful and well-loved superheroes of the world. They were missing some of their heart and soul thanks to the absence of Ultragod, the Prismatic Commando, and the Nightwalker. Even so, their successors had done a decent job of picking up the slack and were established legends.

I'd never actually disliked the Society of Superheroes or superheroes in general despite my avowed desire to be a supervillain. I hated anti-heroes like Shoot-Em-Up and the Extreme! the same way I hated the religiously hypocritical, but liked guys like Fred Rogers (I didn't know he was a Presbyterian minister until a Netflix documentary). I mean, you had to be a particularly obnoxious jackass to dislike people who dedicated their lives to helping others. I just couldn't stand the people who became superheroes because they liked the fame or the violence (or both).

The problem was somewhere along the line I'd become my own antithesis. I was more like Shoot-Em-Up than I was Ultragod. I'd killed a lot of people in my early days as a supervillain and that wasn't something you could take back. Okay, I was better than Shoot-Em-Up if for no other reason than I wasn't fond of underage prostitutes, but it sounded more dramatic if I made a comparison between myself and the man I hated most on Earth. I was an anti-hero, not an anti-villain, and the blood on my hands was never going to wash away. Just, you know, a lot of it was Hitler's and Nazi blood—that I was okay with. Okay, I had a point here somewhere, just give me a second to find it.

Screw it. I looked up at the icons of heroism around me and gave my answer. "I refuse to join any club that would have me as a member."

The High Council looked at me perplexed with Gabrielle looking horrified. The one exception being Guinevere who burst out laughing.

"Excuse me?" Aquarius asked, looking at her strangely.

Guinevere covered her mouth. "I'm sorry, that's just a Groucho Marx quote. I love him."

Yeah, a reminder these guys had been around a long time. I liked Guinevere in the same way that I liked dinosaurs. They were pretty awesome, and I sometimes worked with them, but they weren't people I was particularly friendly with.

Guinevere was an Indian-American woman with long black hair and a body that was simultaneously muscular and beautiful. Guinevere wore leather armor that resembled a rather fashionable suit of plate mail with a skirt. Her body wasn't her original one but unlike Spellbinder and Mandy, the donor had apparently been willing. It was a superhero thing so, of course, that meant it was insane. This from the man whose undead wife was possessed by the ghost of his henchman's sister while he dated both the world's other greatest superheroine and his high school girlfriend.

"You've saved the world on multiple occasions, Gary. You're not as bad as everyone says," Gabrielle said.

"You take that back!" I said, faux-horrified. "That is a very hurtful thing to say to your double fiancé."

"Double fiancé?" Nightwoman asked.

"We're engaged again," Gabrielle said.

"Hopefully with less brainwashing and mind-rape," I muttered.

"What was that?" Gabrielle asked. "Said the woman with Ultra-hearing."

"Just thanking you for the fact I can use this in court to cop an insanity plea," I said, cheerfully.

"I don't think you appreciate the magnitude of the offer we're making," Aquarius said, staring down at me with deep piercing eyes. The half-Korean superhero was a mountain of muscle and his right arm was living coral from where he'd cut off his hand in order to rescue a group of trapped porpoises. Hardcore. Stupid, but hardcore.

"I know you offered Merciful this exact offer and he royally screwed up the world and my life," I said.

Gabrielle sighed. "They offered Merciful a position because they thought he was you."

I wasn't happy about the fact Gabrielle had clearly reconciled with her adopted family without telling me about it. I should have known since family was a hard drug to kick. It was an addiction that very few people managed to break and only a handful benefited from doing so.

"Yeah," I muttered. "But, guys, you need to know that I've killed a bunch of people. Including a Federal agent this morning and the Chief of Staff an hour ago. I'm radioactive and I don't mean in the 'give you superpowers' sense but the 'cancerous tumor' kind."

"I contacted New Avalon with my powers," Isis said. "Apparently, an A.I. uploaded massive amounts of evidence against the late Steve Duck. President Trust has retroactively fired him. Also, the late Reginald Smith turns out to have been a P.H.A.N.T.O.M infiltrator all along."

I blinked then threw my hands in the air. "Whoo hoo! If he was a Nazi, that's instant protection from legal consequences."

"How I wish that were true," Guinevere muttered. She was still fighting a lawsuit about punching a bunch of white supremacists protesting a friend's funeral.

"Either way, we don't want you to publicly join," Aquarius said. "Even if it were possible to clean up your history of things like killing the President."

"He wasn't the President. He was, like, annulled," I corrected. "Also, he was born in the future, so that's like constitutionally not illegal according to the legal teams of shut up, I'm right and don't question me on this."

"Wait, what?" Gabrielle said.

"It's how my father usually got me to stop asking questions," I explained. "I fully intend to pass it on to my own hyper-intelligent children."

"You don't want Gary to be a public member?" Gabrielle asked, her voice containing just a hint of anger. Which I knew her well enough to know meant she was exceptionally ticked off.

"No," Aquarius said. "But it's more complicated than that."

"You want to offer me membership but not actually anywhere close enough that I might tarnish your image," I said, getting it. "Thank you, I was worried you guys had lost your minds."

"Gary, this is a mockery," Gabrielle said, putting her hands on her hips.

"No, letting me into the Society of Superheroes would be a mockery," I said. "It's more insane than that time you tried to get me to watch Eurovision with you and I thought I'd dropped acid."

"It's an underrated display of cultural diversity," Gabrielle said, her voice serious.

"No one believes that, especially not in Europe!" I snapped.

Aquarius, who I believed was probably the person who wanted me here least, cleared his throat. "It's because we'd like you to go undercover, Gary."

"Just not with Gabrielle," Captain Ultra said, sounding both jealous and contemptuous.

Yeah, I really didn't like that guy.

Gabrielle just rolled her eyes. "What do you mean?"

"I think that's my line, Gabby."

Guinevere cleared her throat. "After much debate, it's been pointed out that maybe our policy toward supervillains being completely irredeemable reprobates might have been a premature judgment, if not self-defeating."

"Is the Eighties retro? If it's an option, I'd like to be an Eighties *retro*bate," I said, starting to hum Huey Lewis' *Back in Time*.

"He's not taking this seriously," Captain Ultra said. "We should forget this and find a better candidate or abandon the plan altogether."

"Clever, using reverse-psychology on me to make me want to join," I said, staring at him.

"We're not using reverse—"

"Alright, I accept," I said, frowning. "I'll also eat my veggies and go to school! That'll show you."

Amanda smiled. "Gary, you are the best archnemesis ever."

"And yet you didn't invite me to your wedding," I said, shaking my head. "Really? I could have stolen the best sort of wedding presents. Maybe got you a Devil's food cake."

"I expected you to crash it," Amanda said. "Also, where you go, Cindy follows."

"Yo!" Cindy said, walking up. "So is Gary done mocking your offer to join the Society of Superheroes?"

"Speak of the Bitch," Amanda said.

"That doesn't apply anymore. My werewolfism is cured!" Cindy said, sounding disappointed.

I stared at her. "What?"

"Yeah, it sucks," Cindy said, frowning. "It feels like one of those gimmicks they throw at characters whose sales are flagging but they can't actually think of something new. You know like Guinevere loses her powers then becomes a martial artist or the time Gabrielle dated a horse."

"We're not fictional characters, Cindy," I said. "Also, she's still dating a horse."

"Hey!" Gabrielle snapped. "That's private."

Captain Ultra covered his eyes with one hand and muttered something sexist that made me want to punch him in the face.

"Says the guy who talks to gods who rewrite reality for fun," Cindy said. "Also, really, Gabby?"

"So," I interrupted the pair, then turned back to Guinevere then Amanda. "What is it that you want me to do?"

"We want you to remain a supervillain in public," Guinevere explained. "You can commit crimes against property but not civilians. Your purpose will be to try to weed out those supervillains who are redeemable from those who are genuinely evil."

"And then what?" I asked, not sure I believed her.

"You offer them a better opportunity," Guinevere said.

"Provide them options to be more than just killers and thieves. To be inventors, protectors, and eccentrics rather than enemies of the people."

"A lot of supervillains are that way because they're friends of the people," I said. "Because they want to strike back at the system."

"I'm pretty sure that's just you," Cindy said. "Also, the guy with the magnetism powers that Jane says protects Supers."

"He's not real," I said, contemplating their offer. "Hopefully."

"Just saying money would work for bringing a lot of the quote-unquote bad guys over," Cindy said. "At the end of the day, we all agree that it's really just about fame and fortune and our superiority over the little people. Heroes and villains both."

"No, we don't," Amanda said.

Captain Ultra at least looked guilty.

Guinevere just looked tired. "There's something else."

Gabrielle looked down. "I was also hoping you'd become the protector of Atlas City."

Captain Ultra looked revolted by the prospect.

I tried to process that but couldn't. "You want me to become protector of Ultragod's city?"

Guinevere nodded. "Falconcrest City's crime rate and super-villains are under control and we're negotiating for a repeal of the laws against superheroism in the United States. However, you don't have to worry about that as an outlaw."

"Outlawwwwww!" Cindy said, making an air guitar gesture. "Sounds so much better than criminal."

It was a ridiculous offer, even if it had been made to someone besides me. Atlas City was one of the largest cities in America, the New Angeles of the South, and a metropolis intrinsically linked to superheroism. It was also vital to the American economy as it was one of the few places with regular traffic to outer space as well as tech companies researching bleeding-edge super-science. Plenty of Supers who didn't want to be superheroes or villains fled to the city to enjoy its more tolerant accepting atmosphere. Atlas City was also a place riddled with crime thanks to the pro-liferation of Black Market supertech and the fact it had been sub-ject to near-constant terror attacks by, well, Tom Terror.

"Aren't you the protector of Atlas City, Gabrielle?" I asked. Gabrielle didn't respond for a moment. "I have my own legacy to look after. The Shadow Seven...teen, are always at work in countries that don't have heroes of their own."

"Also, trying to redeem villains," I pointed out. "Just how much of your workload would I be taking on?"

"A lot," Gabrielle said. "I have a big cape to fill."

"Which means you're going to be gone even more than before," I said, realizing why she was doing this.

"You'll be fine," Gabrielle said.

"We both will," Cindy said, snarking from the sidelines. "By the way, when does Valkyrie Girl turn eighteen?"

Cindy was then encased in an opaque soundproof Ultra-Force bubble. There were a few bumps rising from the inside where Cindy was clearly trying to beat her way out.

"Oops," Gabrielle said, looking at the bubble. "I wonder who could have done that."

"Just leave some airholes," I said. "We don't want her to end up like Bandito the Super Dog."

If the magical dog owner hadn't been killed by his pup's archnemesis afterward, I would have killed him myself.

"My construct bubbles have a membrane-esque exterior," Gabrielle asked. "They can also generate artificial life support in space."

"Dramatically convenient!" I said, cheerfully. This was a hard decision and one I wasn't sure I wanted to embrace. "The people of Atlas City will never accept me as their protector. They barely accepted Gabrielle."

"They never accepted me," Captain Ultra said, the bitterness in his voice palpable. "You will be hated and loathed by the public, even when you save them. Moses Anders was an icon and I will never understand his love for you. In the end, no matter what you do, they will treat you as a supervillain intruding on their city."

"Good," I said, simply. "I wouldn't have it any other way. I'll take the job."

"Face it, tiger, you just hit the jackpot," Cindy said, having somehow escaped the Ultra-Force bubble.

Gabrielle did a double take. "How the hell—"

Cindy also had my cocoa mug, which had magically refilled.

"We can't use that without getting sued," I said, simply. "Also, I'm not getting a new superhero name."

"The Salacious Spidermonkey is a brand we need to trademark," Cindy said. "There's marketing gold there."

I laughed.

Why was the voice in the back of my head positively screaming now?

CHAPTER TWENTY-SEVEN

YOU BROKE MY HEART, FREDO

And so ended the career of Merciless: The Supervillain without MercyTM and so began the career of Merciless: Undercover SuperheroTM. I was going to have to adapt a lot of my licenses and update my marketing agreements. I'd just gotten my second comic, *The Magnificent Merciless*, and a backup feature in *Tales of Misery*.

It was the end of an era.

Gabrielle put her hand on my shoulder. "Are you okay, Gary?"

"I'm just trying to figure out if this is progress or a step back." I took a deep breath. "I became a supervillain because I was trying to honor Keith. Now I'm finally stepping out of that role."

"Your brother wasn't someone to admire," Aquarius said in his deep manly baritone.

"Stay out of this, Tony the Tuna," I said, glaring.

Aquarius raised an eyebrow that contained a century of raw underwater fury.

I hid behind Gabrielle.

Gabrielle rolled her eyes. "Gary, you've beaten Entropicus."

That was a grossly inaccurate statement in the same sense that one football player beat the other team, but I appreciated her support. Nevertheless, I wasn't about to get on the bad side of Underwater Barbarian Man.

"The dude can talk to fish! Do you know how terrifying that is? Like, imagine a shark attacking you on land!" I said. "I mean, yes, it'll end badly for the shark, but land sharks!"

Truth be told, Keith probably would have agreed with Aquarius. When I'd met his spirit in the afterlife, he'd given me a reality check that the life of a supervillain wasn't a glamorous one. It had cost him time with his wife, his daughter, and ultimately his life. I probably should have stopped right there but I felt I could manage it. I'd been wrong.

Gabrielle shook her head. "You'll make a fine superhero, Gary."

I hugged Gabrielle and kissed her. "You always were the best liar among us. It's why I never suspected you were Guinevere."

"Wait, what?" Guinevere said, looking as confused as Gabrielle.

"You almost had me fooled but Guinevere's public identity of Guinevere Avalon has a ponytail and Gabrielle Anders doesn't! Clearly Ultragoddess is just a clever ruse."

"Gary, are you on drugs?" Gabrielle asked.

"Infrequently," I said, smiling then turning around. "I'm going to go get myself something a bit stronger. Do you want anything?"

"No, I'm fine," Gabrielle said nodding. "Thank you again for this."

"Anything," I said, turning around and walking away.

Cindy followed me. "You know I'm really rooting for you two. I love her every bit as much as I love you, despite how often she cheats on you."

"It's not cheating, it's polyamory," I said.

"We knew about you being with her before it happened," Cindy said. "Me and evil demonically possessed corpse woman, a.k.a. Not-Mandy. That's polyamory."

"Yes, I know that," I said, not needing that spelled out. "I was there."

"Did you know about her other boyfriends when she was with them?" Cindy asked.

I glared at her. "Gabrielle has trust issues. I have issues with murdering people. Marriage is about compromise."

"I'm just saying that you should get some issues sorted out before you take the final plunge. This is the second time you've tried with Gabrielle and the definition of insanity is trying repeatedly to get a new result after repeated failures. Which is why the sanest people in the world are quitters."

"I am so glad our daughter benefits from your wisdom," I said, sarcastically.

"I wish I could be a better mom, but my only strategy so far is to do the exact opposite of everything my mom did. It works sometimes but not always. Anyway, I know Gabrielle has trust issues and it's because she's always Ultragoddess even when she's wearing glasses. She never lets her guard down even with you. I never understood those people who date under a secret identity. That's just starting with the premise of lying to your partner."

"Yeah, well, then you're just one bad breakup from Mr. Chaos murdering your entire family," I said. "That happened, you know."

"Yeah, to Acro-Bat," Cindy said. "I didn't say it wasn't practical. I just said it didn't work great. This whole undercover thing is going to tax you, Gary. People are going to feel betrayed by you when they find out you're working for the Society of Superheroes."

"Supervillains aren't one big happy family, Cindy," I said, admitting something I'd known for a long time. "Honor among thieves turned out to be a crock."

"I think that phrase was always meant to be ironic," Cindy pointed out. "It's why the whole Prisoner's Dilemma is a thing in the first place. You have made people better, though. I think you should do this, but do it for the people you're going to help and not to impress Gabrielle. Henceforth known as Merciless Babymama number two."

"She is not known as that," I said. "Also, you know she can hear you, right?"

"Yes, because there's any doubt in the world that I'll say what's on my mind."

She had a point there. "Never change, Cindy."

"Don't worry, I won't. Once you find me the secret of immortality because someone had to eat the last golden apple. Not naming names but it was you."

"How terrible of me."

Cindy leaned in and whispered. "Also, bluntly, being a werewolf doesn't come with immortality. I was hoping this was an Underworld thing where we don't age like vampires, but it's actually just a fuzzy thing."

"I thought you were cured."

"Pfft. That's only to fool the Society of Superheroes idjits," Cindy said, continuing to whisper.

"Gabrielle can hear things from space. Fifteen feet away and whispering isn't going to help."

"Pfft," Cindy said. "That's only if she's listening."

"Which I am!" Gabrielle said, shouting from the group she was with.

Cindy turned her head and stuck out her tongue. "That is very rude!"

"It is a sad-sad day when I am the mature one in the room," I muttered.

"Yeah, well, it hasn't happened yet, Mr. 'I Seriously Suggested a Darth Vader theme for the master bedroom'."

I opened my mouth then closed it. "Fair enough."

Moments later, two ceramic mugs full of beer were presented to us by a pair of metal tentacles. "*Guten tag*, my brothers and sisters."

I took the beer and looked up to see Tina Terror, or, at least the robot version of Cindy, wearing a lab coat over a form-fitting one-piece swimsuit. Because superheroes, am I right? She was also wearing Niki Tesla's steampunk goggles and had her multiplicity rig.

"Niki?" I asked, blinking.

"Oh, hell no!" Cindy said. "Gary, you are not building a robot me for a twins fantasy. I don't have many limits but that's one of them. Wait, how much are you offering?"

"Why does everyone think I'm a pervert?" I asked.

Cindy and Niki cocked their heads to one side in unison.

"Aside from all the reasons," I replied, taking a sip of the beer. It was a deep Earthy brew. "Still not my thing. The incest subtext is a turnoff."

"Too much information, Gary," Niki said. "So, I'm really

amazed by the sexual features available in this android body. I'm going to have to try them all."

Cindy shook with rage. "*What the hell* are you doing in my body?"

"It's not your body," Niki said, simply. "It's just a knock-off of yours. Honestly, I thought a lot of these proportions were fake. Must be surgical. Anywho, when Gary freed me from P.H.A.N.T.O.M's control, I had to transfer my consciousness to a wireless vessel capable of holding my vast intellect. It turned out a shutdown sex doll in the lab where Gary was held was about the only thing worthwhile. Turns out there's not actually that much in the way of Internet service at the center of the Earth. Also, our coverage doesn't reach the surface."

"You should see what I pay for my cellphone plan," I said. "Also, magic."

"Magic is just nature's way of giving us the finger," Niki said. "In any case, Cindy, this is as hard on you as it is on me."

"I'm fairly sure that's not true," Cindy said. "At all."

"Yes, it's not how I'd prefer to pass the Bechdel Test in our first conversation in years either," Niki replied. "However, I can make it up to you."

"How?" Cindy deadpanned.

"Money!" Niki answered. "The cause and solution to all of life's problems. Much like alcohol, sex, drugs, and firearms."

Cindy's demeanor changed upon the mention of the other 'm' word. "I'm listening. I need to warn you that Gary is a superhero now, though."

I did a literal facepalm. "What part of undercover do you not understand?"

"Well, obviously the core concept!" Cindy snapped, having binge-watched *Archer* with me. "Who goes undercover as themselves? This is a setup!"

Okay, she had a point there.

"Wait, you're not already a superhero?" Niki asked, confused.

"Wait, what?" I asked.

"I just thought you were being ironic," Niki replied. "I mean, you hang around with Ultragoddess. You barely commit any crimes. You also kill villains all the time. I feel like the ship has sailed on your bad guyness."

"Maybe it's all part of my master plan to make you think I'm a superhero pretending to be a villain while actually—" I started to say.

"Stop," Niki said, raising her hand. "Don't care. Unsubscribe. All you need to know is I have wreaked a terrible vengeance on P.H.A.N.T.O.M's finances. In addition to exposing their allies wherever I could, I've also emptied all their bank accounts and liquidated their stock. Like three countries have collapsed because of it and while that's bad, they were controlled by terrorists so let's just pretend that won't cause more problems in the long run."

"How much are we talking?" I asked.

"A lot," Nikki said. "I've donated ninety percent of it to fighting global climate change."

Both Cindy and I gagged.

"And another five percent to funding STEM projects to benefit human advancement," Nikki said, without missing a beat.

Cindy looked ill.

"But the remaining five percent is still damn huge, and I intend to spend it on myself. I'm also willing to split it with you guys," Nikki said. "You know, to keep you in the lifestyle of decadent luxury you're accustomed to."

"It's all I've ever wanted," Cindy said, nodding.

"I should donate my share to the victims of Tom Terror," I said, solemnly.

"Seriously?" Cindy asked.

"Hell no!" I snapped. "I'm a parent, which allows me to justify accumulating as much money as possible for the benefit of my kids. Guilt free."

"Oh, is that how that scam works? It suddenly makes a lot more sense," Cindy said, nodding. "Still, I wish you'd donated some of that to handling healthcare for all."

Nikki snorted as she stole someone else's beer. "Of course, you would say that."

"Excuse me?" Cindy asked.

"Well, you're an M.D." Nikki made air quotes. "Not a *real* doctor."

Cindy charged and began fighting with her doppelgänger. Blonde Cindy and Red Cindy punched at each other, neither using their superpowers.

I watched for a second and sipped my beer. "Yeah, okay, maybe I could get into—"

Both women stopped to glare at me.

"Right, I will now go be anywhere else in the universe," I said, turning around to walk away.

There were a lot of confused looks at my continued presence. Apparently, the High Council was keeping my redemption (was that what it was?) on the D-Low. Strangely, not everyone was exactly disapproving. I'd thought all heroes had been approving of Merciful, my opposite, while hating the villain me. Instead, there seemed to be a mixture of emotions regarding me. Most of them seemed happy to see me, if I was honest, which was a weird feeling. Then again, maybe I was projecting. Perhaps, and this is just crazy-talk, I know, but most superheroes weren't completely ungrateful bastards. People who appreciated the fact I helped them escape a bunch of subterranean Nazis. Wow, I used the words 'subterranean Nazis' unironically. I guess that meant I was a real supervillain (hero?) now.

Really, all I wanted to do was go back to my kids and take a break for the next week. I had been out of the supervillain game for a year and this mission had been a lot harder than I'd expected. The thing was, I didn't think I could go back to civilian life either. The simple fact was that the government had been a hair's breadth from coming for my kids, and if you weren't on one side or the other in the war of good versus evil, then you were going to get hit from both sides. I figured that I might as well be one of the good guys, even if it was inherently less cool. Redemption was a choice and I was taking it. At least I didn't have to get zapped by the Emperor after throwing him down a reactor shaft.

I waved at Lisa, Mr. Inventor (I just couldn't call him Galahad, even in my head), and Reyan who were at the donut table. Both Leia and Mindy were sitting beside them, which told me things were going well. I was about to join them when I saw Diabloman poke his head out from the side of the elevator I'd used to reach the room and wave to me. Blinking, I shrugged and walked toward my luchador friend. He was wearing a workout jumpsuit that resembled the outfit of a professional wrestler, as well as a strange pair of golden bracelets that were inscribed with Nub'Ab'Sal writing.

"Wassup?" I said, looking at my best friend. "Not joining the party?"

"I would not be welcome there," Diabloman said, pushing the button for the throne room (marked "T").

The doors closed to the elevator and it started to descend to the Hollow Earth. I wasn't looking forward to it turning upside down again.

"They believe in redemption, D," I said, trying to convince myself of it. "You've saved the world multiple times."

"I have also killed heroes," Diabloman said. "Not just men and women, but children. My crimes are not like yours, Merciless. They are unforgivable and evil. My attempts at atonement have always been vapor and air."

I didn't like to think about the terrible things Diabloman had done. Because, yeah, I pretty much believed anyone who hurt kids did deserve to die. Diabloman had been raised by a murderous evil cult, though, and he'd done whatever he could to make up for his crimes. It made me an enormous hypocrite, but I wanted to help him. I had to believe there was a chance for everybody who wasn't a fascist.

"I wished you out of hell, Diabloman. You have a fresh start," I said, pausing. "Which is another sentence that makes me realize how far we've come together. I'm a real supervillain now and I owe it all to you."

Diabloman's expression was usually visible underneath his mask. It clung tight enough to his face that I could make out the contours of his cheeks, lips, and mouth. "Redemption is not something the gods decide on. It is something that must exist in one's heart. I can never achieve it unless I gain my sister's forgiveness."

I frowned. "Your sister is… not in a good place. You killed her lover. You killed her—"

"I know my crimes," Diabloman said, the barest hint of edge in his voice.

"But if you want to try to bring her back then I'm game," I said, frowning. "I'll try and forgive what she did."

I wouldn't, but I would pretend for Diabloman's sake.

Diabloman smiled under his mask. "You were always the best of us, Merciless. It is a shame you are more Robin Hood and Joaquin Murrieta than the banditos I grew up knowing."

"Are you feeling alright, D?"

"No," Diabloman said.

He then punched me in the chest, face, and stomach before powerbombing me against the floor of the elevator before I could react. The last thing I saw was his boot descending on my face.

CHAPTER TWENTY-EIGHT

THE REAL CLIMAX

The Chaos and Death Orbs hovered over my head, one blackest obsidian and the other a beautiful shade of red. I was floating in an endless void and they spoke to me with the voices of Mindy and Leia. Gradually, they shifted into becoming my two future daughters and looked down on me with frustrated gazes.

"Well, you've screwed it up again, Dad," Mindy said.

"We're trying to help you here," Leia said. "Yet, every time we do, you manage to screw things up worse."

"That's kind of my specialty," I said, not feeling particularly comfortable about my situation. "Maybe I don't want help, though. You think of that? Maybe I want to make it on my own."

"No one makes it on their own," Mindy replied. "We're all interconnected."

"It's the last age of the superhero," Leia replied. "The Nickel Age after the Golden, Silver, and Iron Ages. Like the Wild West, superheroes were never supposed to last forever. They were meant to be a stop gap until the world learned how to deal with the marvels among them. Eventually, superpowers were going to be something that technology caught up to. Flying guys with super-strength, giant robots, and alien invasions are things that will be handled by governments soon. There will be law enforcement wielding mass-produced power armor, soldiers with stem-cell based superpowers, and—"

"Exterminators?" I asked. "The government can't handle these things because they aren't heroes. They're politicians.

They're so interested in preserving the status quo, they've forgotten what it's like to try to make the world a better place. That we can do better. It's why I used to identify as an anarchist. I believed you had to smash down the system in order to build a newer, better one."

"Used to?" Mindy asked.

I stared at them. "I had more to lose after you were born."

"The clock is ticking," Leia said, lifting a digital phone that showed a countdown. You can save the world, but you have to take extreme measures to do it."

"I hate the Extreme!" I snapped, feeling my head.

I saw multiple futures ahead of me: one of them was a blasted-out ruin where humans and Supers destroyed one another in a war that no one won, another was a future where Supers won only to die out because the weak were culled rather than protected, and a third was the planet where Supers were finally eliminated only for humanity to have no defense when the next invasion by Entropicus occurred. There was a fourth, though, where I imposed peace. A world I'd seen in a vision before, ruled by Emperor Gary, and it was one that eventually grew the hell up and got its act together.

"Show me another," I said, simply.

"There is no other," Leia said.

"Show me another," I repeated.

"Why won't you accept what you have to do?" Mindy asked, sounding almost scared.

"Because I believe people can be more like Ultragod than me," I said. "More like Guinevere than the Nightmistress."

"I notice you don't mention Ultragoddess."

"No one should ever worship their partner," I said. "Which, thankfully, is something no one will ever have to do with me. I'm a worship-free demigod."

Both Leia and Mindy frowned.

"We've had this conversation before," Mindy muttered in a slightly eerie tone.

"Always the same answer," Cindy muttered.

That was when they showed me a glimpse of a beautiful Earth covered in brilliant high-tech architecture, sprinkled with retro designs. Supers and humans lived together in harmony. There were still villains, but they were dastardly rather than evil. People looked up to the sky and saw not someone to be jealous of but to aspire to emulate. It was the kind of world where heroes got kittens out of trees and bad guys like the Cream Pie Bandit tried to steal all the cakes at the state fair. It was the world that my doppelgänger, Merciful, was from. It was also a place where I'd been a hero rather than a villain.

"I like this one," I said, simply. "You know, maybe a little less Archie and Sabrina. Wait, that joke no longer works thanks to both getting gritty reboots. Is nothing sacred? What's next, *Back to the Future* with guns?"

"Meet us halfway, Dad," Mindy said.

"Are you my daughters?" I asked. "Or are you just the Primal Orbs using their image? Was the Chaos Orb always trying to lure me down to get it?"

"We're both," Leia said. "The stones came to us when you—"

"Died," Mindy finished for her sister.

I stared at them. "That's what this is all about? You guys are contacting me because I die sometime in the future and you think taking over the world is a better alternative?"

Mindy looked at me then her sister. "Yeah, kinda."

"I'd rather have you than any other world in our future," Leia said. "So, you have at least some worshipers. Blame yearly Disneyland trips with no waiting at the rides."

"That required me to pretend we were guests of the Pope," I said, smiling. "Guys, you don't have to worry, what will be will be."

"That's, unfortunately, not something we can leave to chance," Mindy said. "You're our secondary priority, Dad. The world needs to be saved from the Universal Flaw. You've had better success than anyone in fighting it. However, if you won't do what needs to be done, then we'll find someone else."

"And we'll save you some other way," Leia added.

"Wait, I—"

That was when everything changed, and I found myself waking up from my second ass-beating of the day. I had a bright light in front of my face and had to look to one side. "Guys, I don't mean to complain, but you realize that being knocked unconscious is actually really bad for the brain. I mean, forget what television has taught you, if you don't wake up after thirty minutes then you probably aren't going to."

"I'm sorry, Gary," I heard Diabloman say nearby.

"*Et tu*, Diabloman?" I asked, keeping my eyes closed. "Really?"

I wasn't even mad. Just confused. Superheroes fought each other all the time and the very fact that I'd woken up was a sign this wasn't too serious. The fact Tom Terror had kept me alive was something I was ignoring because it implied something I didn't want to face: that Diabloman was no longer my friend.

"Turn on the polarizers," Maria's voice spoke.

My blood ran cold. "Yeah, I knew I was forgetting something."

The blinding light around me dimmed and I gradually came to view what was an observation deck made of shining chrome metal and control panels with jewels for buttons. It had the same sort of lunatic futurism most Ultranian technology had. There were huge twelve-foot-tall windows surrounding the circular chamber and all of them showed nothing but a brilliant white light.

We were in the Inner Sun. Literally, the Ultranians had apparently built a kind of space station that they made either indestructible or covered in a force shield that allowed them to put it in the heart of a sun. A sun that didn't quite work the same way as the one the Earth orbited but was still damn hot. Talk about impractical designs. On the other hand, it explained why Tom Terror hadn't been able to take over the source of all magic. If he'd known about this place, he would have been here.

Standing there, in the Overlord armor with the helmet removed, was Maria in Mandy's body. Diabloman stood at her side, looking guilty. I also saw Ken. At least, I presumed it was Ken since it looked like him in twenty years with the body of Michael Clarke Duncan. He was wearing a suit of armor with a long red cape, a horned helmet straight from *Skyrim*, and he had a tiny hammer in one hand. I was glad Ken had gotten his original body back but less than pleased he was working for Maria now.

I was, once more, strapped to a table. In fact, I believed it was the exact same table as before. Apparently, Maria had picked up on the fact that Odin had given her a fake spear and infiltrated Skull Castle on her own. She'd picked up my suit of armor and made arrangements to kidnap me. All it had required was for my best friend to choose blood over loyalty.

Okay, now I was mad.

"So, you've decided to go full supervillain, Maria?" I asked, not really all that surprised. "I mean, we all saw this coming. Right?"

Maria looked at me. "Don't be a child, Gary. We both know there's no actual difference between superheroes and villains. It's all a matter of perspective."

"Case in point, something a supervillain would say," I said, unhappily. "So, can we get on to the killing me part?"

"Do you have a death wish, Gary?" Diabloman asked.

I thought about the question before answering it. "No, I don't. I'm not afraid of death, it's true, but I'm happier than I've been in a long time. I have two wonderful children and an upcoming marriage to look forward to."

"Pfft, like that will last," Maria said. "She'll find an excuse to leave you behind. Just like she did before."

"Says the literal rapist," I said, simply. "The world needs a better class of superhero than you. Thankfully, we have Bow Girl—who is thirty-eight and still fits into the costume well. I think the Society of Superheroes needs to work on phasing out anyone over the age of twenty being called girl, boy, lass, or lad. After a certain point, it just becomes embarrassing."

Maria made strangling gestures with her hands then took a deep breath. "I'm not here to hurt you."

"Oh?" I asked.

Maria gestured with the side of her head. "Release him."

Ken walked over and pulled open my restraints one by one. "Sorry about this. It's just when I had a choice between brainwashed into being a white psychopathic murderer and getting fixed, I chose the latter."

"It's alright," I said, giving him two thumbs up. "I'll pretend you were brainwashed. It's like the ultimate Get out of Jail Free card."

"Appreciate it," Ken said, nodding. "I promise to let you escape your next heist."

I didn't tell him I was defecting to the other team because I fully intended to kick his ass after this was done. You know, after I somehow disabled his incredible strength and invulnerability. No wait, he was just a fourteen-year-old kid. You couldn't hold them to the same standards as the rest of us. Especially when a beautiful woman was asking.

I couldn't turn insubstantial and escape because, well, we were in the middle of a sun. I also didn't want to damage any of the equipment inside. So, instead, I just stood up and walked toward Maria. "What is it you want?"

"It is a complicated issue—" Diabloman started to say.

"Shut up," I said, simply. "We're not talking anymore."

I wasn't sure we ever would again.

"The body I inhabit likes you, Gary," Maria said, frowning in a way reminiscent of Mandy.

"The body you inhabit is soulless," I said.

"Soulless but still possessed of a will of its own," Maria said.

"That is, by definition, the opposite of soulless," I said.

Maria made a dismissive wave. "It doesn't matter. What matters is I'm willing to make restitution for what I did."

"How's that?" I asked, utterly devoid of mirth. I never thought I would get tired of the fun of supervillainy and crime-committing. However, I was ready to close the book on this chapter of my life. Or wait, was it "turn the page on this chapter of my life"? I forget how the saying goes. Anyway, I had a very simple way to do it.

Kill Maria.

Call me sexist and believe me, I'm usually more woke than this, but I don't actually like killing female baddies. The Nightmistress, Abaddonian gods, Amazons, Zombies and Nazis aside, I've never actually done it. Which sounds like more than it is compared to the number of people I've killed total that is still like ninety percent dudes.

Okay, I had a point here somewhere. Anyway, it's doubly problematic when one of them is your reanimated dead wife possessed by the sister of your now possibly former best friend. However, Maria was going to be a persistent thorn in my side until I dealt with her permanently. Mandy's demonically empowered vampire self also needed to be put down. It's what she'd want.

Probably.

Yeah, now I sounded like I was trying to convince myself I wanted to do what I needed to do. I didn't even understand why I was hesitating. Yet, here I was. Hesitating. That was almost a guarantee of losing in a battle of magic versus magic. I might as well just put my head on the chopping block and let her kill me.

"I want to take over your destiny," Maria said.

"My...destiny," I said, unsure what she said. "What do you mean?"

"I'll be the villain who takes over the world," Maria said. "Who unites the world in opposition to them."

I stared at her. "Where did you even hear about that?"

"Mindy and Leia spoke to me, too," Maria said.

I stared at her. "That's it. This year's trip to Anime Con is off."

"Mindy is not even a year old," Diabloman said. "She wouldn't appreciate it."

"You don't know that," I snapped back. "Wait, I just realized I banished Jane from this universe and my sister is arrested. Goddammit, who am I going to get to babysit for me? Do you think Jane would resent it if I kidnapped her back from her dimension? Maybe I can give her an apology salt lick or something. Or kill the hunter who whacked Bambi's mother."

"Heroes don't kill," Ken said, calling from his side.

I glared at him. "They also don't join psychotic vampire witches out to take over the world."

"I thought you were going undercover," Ken said.

I stared at him. "Does everyone know about that already? The whole point of going undercover is no one knows you're doing it!"

"Cindy knows so it didn't last a minute and a half,"

Diabloman said. "Congratulations on your redemption."

"Which you had a chance at and threw away," I said, looking at him. I was furious with him but not for the reasons I expected. It wasn't the betrayal. Okay, it was a little the betrayal. No, it was the fact he was doing it for his sister. Maria was digging herself a deeper and deeper hole and he was willing to throw himself down it to join her.

"*Sí,*" Diabloman said, simply.

"You realize no one actually takes over the world," I replied, wondering why I was even bothering.

"You could and have," Maria said. "Just agree."

"And then what?" I asked.

"Then we never have to see each other again," Maria replied. "The P.H.A.N.T.O.M Block nations in Eastern Europe are vulnerable to invasion with the death of Tom Terror. I'll start there and move on to other countries no one cares about. With the orichalcum wealth in the Hollow Earth, I'll be able to leverage superpower status for my alliance. In time, people will beg me to rule them."

"And you want to help with this?" I asked Diabloman and Ken.

"I just want to punch Nazis and get paid," Ken said. "Besides, if a superhero goes rogue then the others will have my back until I get a slap on the wrist for it. It's called the Cape Wall."

Diabloman sucked in a breath. "I owe her a debt I must repay."

"You cannot repay," Maria said, her tone acidic. "But I'll let you try. So, Gary, do we have a deal?"

"Yeah, but we have to shake on it," I said, simply. I'd made my decision on how to handle this.

Maria nodded and took my hand.

That's when I sent her soul to hell.

CHAPTER TWENTY-NINE

I REALLY SUCK AT THIS SUPERHERO THING

Yeah, I don't think I'm ever going to achieve redemption. I wasn't going to achieve the Force Ghost by Obi-Wan and Yoda-type where all is forgiven despite a lifetime of evil deeds. I never quite bought that for Anakin Skywalker anyway. It seemed George Lucas, the Force, and Catholicism had a lot in common about how easy it was to wash away sin. For me, I was very old school and believed once you did the crime you had to serve your time. Strangely, this didn't stop me from doing the crime and trying to avoid the latter whatever the cost. So, I'm honest in my dishonesty.

I'm ninety percent sure that sending someone's soul to hell is up there for things superheroes don't do. Not even Hellrider would do it (okay, maybe him). I felt like I'd proved I wasn't worthy of being a hero. Even an undercover one. What can I say, the Dark Side is tempting in a way that the Light Side is not.

"Sorry, Maria," I said, not sorry in the slightest.

"You bastard." Maria's eyes widened in the second between my using the Death Orb and her soul getting sucked into the object before being punted off to an unpleasant afterlife. "What have you done?"

"I send souls to their afterlives," I said, squeezing her hand as the necromantic power united us both. "It's kind of what I do."

"I… want to live."

I closed my eyes. "You've been dead a long time."

I should have recognized the signs, but I hadn't. Maria went insane because she hadn't been able to find peace in death, but that was because she'd become a ghost rather than going off to her natural destination as a hero. She'd been too tied to the world due to her need for revenge against Diabloman, her anger at her teammates for not saving her, and the resentment she felt for the people she was saving at the cost of her own life.

Did she deserve Hell? Honestly, I didn't think anyone deserved hell. However, hell came in a wide variety of sizes, shapes, and colors. There were places that were your last stop, do not pass Go, do not collect $200. There were places that functioned more like the Catholic Purgatory or the Buddhist Hells where they eventually burned the bad out of you. There was one other type of hell and that was the worst one: the place you created for yourself from your nightmares, self-hatred, anger, and refusal to face your own flaws.

That was Maria's destination.

"You will never know happiness, Merciless," Maria said, struggling to resist having her spirit torn from her host body. "You're a plague."

"Yeah," I said, wondering what it looked like to the other two people in the room. For them, it had to look like we were glowing with eldritch energies. I could see Diabloman try to approach, only to be shoved back by an invisible barrier. "But so are you."

"Damn—" Maria started to say before she was gone. Her spirit passed through mine into the Death Orb and into the Great Beyond.

I felt her pain as it happened and got a sense of what her prison would be like. It was a nightmare that was forged from her desire to serve herself rather than the selflessness she'd known in life. To get revenge, to find love (even if the sex wasn't important), and to live in a way she'd been denied. Normal everyday wants and needs that had been denied her as a super-hero—but that had become all-consuming obsessions.

That was why she'd settled into Mandy's life; it had given her the family she'd always wanted. Maria thought she could just settle into another woman's life and take it over—no matter how ill-fitting it was. There was potential for redemption there. Maybe in a few decades I'd let her out of the dimension of darkness and regret I had condemned her to. But not before.

"*Requiescat in infernus,*" I said in Latin. I'm pretty sure you can infer the meaning.

Much to my surprise, Vamp Mandy (for lack of a better term—cut me some slack here) didn't die. Instead, the undead revenant I'd made of my wife stood there as if she was coming out of a trance. Her eyes turned an iridescent yellow and narrowed as she looked at me. She then grabbed my throat with one of her armored gauntlets and lifted me off the ground. The gauntlets, like all the armor, were made of extra-dimensional metal that drained away my magic just by being near it.

"You!" Vamp Mandy screamed. "You condemned me to this hell of being a prisoner in my own body!"

Ken looked to Diabloman as if this was the most normal thing in the world. "Do you know what's going on?"

"You cannot kill him!" Diabloman charged at Vamp Mandy, slamming into her armored form as all his tattoos glowed.

"Ah, thanks, D," I said, flying out of Vamp Mandy's grip.

"Because I'm going to!" Diabloman snarled with rage.

I was disappointed but not surprised. If I was a superhero, I would have made some sort of apology or tried to justify myself. Instead, I just accepted the fact our friendship was broken. He'd betrayed me and I'd done something unforgivable to the person he'd betrayed me for. Well, I was no stranger to dealing with the consequences of my actions and was prepared to deal with them here. I just hoped I didn't have to kill my friend.

"Imbecile," Vamp Mandy said, smacking Diabloman across the room with one power-armored fist. "I am stronger than you without this armor."

"I have slain heroes and gods," Diabloman shouted, rising and raising his fists. "I am the champion of the gods the Devil prays to! You shall not defeat me!"

Diabloman then turned around and charged at the windows. I realized in that moment he was going to smash them to pieces and expose us all to the interior of the Inner Sun. It was a suicide move and one that showed he had nothing left to live for. A foolish notion since his daughter was outside, proud of her father showing the world he could be a hero.

"No, D, don't!" I shouted at him, raising my fist. With the Death Orb, I could kill just about anyone and my emotions were running hot enough that it was close to fully charged. I wanted to live but I couldn't kill him.

Couldn't kill my friend.

Ken charged at him with superspeed, but Diabloman managed to grab him by the cape and hurl him against the wall. It cracked under his attack, allowing burning beams of light through. They were only a fraction of the heat outside but fully capable of frying us like vampires. Which, honestly, was a bit of irony I didn't realize until the moment I thought it.

"Hiss!" Vamp Mandy said, covering her face with a metal arm.

"This was the way it was meant to be, Merciless!" Diabloman said, shouting at the top of his lungs. "I was born to be a taker of life and not giver. I destroyed a whole universe. No one can be redeemed from that, no matter what good deeds they may do after or what cosmic wishes may be expended on their behalf. Hell is—"

"Oh do shut the hell up," I said, pointing a finger with my left hand at him and generating a glowing beam of prismatic energy that sucked all of the energy flying in through the walls before engulfing Diabloman.

He vanished in an explosion of brilliant rainbow colors.

Ken got up off the ground and looked over at me. "What the hell did you just do?"

"I sent him to Albuquerque," I said, feeling the Chaos Orb pulse inside my hand. It didn't like being directed in its magic. I could wield its power, but I suspected it was a power that wanted to wield me instead. Well, I was used to being unable to control myself, so this wouldn't be anything new. "Maybe he'll pass Bugs Bunny on the way there."

"Huh?" Ken asked.

"Shut up and look for something resembling duct tape!" I snapped, seeing the light beams return through the cracks. Each of them was like a death ray shooting a continuous beam around us and I had to duck my head to maneuver around them. Worse, the walls of the control room were starting to crack around us and it looked like this entire place was going to explode.

"I don't think the Ultranians used duct tape," Ken said, looking around helplessly. "Listen, I'm sorry about all this, but she made me an offer I couldn't refuse."

"Getting your body back?" I asked, searching around frantically and ignoring Vamp Mandy getting up off the ground.

"No," Ken said, frowning. "Spellbinder said she could bring my parents back. Reyan's and mine."

I closed my eyes. "Yeah, I can understand that."

"Sorry," Ken said, clearly expecting to die.

"Yeah, me, too."

I, of course, had a plan. One more trick, but I wasn't sure if it was going to work. I wanted to try to use the Chaos Orb, which was raw, undiluted magic in its purest form, to teleport Ken and me from this place. The problem was I felt that it had a will inside it. It had already just teleported Diabloman to "safety" and didn't like repeating its tricks. I didn't know if I was anthropomorphizing the orbs too much, that maybe I was just crazy and hallucinating things like my daughters speaking to them, but I was kind of in a spot.

So, I was willing to try anything. "Listen, Cersei, isn't it more chaotic to do something twice than always refuse to do something a second time?"

Yes, I named the Chaos Orb Cersei. I immediately got a bunch of annoyance from the Death Orb that I hadn't given her a name. I told her I'd get back on that. Either way, I felt the orbs glow in my hand as the walls around us began to collapse.

"Get over here!" I shouted to Ken.

Ken didn't hesitate and was at my side in an instant, even as he almost burned himself by nearly running into one of the light beams. The room was becoming an inferno and I only avoided being cooked by the ambient heat by turning insubstantial.

"Gary!" Vamp Mandy hissed to one side.

Leaving Vamp Mandy here to be destroyed was an elegant solution to the fact I hadn't been willing or able to kill her until this point. Mandy had been someone who wanted to be a hero. She wasn't a killer, unless the monster was undead, and Vamp Mandy had hundreds of deaths to her name. Yeah, most of them were complete bastards but we were trying to cut down on murdering people in general.

Being trapped at the heart of a sun would be a quick and painless way of dying. It surprised me how much I cared about that, given I'd gone to elaborate lengths to reassure myself Vamp Mandy was just a shell. So, of course, I reached out and grabbed her metal hand and teleported her away as well before the Ultranian station detonated in an explosion of mystical light.

The three of us appeared on the surface of the Hollow Earth a few hundred miles away from the Inner Sun that, thankfully, wasn't exploding or shooting out fireballs. Whatever the Ultranian station was designed to monitor or fix didn't seem to influence whether the Inner Sun was still going to remain stable. It would kind of suck after all to survive that place exploding, only for the entire Hollow Earth to be destroyed due to normal physics suddenly applying in the Earth's core again. That probably would have resulted in the death of not just everyone living here but also on the surface of the Earth, too.

We were in the middle of a field of large manure piles from a herd of nearby brachiosaurs. It was not the best place we could have landed but I was thinking any port in a storm. I wasn't looking forward to hiking wherever I had to in order to reunite with everyone else. Then I remembered I could fly and decided to stop whining. Also, I was really hoping Captain Dumbass would give me a lift.

"You saved my life," Ken said, blinking. "That was really cool of you."

"Yeah, I'm just awesome," I muttered under my breath. "Kid, as a general rule, you're going to find that allying with supervillains has a lot more in the way of consequences than I think you were prepared for."

"Yeah," Ken said, looking down. "Can I pretend my brain was fried by Nazi brainwashing and everything is good now?"

"Sure," I said, not looking at Vamp Mandy.

"Good," Ken said, before flying into the air.

"Son of a bitch," I muttered, watching him fly off. "He didn't even offer to give me a ride. You okay, Vamp Mandy?"

"Call me Mandy."

"No."

"Fine." Vamp Mandy was tearing pieces of her armor off. Her face had been badly burned but was regenerating before my eyes. I hoped that didn't mean she was feeling peckish.

"Yes, I am," she said.

"We cool?" I asked, deliberately evoking *Pulp Fiction*. I wasn't in the mood to quote *Star Wars*.

"Are you going to hunt me in the future?" Vamp Mandy asked.

I sucked in my breath. "No, I'm sentimental that way. Even for soulless abominations."

I was surprisingly glad to have her back. I didn't think we were going to become besties but there was a peace with what Mandy had become, or at least a part of her. I was prepared to let her go the way I'd let go of Keith and Cloak. I wasn't sure about Diabloman, but I was glad he'd survived as well, even if we were now enemies.

"Demon, not soulless," Mandy corrected.

I turned around to look at her. Her injuries were completely healed, and she was in a slightly charred bodysuit. "Well, excuse me all to hell."

"Demons are made from the regrets of humans. Things they hate about themselves and leave behind when they ascend to become divine beings. You should wonder, Gary, why I still care for you so much. Was it because your wife's love for you was so strong or was it something she left behind."

"Ouch."

"It means you might have been the most important thing in the world to her," Vamp Mandy said. "Something she needed to let go of if she was to ascend."

"You're really terrible at this reassuring thing."

"Well, I am made of pure evil."

I looked at her. "Just don't do anything too horrifying, alright? I'm sorry for what I did. Trying to turn back the clock."

Vamp Mandy snorted. "Gary, you're not responsible for

everything. I made my choice to sacrifice myself. You can forgive yourself."

I, not Mandy.

I shook my head. "And then what?"

"Go be a hero," Mandy said. "You always were meant to be one. Cloak saw it. I saw it. Let the world see it."

"And if I suck at it?"

"Oh, you will, I'm sure. But it'll be entertaining as hell."

Merciless will return in:
THE KINGDOM OF SUPERVILLAINY
Book Seven of The Supervillainy Saga

About the Author

C.T. Phipps is a lifelong student of horror, science fiction, and fantasy. An avid tabletop gamer, he discovered this passion led him to write and turned him into a lifelong geek. He is a regular blogger and also a reviewer for The Bookie Monster.

Bibliography

The Rules of Supervillainy (Supervillainy Saga #1)
The Games of Supervillainy (Supervillainy Saga #2)
The Secrets of Supervillainy (Supervillainy Saga #3)
The Kingdom of Supervillany (Supervillainy Saga #4)
The Science of Supervillainy (Supervillainy Saga #5)
The Tournament of Supervillainy (Supervillainy Saga #6)

I Was a Teenage Weredeer (The Bright Falls Mysteries, Book 1)
An American Weredeer in Michigan (The Bright Falls Mysteries, Book 2)

Esoterrorism (Red Room, Vol. 1)
Eldritch Ops (Red Room, Vol. 2)

Agent G: Infiltrator (Agent G, Vol. 1)
Agent G: Saboteur (Agent G, Vol. 2)
Agent G: Assassin (Agent G, Vol. 3)

Cthulhu Armageddon (Cthulhu Armageddon, Vol. 1)
The Tower of Zhaal (Cthulhu Armageddon, Vol. 2)

Lucifer's Star (Lucifer's Star, Vol. 1)
Lucifer's Nebula (Lucifer's Star, Vol. 2)

Straight Outta Fangton (Straight Outta Fangton, Vol. 1)
100 Miles and Vampin' (Straight Outta Fangton, Vol. 2)

Wraith Knight (Wraith Knight, Vol. 1)
Wraith Lord (Wraith Knight, Vol. 2)

Curious about other Crossroad Press books?
Stop by our site:
http://www.crossroadpress.com
We offer quality writing
in digital, audio, and print formats.

www.ingramcontent.com/pod-product-compliance
Lightning Source LLC
Chambersburg PA
CBHW060416180626
46817CB00007B/2594